HALFWAY TO GALACTIC RULE

In *The Currents of Space*, Trantor has begun forming its great Empire, but only half of the worlds of the Galaxy recognize its rule. Now the time for conquest by force is over, and diplomacy must take over. But when all life on one small kingdom is being risked by power-mad fools, what are the limits of patience?

THE GALACTIC EMPIRE NOVELS

These three novels by Isaac Asimov show the development of the Galactic Empire, whose decay gave rise to the Foundation. They span the time from the first star kingdoms to the full flowering of the Empire that ruled all the Galaxy. Each is a complete, independent novel. Together they provide facts, history, and human developments that are often only hinted at in the Foundation Series. Much of the material in the bestselling *Foundation's Edge* derives directly from background material to be found in these marvelous precursor novels.

By Isaac Asimov
Published by Ballantine Books:

THE CLASSIC FOUNDATION SERIES:
   Foundation
   Foundation and Empire
   Second Foundation
   Foundation's Edge
   Foundation and Earth

THE GALACTIC EMPIRE NOVELS:
   The Stars, Like Dust
   The Currents of Space
   Pebble in the Sky

THE ROBOT NOVELS:
   The Caves of Steel
   The Naked Sun
   The Robots of Dawn
   Robots and Empire

I, ROBOT

THE GODS THEMSELVES

THE END OF ETERNITY

THE BICENTENNIAL MAN and Other Stories

NIGHTFALL and Other Stories

NINE TOMORROWS

THE MARTIAN WAY and Other Stories

THE WINDS OF CHANGE and Other Stories

THE EARLY ASIMOV—Book One

THE EARLY ASIMOV—Book Two

THE LUCKY STARR ADVENTURES:
Writing as Paul French
   David Starr—Space Ranger
   Lucky Starr and the Pirates of the Asteroids
   Lucky Starr and the Oceans of Venus
   Lucky Starr and the Big Sun of Mercury
   Lucky Starr and the Moons of Jupiter
   Lucky Starr and the Rings of Saturn

ISAAC ASIMOV

THE CURRENTS OF SPACE

A Galactic Empire Novel

A DEL REY BOOK

BALLANTINE BOOKS • NEW YORK

CONTENTS

PROLOG
A YEAR BEFORE

The man from Earth came to a decision. It had been slow in coming and developing, but it was here.

It had been weeks since he had felt the comforting deck of his ship and the cool, dark blanket of space about it. Originally, he had intended a quick report to the local office of the Interstellar Spatio-analytic Bureau and a quicker retreat to space. Instead, he had been held here.

It was almost like a prison.

He drained his tea and looked at the man across the table. He said, "I'm not staying any longer."

The other man came to a decision. It had been slow in coming and developing, but it was here. He would need time, much more time. The response to the first letters had been nil. They might have fallen into a star for all they had accomplished.

That had been no more than he had expected, or, rather, no less. But it was only the first move.

It was certain that, while future moves developed, he could not allow the man from Earth to squirm out of reach. He fingered the smooth black rod in his pocket.

He said, "You don't appreciate the delicacy of the problem."

The Earthman said, "What's delicate about the destruction of a planet? I want you to broadcast the details to all of Sark; to everyone on the planet."

"We can't do that. You know it would mean panic."

"You said at first you would do it."

"I've thought it over and it just isn't practical."

The Earthman turned to a second grievance. "The representative of the I.S.B. hasn't arrived."

"I know it. They are busy organizing proper procedures for this crisis. Another day or two."

"Another day or two! It's always another day or two! Are they so busy they can't spare me a moment? They haven't even seen my calculations."

"I have offered to bring your calculations to them. You don't want me to."

"And I still don't. They can come to me or I can go to them." He added violently, "I don't think you believe me. You don't believe Florina will be destroyed."

"I believe you."

"You don't. I know you don't. I see you don't. You're humoring me. You can't understand my data. You're not a Spatio-analyst. I don't even think you're who you say you are. Who are you?"

"You're getting excited."

"Yes, I am. Is that surprising? Or are you just thinking, Poor devil, Space has him. You think I'm crazy."

"Nonsense."

"Sure you do. That's why I want to see the I.S.B. They'll know if I'm crazy or not. They'll know."

The other man remembered his decision. He said, "Now you're not feeling well. I'm going to help you."

"No, you're not," shouted the Earthman hysterically, "because I'm going to walk out. If you want to stop me, kill me, except that you won't dare. The blood of a whole world of people will be on your hands if you do."

The other man began shouting, too, to make himself heard. "I won't kill you. Listen to me, I won't kill you. There's no need to kill you."

The Earthman said, "You'll tie me up. You'll keep me here. Is that what you're thinking? And what will you do when the I.S.B. starts looking for me? I'm supposed to send in regular reports, you know."

"The Bureau knows you're safely with me."

"Do they? I wonder if they know I've reached the planet at all? I wonder if they received my original message?" The Earthman was giddy. His limbs felt stiff.

The other man stood up. It was obvious to him that his decision had come none too soon. He walked slowly about the long table, toward the Earthman.

He said soothingly, "It will be for your own good." He took the black rod from his pocket.

The Earthman croaked, "That's a psychic probe." His words were slurred, and when he tried to rise, his arms and legs barely quivered.

He said, between teeth that were clenching in rigor, "Drugged!"

"Drugged!" agreed the other man. "Now look, I won't hurt you. It's difficult for you to understand the true delicacy of the matter while you're so excited and anxious about it. I'll just remove the anxiety. Only the anxiety."

The Earthman could no longer talk. He could only sit there. He could only think numbly, Great Space, I've been drugged. He wanted to shout and scream and run, but he couldn't.

The other had reached the Earthman now. He stood there,

looking down at him. The Earthman looked up. His eyeballs could still move.

The psychic probe was a self-contained unit. Its wires needed only to be fixed to the appropriate places on the skull. The Earthman watched in panic until his eye muscles froze. He did not feel the fine sting as the sharp, thin leads probed through skin and flesh to make contact with the sutures of his skull bones.

He yelled and yelled in the silence of his mind. He cried, No, you don't understand. It's a planet full of people. Don't you see that you can't take chances with hundreds of millions of living people?

The other man's words were dim and receding, heard from the other end of a long, windy tunnel. "It won't hurt you. In another hour you'll feel well, really well. You'll be laughing at all this with me."

The Earthman felt the thin vibration against his skull and then that faded too.

Darkness thickened and collapsed about him. Some of it never lifted again. It took a year for even parts of it to lift.

1. THE FOUNDLING

Rik put down his feeder and jumped to his feet. He was trembling so hard he had to lean against the bare milk-white wall.

He shouted, "I remember!"

They looked at him and the gritty mumble of men at lunch died somewhat. Eyes met his out of faces indifferently clean and indifferently shaven, glistening and white in the imperfect wall illumination. The eyes reflected no great interest, merely the reflex attention enforced by any sudden and unexpected cry.

Rik cried again, "I remember my job. I had a job!"

Someone called, "Shoddop!" and someone else yelled, "Siddown!"

The faces turned away, the mumble rose again. Rik stared blankly along the table. He heard the remark, "Crazy Rik," and a shrug of shoulders. He saw a finger spiral at a man's temple. It all meant nothing to him. None of it reached his mind.

Slowly he sat down. Again he clutched his feeder, a spoonlike affair, with sharp edges and little tines projecting from the front curve of the bowl, which could therefore with equal clumsiness cut, scoop and impale. It was enough for a millworker. He turned it over and stared without seeing at his number on the back of the handle. He didn't have to see it. He knew it by heart. All the others had registration numbers, just as he had, but the others had names also. He didn't. They called him Rik because it meant something like "moron" in the slang of the kyrt mills. And often enough they called him "Crazy Rik."

But perhaps he would be remembering more and more now. This was the first time since he had come to the mill that he had remembered anything at all from before the beginning. If he thought hard! If he thought with all his mind!

All at once he wasn't hungry; he wasn't the least hungry. With a sudden gesture, he thrust his feeder into the jellied briquet of meat and vegetables before him, pushed the food away, and buried his eyes in the heels of his palms. His fingers thrust and clutched at his hair and painstakingly he tried to follow his mind into the pitch from which it had extracted a single item—one muddy, undecipherable item.

Then he burst into tears, just as the clanging bell announced the end of his lunch shift.

Valona March fell in beside him when he left the mill that evening. He was scarcely conscious of her at first, at least as an individual. It was only that he heard his footsteps matched. He stopped and looked at her. Her hair was something between blonde and brown. She wore it in two thick plaits that she clamped together with little magnetized green-stoned pins. They were very cheap pins and had a faded look about them. She wore the simple cotton dress which was all that was needed in that mild climate, just as Rik himself needed only an open, sleeveless shirt and cotton slacks.

She said, "I heard something went wrong lunchtime."

She spoke in the sharp, peasant accents one would expect. Rik's own language was full of flat vowels and had a nasal touch. They laughed at him because of it and imitated his way of speaking, but Valona would tell him that that was only their own ignorance.

Rik mumbled, "Nothing's wrong, Lona."

She persisted. "I heard you said you remembered something. Is that right, Rik?"

She called him Rik too. There wasn't anything else to call him. He couldn't remember his real name. He had tried desperately enough. Valona had tried with him. One day she had obtained a torn city directory somehow and had read all the first names to him. None had seemed more familiar than any other.

He looked her full in the face and said, "I'll have to quit the mill."

Valona frowned. Her round, broad face with its flat, high cheekbones was troubled. "I don't think you can. It wouldn't be right."

"I've got to find out more about myself."

Valona licked her lips. "I don't think you should."

Rik turned away. He knew her concern to be sincere. She had obtained the mill job for him in the first place. He had had no experience with mill machinery. Or perhaps he had, but just didn't remember. In any case, Lona had insisted that he was too small for manual labor and they had agreed to give him technical training without charge. Before that, in the nightmarish days when he could scarcely make sounds and when he didn't know what food was for, she had watched him and fed him. She had kept him alive.

He said, "I've got to."

"Is it the headaches again, Rik?"

"No. I really remember something. I remember what my job was before——Before!"

He wasn't sure he wanted to tell her. He looked away.

The warm, pleasant sun was at least two hours above the horizon. The monotonous rows of workers' cubicles that stretched out and round the mills were tiresome to look at, but Rik knew that as soon as they topped the rise the field would lie before them in all the beauty of crimson and gold.

He liked to look at the fields. From the very first the sight had soothed and pleased him. Even before he knew that the colors were crimson and gold, before he knew that there were such things as colors, before he could express his pleasure in anything more than a soft gurgle, the headaches would flicker away faster in the fields. In those days Valona would borrow a diamagnetic scooter and take him out of the village every idle-day. They would skim along, a foot above the road, gliding on the cushioned smoothness of the counter-gravity field, until they were miles and miles away from any human habitation and there would be left only the wind against his face, fragrant with the kyrt blossoms.

They would sit beside the road then, surrounded by color and scent, and between them share a food briquet, while the sun glowed down upon them until it was time to return again.

Rik was stirred by the memory. He said, "Let's go to the fields, Lona."

"It's late."

"Please. Just outside town."

She fumbled at the thin money pouch she kept between herself and the soft blue leather belt she wore, the only luxury of dress she allowed herself.

Rik caught her arm. "Let's walk."

They left the highway for the winding, dustless, packed-sand roads half an hour later. There was a heavy silence between them and Valona felt a familiar fear clutching at her. She had no words to express her feelings for him, so she had never tried.

What if he should leave her? He was a little fellow, no taller than herself and weighing somewhat less, in fact. He was still like a helpless child in many ways. But before they had turned his mind off he must have been an educated man. A very important educated man.

Valona had never had any education besides reading and writing and enough trade-school technology to be able to handle mill machinery, but she knew enough to know that all people were not so limited. There was the Townman, of course, whose great knowledge was so helpful to all of them. Occasionally Squires came on inspection tours. She had never seen them close up but once, on a holiday, she had visited the City and seen a group of incredibly gorgeous creatures at a distance. Occasionally the millworkers were allowed to listen to what educated people sounded like. They spoke differently, more fluently, with longer words and softer tones. Rik talked like that more and more as his memory improved.

She had been frightened at his first words. They came so suddenly after long whimpering over a headache. They were pronounced queerly. When she tried to correct him he wouldn't change.

Even then she had been afraid that he might remember too much and then leave her. She was only Valona March. They called her Big Lona. She had never married. She never would. A large, big-footed girl with work-reddened hands like herself could never marry. She had never been able to do more than look at the boys with dumb resentment when they ignored her at the idle-day dinner festivals. She was too big to giggle and smirk at them.

She would never have a baby to cuddle and hold. The others girls did, one after the other, and she could only crowd about for a quick glimpse of something red and hairless with screwed-up eyes, fists impotently clenched, gummy mouth——

"It's your turn next, Lona."

"When will you have a baby, Lona?"

She could only turn away.

But when Rik had come, he was like a baby. He had to

be fed and taken care of, brought out into the sun, soothed to sleep when the headaches racked him.

The children would run after her, laughing. They would yell, "Lona's got a boy friend. Big Lona's got a crazy boy friend. Lona's boy friend is a rik."

Later on, when Rik could walk by himself (she had been as proud the day he took his first step as though he were really only one year old, instead of more like thirty-one) and stepped out, unescorted, into the village streets, they had run about him in rings, yelling their laughter and foolish ridicule in order to see a grown man cover his eyes in fear, and cringe, with nothing but whimpers to answer them. Dozens of times she had come charging out of the house, shouting at them, waving her large fists.

Even grown men feared those fists. She had felled her section head with a single wild blow the first day she had brought Rik to work at the mill because of a sniggering indecency concerning them which she overheard. The mill council fined her a week's pay for that incident, and might have sent her to the City for further trial at the Squire's court, but for the Townman's intervention and the plea that there had been provocation.

So she wanted to stop Rik's remembering. She knew she had nothing to offer him; it was selfish of her to want him to stay mind-blank and helpless forever. It was just that no one had ever before depended upon her so utterly. It was just that she dreaded a return to loneliness.

She said, "Are you sure you remember, Rik?"

"Yes."

They stopped there in the fields, with the sun adding its reddening blaze to all that surrounded them. The mild, scented evening breeze would soon spring up, and the checkerboard irrigation canals were already beginning to purple.

He said, "I can trust my memories as they come back, Lona. You know I can. You didn't teach me to speak, for instance. I remembered the words myself. Didn't I? Didn't I?"

She said reluctantly, "Yes."

"I even remember the times you took me out into the fields before I could speak. I keep remembering new things all the time. Yesterday I remembered that once you caught a kyrt fly for me. You held it closed in your hands and made me put my eye to the space between your thumbs so that I could see it flash purple and orange in the darkness. I laughed and tried to force my hand between yours to get it, so that it flew away and left me crying after all. I didn't know it was a kyrt fly then, or anything about it, but it's all very clear to me now. You never told me about that, did you, Lona?"

She shook her head.

"But it did happen, didn't it? I remember the truth, don't I?"

"Yes, Rik."

"And now I remember something about myself from before. There must have been a *before*, Lona."

There must have been. She felt the weight on her heart when she thought that. It was a different before, nothing like the now they lived in. It had been on a different world. She knew that because one word he had never remembered was kyrt. She had to teach him the word for the most important object on all the world of Florina.

"What is it you remember?" she asked.

At this, Rik's excitement seemed suddenly to die. He hung back. "It doesn't make much sense, Lona. It's just that I had a job once, and I know what it was. At least, in a way."

"What was it?"

"I analyzed Nothing."

She turned sharply upon him, peering into his eyes. For a moment she put the flat of her hand upon his forehead, until he moved away irritably. She said, "You don't have a headache again, Rik, have you? You haven't had one in weeks."

"I'm all right. Don't you go bothering me."

Her eyes fell, and he added at once, "I don't mean that

you bother me, Lona. It's just that I feel fine and I don't
want you to worry."

She brightened. "What does 'analyzed' mean?" He knew
words she didn't. She felt very humble at the thought of
how educated he must once have been.

He thought a moment. "It means—it means 'to take
apart.' You know, like we would take apart a sorter to find
out why the scanning beam was out of alignment."

"Oh. But, Rik, how can anyone have a job not analyzing
anything? That's not a job."

"I didn't say I didn't analyze anything. I said I analyzed
Nothing. With a capital N."

"Isn't that the same thing?" It was coming, she thought.
She was beginning to sound stupid to him. Soon he would
throw her off in disgust.

"No, of course not." He took a deep breath. "I'm afraid
I can't explain though. That's all I remember about that.
But it must have been an important job. That's the way it
feels. I *couldn't* have been a criminal."

Valona winced. She should never have told him that.
She had told herself it was only for his own protection that
she warned him, but now she felt that it had really been to
keep him bound tighter to herself.

It was when he had first begun to speak. It was so sudden
it had frightened her. She hadn't even dared speak to the
Townman about it. The next idle-day she had withdrawn
five credits from her life-hoard—there would never be a
man to claim it as dowry, so that it didn't matter—and
taken Rik to a City doctor. She had the name and address
on a scrap of paper, but even so it took two frightening
hours to find her way to the proper building through the
huge pillars that held the Upper City up to the sun.

She had insisted on watching and the doctor had done
all sorts of fearful things with strange instruments. When
he put Rik's head between two metal objects and then made
it glow like a kyrt fly in the night, she had jumped to her

feet and tried to make him stop. He called two men who dragged her out, struggling wildly.

Half an hour afterward the doctor came out to her, tall and frowning. She felt uncomfortable with him because he was a Squire, even though he kept an office down in the Lower City, but his eyes were mild, even kind. He was wiping his hands on a little towel, which he tossed into a wastecan, even though it looked perfectly clean to her.

He said, "Where did you meet this man?"

She had told him the circumstances cautiously, reducing it to the very barest essentials and leaving out all mention of the Townman and the patrollers.

"Then you know nothing about him?"

She shook her head. "Nothing before that."

He said, "This man has been treated with a psychic probe. Do you know what that is?"

At first she had shaken her head again, but then she said in a dry whisper, "Is it what they do to crazy people, Doctor?"

"And to criminals. It is done to change their minds for their own good. It makes their minds healthy, or it changes the parts that make them want to steal and kill. Do you understand?"

She did. She grew brick-red and said, "Rik never stole anything or hurt anybody."

"You call him Rik?" He seemed amused. "Now look here, how do you know what he did before you met him? It's hard to tell from the condition of his mind now. The probing was thorough and brutal. I can't say how much of his mind has been permanently removed and how much has been temporarily lost through shock. What I mean is that some of it will come back, like his speaking, as time goes on, but not all of it. He should be kept under observation."

"No, no. He's got to stay with me. I've been taking good care of him, Doctor."

He frowned, and then his voice grew milder. "Well, I'm thinking of you, my girl. Not all the bad may be out of his mind. You wouldn't want him to hurt you someday."

At that moment a nurse led out Rik. She was making

little sounds to quiet him, as one would an infant. Rik put a hand to his head and stared vacantly, until his eyes focused on Valona; then he held out his hands and cried, feebly, "Lona——"

She sprang to him and put his head on her shoulder, holding him tightly. She said to the doctor, "He wouldn't hurt me, no matter what."

The doctor said thoughtfully, "His case will have to be reported, of course. I don't know how he escaped from the authorities in the condition he must have been in."

"Does that mean they'll take him away, Doctor?"

"I'm afraid so."

"Please, Doctor, don't do that." She wrenched at the handkerchief, in which were the five gleaming pieces of credit-alloy. She said, "You can have it all, Doctor. I'll take good care of him. He won't hurt anyone."

The doctor looked at the pieces in his hand. "You're a millworker, aren't you?"

She nodded.

"How much do they pay you a week?"

"Two point eight credits."

He tossed the coins gently, brought them together in his closed palm with a tinkle of metal, then held them out to her. "Take it, girl. There's no charge."

She accepted them with wonder. "You're not going to tell anyone, Doctor?"

But he said, "I'm afraid I have to. It's the law."

She had driven blindly, heavily, back to the village, clutching Rik to her desperately.

The next week on the hypervideo newscast there had been the news of a doctor dying in a gyro-crash during a short failure in one of the local transit power-beams. The name was familiar and in her room that night she compared it with that on the scrap of paper. It was the same.

She was sad, because he had been a good man. She had received his name once long before from another worker as a Squire doctor who was good to the mill hands and had saved it for emergencies. And when the emergency had come he had been good to her too. Yet her joy drowned the sorrow. He had not had the time to report Rik. At least, no one ever came to the village to inquire.

Later, when Rik's understanding had grown, she had told him what the doctor had said so that he would stay in the village and be safe.

Rik was shaking her and she left her reveries.

He said, "Don't you hear me? I couldn't be a criminal if I had an important job."

"Couldn't you have done wrong?" she began hesitantly. "Even if you were a big man, you might have. Even Squires——"

"I'm sure I haven't. But don't you see that I've got to find out so that others can be sure? There's no other way. I've got to leave the mill and village and find out more about myself."

She felt the panic rise. "Rik! That would be dangerous. Why should you? Even if you analyzed Nothing, why is it so important to find out more about it?"

"Because of the other thing I remember."

"What other thing?"

He whispered, "I don't want to tell you."

"You ought to tell somebody. You might forget again."

He seized her arm. "That's right. You won't tell anyone else, will you, Lona? You'll just be my spare memory in case I forget."

"Sure, Rik."

Rik looked about him. The world was very beautiful. Valona had once told him that there was a huge shining sign in the Upper City, miles above it even, that said: "Of all the Planets in the Galaxy, Florina is the Most Beautiful."

And as he looked about him he could believe it.

He said, "It is a terrible thing to remember, but I always

remember correctly, when I do remember. It came this afternoon."

"Yes?"

He was staring at her in horror. "Everybody in the world is going to die. Everybody on Florina."

2. THE TOWNMAN

Myrlyn Terens was in the act of removing a book-film from its place on the shelf when the door-signal sounded. The rather pudgy outlines of his face had been set in lines of thought, but now these vanished and changed into the more usual expression of bland caution. He brushed one hand over his thinning, ruddy hair and shouted, "One minute."

He replaced the film and pressed the contact that allowed the covering section to spring back into place and become indistinguishable from the rest of the wall. To the simple millworkers and farmhands he dealt with, it was a matter of vague pride that one of their own number, by birth at any rate, should own films. It lightened, by tenuous reflection, the unrelieved dusk of their own minds. And yet it would not do to display the films openly.

The sight of them would have spoiled things. It would have frozen their none too articulate tongues. They might boast of their Townman's books, but the actual presence of them before their eyes would have made Terens seem too much the Squire.

There were, of course, the Squires as well. It was unlikely in the extreme that any of them would visit him socially at his house, but should one of them enter, a row of films in sight would be injudicious. He was a Townman and custom gave him certain privileges but it would never do to flaunt them.

He shouted again, "I'm coming!"

This time he stepped to the door, closing the upper seam of his tunic as he went. Even his clothing was somewhat Squirelike. Sometimes he almost forgot he had been born on Florina.

Valona March was on the doorstep. She bent her knees and ducked her head in respectful greeting.

Terens threw the door wide. "Come in, Valona. Sit down. Surely it's past curfew. I hope the patrollers didn't see you."

"I don't think so, Townman."

"Well, let's hope that's so. You've got a bad record, you know."

"Yes, Townman. I am very grateful for what you have done for me in the past."

"Never mind. Here, sit down. Would you like something to eat or drink?"

She seated herself, straight-backed, at the edge of a chair and shook her head. "No, thank you, Townman. I have eaten."

It was good form among the villagers to offer refreshment. It was bad form to accept. Terens knew that. He didn't press her.

He said, "Now what's the trouble, Valona? Rik again?"

Valona nodded, but seemed at a loss for further explanation.

Terens said, "Is he in trouble at the mill?"

"No, Townman."

"Headaches again?"

"No, Townman."

Terens waited, his light eyes narrowing and growing sharp. "Well, Valona, you don't expect me to guess your trouble, do you? Come, speak out or I can't help you. You do want help, I suppose."

She said, "Yes, Townman," then burst out, "How shall I tell you, Townman? It sounds almost crazy."

Terens had an impulse to pat her shoulder, but he knew she would shrink from the touch. She sat, as usual, with her large hands buried as far as might be in her dress. He noticed that her blunt, strong fingers were intertwined and slowly twisting.

He said, "Whatever it is, I will listen."

"Do you remember, Townman, when I came to tell you about the City doctor and what he said?"

"Yes, I do, Valona. And I remember I told you particularly that you were never to do anything like that again without consulting me. Do *you* remember that?"

She opened her eyes wide. She needed no spur to recollect his anger. "I would never do such a thing again, Townman. It's just that I want to remind you that you said you would do everything to help me keep Rik."

"And so I will. Well, then, have the patrollers been asking about him?"

"No. Oh, Townman, do you think they might?"

"I'm sure they won't." He was losing patience. "Now, come, Valona, tell me what is wrong."

Her eyes clouded. "Townman, he says he will leave me. I want you to stop him."

"Why does he want to leave you?"

"He says he is remembering things."

Interest leaped into Terens' face. He leaned forward and almost he reached out to grip her hand. "Remembering things? What things?"

Terens remembered the day Rik had first been found. He had seen the youngsters clustered near one of the irrigation ditches just outside the village. They had raised their shrill voices to call him.

"Townman! Townman!"

He had broken into a run. "What's the matter, Rasie?" He had made it his business to learn the youngsters' names when he came to town. That went well with the mothers and made the first month or two easier.

Rasie was looking sick. He said, "Looky here, Townman."

He was pointing at something white and squirming, and it was Rik. The other boys were yelling at once in confused explanation. Terens managed to understand that they were playing some game that involved running, hiding and pursuing. They were intent on telling him the name of the game, its progress, the point at which they had been interrupted, with a slight subsidiary argument as to exactly which individual or side was "winning." All that didn't matter, of course.

Rasie, the twelve-year-old black-haired one, had heard the whimpering and had approached cautiously. He had expected an animal, perhaps a field rat that would make good chasing. He had found Rik.

All the boys were caught between an obvious sickness and an equally obvious fascination at the strange sight. It was a grown human being, nearly naked, chin wet with drool, whimpering and crying feebly, arms and legs moving about aimlessly. Faded blue eyes shifted in random fashion out of a face that was covered with a grown stubble. For a moment the eyes caught those of Terens and seemed to focus. Slowly the man's thumb came up and inserted itself into his mouth.

One of the children laughed. "Looka him, Townman. He's finger-sucking."

The sudden shout jarred the prone figure. His face reddened and screwed up. A weak whining, unaccompanied by tears, sounded but his thumb remained where it was. It showed wet and pink in contrast to the rest of the dirt-smeared hand.

Terens broke his own numbness at the sight. He said, "All right, look, fellows, you shouldn't be running around here in the kyrt field. You're damaging the crop and you know what that will mean if the farm hands catch you. Get going, and keep quiet about this. And listen, Rasie, you run to Mr. Jencus and get him to come here."

Ull Jencus was the nearest thing to a doctor the town had. He had passed some time as apprentice in the offices of a real doctor in the City and on the strength of it he had been relieved of duty on the farms or in the mills. It didn't work out too badly. He could take temperatures, administer pills, give injections and, most important, he could tell when some disorder was sufficiently serious to warrant a trip to the City hospital. Without such semiprofessional backing, those unfortunates stricken with spinal meningitis or acute appendicitis might suffer intensively but usually not for long. As it was, the foremen muttered and accused Jencus in everything but words of being an accessory after the fact to a conspiracy of malingering.

Jencus helped Terens lift the man into a scooter cart and, as unobtrusively as they might, carried him into town.

Together they washed off the accumulated and hardened grime and filth. There was nothing to be done about the hair. Jencus shaved the entire body and did what he could by way of physical examination.

Jencus said, "No infection I c'n tell of, Townman. He's been fed. Ribs don't stick out too much. *I* don't know what to make of it. How'd he get out there, d'you suppose, Townman?"

He asked the question with a pessimistic tone as though no one could expect Terens to have the answer to anything. Terens accepted that philosophically. When a village has lost the Townman it has grown accustomed to over a period of nearly fifty years, a newcomer of tender age must expect a transition period of suspicion and distrust. There was nothing personal in it.

Terens said, "I'm afraid I don't know."

"Can't walk, y'know. Can't walk a step. He'd have to be *put* there. Near's I c'n make out, he might's well be a baby. Everything else seems t'be gone."

"Is there a disease that has this effect?"

"Not's I know of. Mind trouble might do it, but I don't know nothing 'tall about that. Mind trouble I'd send to the City. Y'ever see this one, Townman?"

Terens smiled and said gently, "I've just been here a month."

Jencus sighed and reached for his handkerchief. "Yes. Old Townman, he was a fine man. Kept us well, he did. *I* been here 'most sixty years, and never saw this fella before. Must be from 'nother town."

Jencus was a plump man. He had the look of having been born plump, and if to this natural tendency is added the effect of a largely sedentary life, it is not surprising that he tended to punctuate even short speeches by a puff and a rather futile swipe at his gleaming forehead with his large red handkerchief.

He said, "Don't 'xactly know what t'say t'the patrollers."

The patrollers came all right. It was impossible to avoid that. The boys told their parents; their parents told one another. Town life was quiet enough. Even this would be unusual enough to be worth the telling in every possible combination of informer and informee. And in all the telling, the patrollers could not help but hear.

The patrollers, so called, were members of the Florinian Patrol. They were not natives of Florina and, on the other hand, they were not countrymen of the Squires from the planet Sark. They were simply mercenaries who could be counted on to keep order for the sake of the pay they got and never to be led into the misguidance of sympathy for Florinians through any ties of blood or birth.

There were two of them and one of the foremen from the mill came with them, in the fullness of his own midget authority.

The patrollers were bored and indifferent. A mindless idiot might be part of the day's work but it was scarcely an exciting part. One said to the foreman, "Well, how long does it take you to make an identification? Who is this man?"

The foreman shook his head energetically. "I never saw him, Officer. He's no one around here!"

The patroller turned to Jencus. "Any papers on him?"

"No, sir. He just had a rag 'bout him. Burned it t'prevent infection."

"What's wrong with him?"

"No mind, near's I c'n make out."

At this point Terens took the patrollers aside. Because they were bored they were amenable. The patroller who had been asking the questions put up his notebook and said, "All right, it isn't even worth making a record of. It has nothing to do with us. Get rid of it somehow."

Then they left.

The foreman remained. He was a freckled man, red of hair, with a large and bristly mustache. He had been foreman of rigid principles for five years and that meant his responsibility for the fulfillment of quota in his mill rested heavily upon him.

"Look here," he said fiercely. "What's to be done about this? The damn folk are so busy talking, they ain't working."

"Send him t'City hospital, near's I c'n make out," said Jencus, wielding his handkerchief industriously. "Noth'n' I c'n do."

"To the City!" The foreman was aghast. "Who's going to pay? Who'll stand the fees? He ain't none of us, is he?"

"Not's far's I know," admitted Jencus.

"Then why should *we* pay? Find out who he belongs to. Let *his* town pay."

"How we going t'find out? Tell me that."

The foreman considered. His tongue licked out and played with the coarse reddish foliage of his upper lip. He said, "Then we'll just have to get rid of him. Like the patroller said."

Terens interrupted. "Look here. What do you mean by that?"

The foreman said, "He might as well be dead. It would be a mercy."

Terens said, "You can't kill a living person."

"Suppose *you* tell me what to do then."

"Can't one of the townpeople take care of him?"

"Who'd want to? Would you?"

Terens ignored the openly insolent attitude. "I've got other work to do."

"So have all the folk. I can't have anyone neglecting mill work to take care of this crazy thing."

Terens sighed, and said without rancor, "Now, Foreman, let's be reasonable. If you *don't* make quota this quarter I might suppose it's because one of your workers is taking care of this poor fellow, and I'll speak up for you to the Squires. Otherwise I'll just say that I don't know of any reason you couldn't make quota, in case you don't make it."

The foreman glowered. The Townman had only been here a month, and already he was interfering with men who had lived in town all their lives. Still, he had a card marked with Squire's marks. It wouldn't do to stand too openly against him too long.

He said, "But who'd take him?" A horrible suspicion smote him. "*I* can't. I got three kids of my own and my wife ain't well."

"I didn't suggest that you should."

Terens looked out the window. Now that the patrollers had left, the squirming, whispering crowd had gathered closer about the Townman's house. Most were youngsters, too young to be working, others were farm hands from the nearer farms. A few were millworkers, away from their shifts.

Terens saw the big girl at the very edge of the crowd. He had noticed her often in the past month. Strong, competent, and hard-working. Good natural intelligence hidden under that unhappy expression. If she were a man she might have been chosen for Townman's training. But she was a woman; parents dead, and plain enough she was to preclude romantic side interests. A lone woman, in other words, and likely to remain so.

He said, "What about her?"

The foreman looked, then roared, "Damn it. She ought to be at work."

"All right," soothed Terens. "What's her name?"

"That's Valona March."

"That's right. I remember now. Call her in."

From that moment Terens had made himself an unofficial guardian of the pair. He had done what he could to obtain additional food rations for her, extra clothing coupons and whatever else was required to allow two adults (one unregistered) to live on the income of one. He had been instrumental in helping her obtain training for Rik at the kyrt mills. He had intervened to prevent greater punishment on the occasion of Valona's quarrel with a section head. The death of the City doctor had made it unnecessary for him to attempt further action there than he had taken, but he had been ready.

It was natural for Valona to come to him in all her troubles, and he was waiting now for her to answer his question.

Valona was still hesitating. Finally she said, "He says everyone in the world will die."

Terens looked startled. "Does he say how?"

"He says he doesn't know how. He just says he remembers that from before he was like, you know, like he is. And he says he remembers he had an important job, but I don't understand what it is."

"How does he describe it?"

"He says he an—analyzes Nothing with a capital N."

Valona waited for comment, then hastened to explain, "Analyze means taking something apart like——"

"I know what it means, girl."

Valona watched him anxiously. "Do *you* know what he means, Townman?"

"Perhaps, Valona."

"But, Townman, how can anyone do anything to Nothing?"

Terens got to his feet. He smiled briefly. "Why, Valona,

don't you know that everything in all the Galaxy is mostly Nothing?"

No light of understanding dawned on Valona, but she accepted that. The Townman was a very educated man. With an unexpected twinge of pride, she was suddenly certain that her Rik was even more educated.

"Come." Terens was holding his hand out to her.

She said, "Where are we going?"

"Well, where's Rik?"

"Home," she said. "Sleeping."

"Good. I'll take you there. Do you want the patrollers to find you on the street alone?"

The village seemed empty of life in the nighttime. The lights along the single street that split the area of workers' cabins in two gleamed without glare. There was a hint of rain in the air, but only of that light warm rain that fell almost every night. There was no need to take special precautions against it.

Valona had never been out so late on a working evening and it was frightening. She tried to shrink away from the sound of her own footsteps, while listening for the possible distant step of the patrollers.

Terens said, "Stop trying to tiptoe, Valona. I'm with you."

His voice boomed in the quiet and Valona jumped. She hurried forward in response to his urging.

Valona's hut was as dark as the rest and they stepped in gingerly. Terens had been born and brought up in just such a hut and though he had since lived on Sark and now occupied a house with three rooms and plumbing, there was still something of a nostalgia about the barrenness of its interior. One room was all that was required, a bed, a chest of drawers, two chairs, a smooth poured-cement floor, a closet in one corner.

There was no need for kitchen facilities, since all meals were eaten at the mill, nor for a bathroom, since a line of community outhouses and shower cells ran along the space behind the houses. In the mild, unvarying climate, windows were not adapted for protection against cold and rain. All four walls were pierced by screened openings and eaves above were sufficient ward against the nightly windless sprinkles.

In the flare of a little pocket light which he held cupped in one palm Terens noted that one corner of the room was marked off by a battered screen. He remembered getting it for Valona rather recently when Rik had become too little of a child or too much of a man. He could hear the regular breathing of sleep behind it.

He nodded his head in that direction. "Wake him, Valona."

Valona tapped on the screen. "Rik! Rik, baby!"

There was a little cry.

"It's only Lona," said Valona. They rounded the screen and Terens played his little light upon their own faces, then upon Rik.

Rik threw an arm up against the glare. "What's the matter?"

Terens sat down on the edge of the bed. Rik slept in the standard cottage bed, he noted. He had obtained for Valona an old, rather rickety cot at the very first, but she had reserved that for herself.

"Rik," he said, "Valona says you're beginning to remember things."

"Yes, Townman." Rik was always very humble before the Townman, who was the most important man he had ever seen. Even the mill superintendent was polite to the Townman. Rik repeated the scraps his mind had gathered during the day.

Terens said, "Have you remembered anything else since you told this to Valona?"

"Nothing else, Townman."

Terens kneaded the fingers of one hand with those of the other. "All right, Rik. Go back to sleep."

Valona followed him out of the house. She was trying

hard to keep her face from twisting and the back of one rough hand slid across her eyes. "Will he have to leave me, Townman?"

Terens took her hands and said gravely, "You must be a grown woman, Valona. He will have to come with me for just a short while but I'll bring him back."

"And after that?"

"I don't know. You must understand, Valona. Right now it is the most important thing in all the world that we find out more about Rik's memories."

Valona said suddenly, "You mean everybody on Florina might die, the way he says?"

Terens' grip tightened. "Don't ever say that to anyone, Valona, or the patrollers may take Rik away forever. I mean that."

He turned away and walked slowly and thoughtfully back to his house without really noticing that his hands were trembling. He tried futilely to sleep and after an hour of that he adjusted the narco-field. It was one of the few pieces of Sark he had brought with him when he first returned to Florina to become Townman. It fitted about his skull like a thin black felt cap. He adjusted the controls to five hours and closed contact.

He had time to adjust himself comfortably in bed before the delayed response shorted the conscious centers of his cerebrum and blanketed him into instantaneous, dreamless sleep.

3. THE LIBRARIAN

They left the diamagnetic scooter in a scooter-cubby outside the City limits. Scooters were rare in the City and
Terens had no wish to attract unnecessary attention. He
thought for a savage moment of those of the Upper City
with their diamagnetic ground-cars and anti-grav gyros. But
that was the Upper City. It was different.

Rik waited for Terens to lock the cubby and fingerprint-
seal it. He was dressed in a new one-piece suit and felt a
little uncomfortable. Somewhat reluctantly he followed the
Townman under the first of the tall bridgelike structures
that supported the Upper City.

On Florina, all other cities had names, but this one was
simply the "City." The workers and peasants who lived in
it and around it were considered lucky by the rest of the
planet. In the City there were better doctors and hospitals,
more factories and more liquor stores, even a few dribbles
of very mild luxury. The inhabitants themselves were some-

what less enthusiastic. They lived in the shadow of the Upper City.

The Upper City was exactly what the name implied, for the City was double, divided rigidly by a horizontal layer of fifty square miles of cementalloy resting upon some twenty thousand steel-girdered pillars. Below in the shadow were the "natives." Above, in the sun, were the Squires. It was difficult to believe in the Upper City that the planet of its location was Florina. The population was almost exclusively Sarkite in nature, together with a sprinkling of patrollers. They were the upper class in all literalness.

Terens knew his way. He walked quickly, avoiding the stares of passers-by, who surveyed his Townman clothing with a mixture of envy and resentment. Rik's shorter legs made his gait less dignified as he tried to keep up. He did not remember very much from his only other visit to the City. It seemed so different now. Then it had been cloudy. Now the sun was out, pouring through the spaced openings in the cementalloy above to form strips of light that made the intervening space all the darker. They plunged through the bright strips in a rhythmic, almost hypnotic fashion.

Oldsters sat on wheeled chairs in the strips, absorbing the warmth and moving as the strip moved. Sometimes they fell asleep and would remain behind in the shade, nodding in their chairs until the squeaking of the wheels when they shifted position woke them. Occasionally mothers nearly blocked the strips with their carriaged offspring.

Terens said, "Now, Rik, stand up straight. We're going up."

He was standing before a structure that filled the space between four square-placed pillars, and from ground to Upper City.

Rik said, "I'm scared."

Rik could guess what the structure was. It was an elevator that lifted to the upper level.

These were necessary, of course. Production was below, but consumption was above. Basic chemicals and raw food staples were shipped into Lower City, but finished plasticware and fine meals were matters for Upper City. Excess population spawned below; maids, gardeners, chauffeurs, construction laborers were used above.

Terens ignored Rik's expression of fright. He was amazed that his own heart beat so violently. Not fright, of course. Rather a fierce satisfaction that he was going up. He would step all over that sacred cementalloy, stamp on it, scuff his dirt upon it. He could do that as a Townman. Of course he was still only a Florinian native to the Squires, but he was a Townman and he could step on the cementalloy whenever he pleased.

Galaxy, he hated them!

He stopped himself, drew a firm breath and signaled for the elevator. There was no use thinking hate. He had been on Sark for many years; on Sark itself, the center and breeding place of the Squires. He had learned to bear in silence. He ought not forget what he had learned now. Of all times, not now.

He heard the whir of the elevator settling at the lower level, and the entire wall facing him dropped into its slot.

The native who operated the elevator looked disgusted. "Just two of you."

"Just two," said Terens, stepping in. Rik followed.

The operator made no move to restore the fallen wall to its original position. He said, "Seems to me you guys could wait for the two o'clock load and move with it. I ain't supposed to run this thing up and down for no two guys." He spat carefully, making sure that the sputum hit lower-level concrete and not the floor of his elevator.

He went on, "Where's your employment tickets?"

Terens said, "I'm a Townman. Can't you see it by my clothes?"

"Clothes don't mean nothing. Listen, you think I'm risking my job because you maybe picked up some uniform somewheres? Where's your card?"

Terens, without another word, presented the standard document-folder all natives had to carry at all times: registration number, employment certificate, tax receipts. It was open to the crimson of his Townman's license. The operator scanned it briefly.

"Well, maybe you picked that up, too, but that's not my business. You got it and I pass you, though Townman's just a fancy name for a native to my way of figgering. What about the other guy?"

"He's in my charge," said Terens. "He can come with me, or shall we call a patroller and check into the rules?"

It was the last thing Terens wanted but he suggested it with suitable arrogance.

"Awrright! Y'don't have to get sore." The elevator wall moved up, and with a lurch the elevator climbed. The operator mumbled direfully under his breath.

Terens smiled tightly. It was almost inevitable. Those who worked directly for the Squires were only too glad to identify themselves with the rulers and make up for their real inferiority by a tighter adherence to the rules of segregation, a harsh and haughty attitude toward their fellows. They were the "uppermen" for whom the other Florinians reserved their particular hate, unalloyed by the carefully taught awe they felt for the Squires.

The vertical distance traveled was thirty feet, but the door opened again to a new world. Like the native cities of Sark, Upper City was laid out with a particular eye to color. Individual structures, whether dwelling places or public buildings, were inset in an intricate multicolored mosaic which, close at hand, was a meaningless jumble, but at a distance of a hundred yards took on a soft clustering of hues that melted and changed with the angle of view.

"Come on, Rik," said Terens.

Rik was staring wide-eyed. Nothing alive and growing! Just stone and color in huge masses. He had never known houses could be so huge. Something stirred momentarily in his mind. For a second the hugeness was not so strange . . . And then the memory closed down again.

A ground-car flashed by.

"Are those Squires?" Rik whispered.

There had been time for only a glance. Hair close-cropped,

wide, flaring sleeves of glossy, solid colors ranging from blue to violet, knickers of a velvety appearance and long, sheer hose that gleamed as if it were woven of thin copper wire. They wasted no glance at Rik and Terens.

"Young ones," said Terens. He had not seen them at such close quarters since he left Sark. On Sark they were bad enough but at least they had been in place. Angels did not fit here, thirty feet over Hell. Again he squirmed to suppress a useless tremble of hatred.

A two-man flatcar hissed up behind them. It was a new model that had built-in air controls. At the moment it was skimming smoothly two inches above surface, its gleaming flat bottom curled upward at all edges to cut air resistance. Still, the slicing of air against its lower surface sufficed to produce the characteristic hiss which meant "patrollers."

They were large, as all patrollers were; broad-faced, flat-cheeked, long, straight black hair, light brown in complexion. To the natives, all patrollers looked alike. The glossy black of their uniforms, enhanced as they were by the startling silver of strategically placed buckles and ornamental buttons, depressed the importance of the face and encouraged the impression of likeness still more.

One patroller was at the controls. The other leaped out lightly over the shallow rim of the car.

He said, "Folder!" stared mechanically and momentarily at it and flipped it back to Terens. "Your business here?"

"I intend consulting the library, Officer. It is my privilege."

The patroller turned to Rik. "What about you?"

"I——" began Rik.

"He is my assistant," interposed Terens.

"He has no Townman privileges," said the patroller.

"I'll be responsible for him."

The patroller shrugged. "It's your lookout. Townmen have privileges, but they're not Squires. Remember that, boy."

"Yes, Officer. By the way, could you direct me to the library?"

The patroller directed him, using the thin, deadly barrel of a needle-gun to indicate direction. From their present angle, the library was a blotch of brilliant vermilion deepening into crimson toward the upper stories. As they approached, the crimson crept downward.

Rik said with sudden vehemence, "I think it's ugly."

Terens gave him a quick, surprised glance. He had been accustomed to all this on Sark, but he, too, found the garishness of Upper City somewhat vulgar. But then, Upper City was more Sark than Sark itself. On Sark, not all men were aristocrats. There were even poor Sarkites, some scarcely better off than the average Florinian. Here only the top of the pyramid existed, and the library showed that.

It was larger than all but a few on Sark itself, far larger than Upper City required, which showed the advantage of cheap labor. Terens paused on the curved ramp that led to the main entrance. The color scheme on the ramp gave the illusion of steps, somewhat disconcerting to Rik, who stumbled, but giving the library the proper air of archaism that traditionally accompanied academic structures.

The main hall was large, cold, and all but empty. The librarian behind the single desk it contained looked like a small, somewhat wrinkled pea in a bloated pod. She looked up and half rose.

Terens said quickly, "I'm a Townman. Special privileges. I am responsible for this native." He had his papers ready and marched them before him.

The librarian seated herself and looked stern. She plucked a metal sliver from a slot and thrust it at Terens. The Townman placed his right thumb firmly upon it. The librarian took the sliver and put it in another slot where a dim violet light shone briefly.

She said, "Room 242."

"Thank you."

The cubicles on the second floor had that icy lack of personality that any link in an endless chain would have.

Some were filled, their glassite doors frosted and opaque. Most were not.

"Two forty-two," said Rik. His voice was squeaky.

"What's the matter, Rik?"

"I don't know. I feel very excited."

"Ever been in a library before?"

"I don't know."

Terens put his thumb on the round aluminum disk which, five minutes before, had been sensitized to his thumbprint. The clear glass door swung open and, as they stepped within, it closed silently and, as though a blind had been drawn, became opaque.

The room was six feet in each direction, without window or adornment. It was lit by the diffuse ceiling glow and ventilated by a forced-air draft. The only contents were a desk that stretched from wall to wall and an upholstered backless bench between it and the door. On the desk were three "readers." Their frosted-glass fronts slanted backward at an angle of thirty degrees. Before each were the various control-dials.

"Do you know what this is?" Terens sat down and placed his soft, plump hand upon one of the readers.

Rik sat down too.

"Books?" he asked eagerly.

"Well." Terens seemed uncertain. "This is a library, so your guess doesn't mean much. Do you know how to work the reader?"

"No. I don't think so, Townman."

"You're sure? Think about it a little."

Rik tried valiantly. "I'm sorry, Townman."

"Then I'll show you. Look! First, you see, there's this knob, labeled 'Catalog' with the alphabet printed about it. Since we want the encyclopedia first, we'll turn the knob to E and press downward."

He did so and several things happened at once. The frosted glass flared into life and printing appeared upon it. It stood out black on yellow as the ceiling light dimmed. Three smooth panels moved out like so many tongues, one before each reader, and each was centered by a tight light-beam.

Terens snapped a toggle switch and the panels moved back into their recesses.

He said, "We won't be taking notes."

Then he went on, "Now we can go down the list of E's by turning this knob."

The long line of alphabetized materials, titles, authors, catalog numbers flipped upward, then stopped at the packed column listing the numerous volumes of the encyclopedia.

Rik said suddenly, "You press the numbers and letters after the book you want on these little buttons and it shows on the screen."

Terens turned on him. "How do you know? Do you remember that?"

"Maybe I do. I'm not sure. It just seems the right thing."

"Well, call it an intelligent guess."

He punched a letter-number combination. The light on the glass faded, then brightened again. It said: "Encyclopedia of Sark, Volume 54, Sol—Spec."

Terens said, "Now look, Rik, I don't want to put any ideas in your head, so I won't tell you what's in my mind. I just want you to look through this volume and stop at anything that seems familiar. Do you understand?"

"Yes."

"Good. Now take your time."

The minutes passed. Suddenly Rik gasped and sent the dials spinning backward.

When he stopped, Terens read the heading and looked pleased. "You remember now? This isn't a guess? You remember?"

Rik nodded vigorously. "It came to me, Townman. Very suddenly."

It was the article on Spatio-analysis.

"I know what it says," Rik said. "You'll see, you'll see." He was having difficulty breathing normally and Terens, for his part, was almost equally excited.

"See," said Rik, "they always have this part."

He read aloud haltingly, but in a manner far more proficient than could be accounted for by the sketchy lessons in reading he had received from Valona. The article said:

"'It is not surprising that the Spatio-analyst is by temperament an introverted and, often enough, maladjusted individual. To devote the greater part of one's adult life to the lonely recording of the terrible emptiness between the stars is more than can be asked of someone entirely normal. It is perhaps with some realization of this that the Spatio-analytic Institute has adopted as its official slogan the somewhat wry statement, "We Analyze Nothing."'"

Rik finished with what was almost a shriek.

Terens said, "Do you understand what you've read?"

The smaller man looked up with blazing eyes. "It said, 'We Analyze Nothing.' That's what I remembered. I was one of them."

"You were a Spatio-analyst?"

"Yes," cried Rik. Then, in a lower voice, "My head hurts."

"Because you're remembering?"

"I suppose so." He looked up, forehead furrowed. "I've got to remember more. There's danger. Tremendous danger! I don't know what to do."

"The library's at our disposal, Rik." Terens was watching carefully, weighing his words. "Use the catalog yourself and look up some texts on Spatio-analysis. See where that leads you."

Rik flung himself upon the reader. He was shaking visibly. Terens moved aside to give him room.

"How about Wrijt's *Treatise of Spatio-analytic Instrumentation*?" asked Rik. "Doesn't that sound right?"

"It's all up to you, Rik."

Rik punched the catalog number and the screen burned brightly and steadily. It said, "Please Consult Librarian for Book in Question."

Terens reached out a quick hand and neutralized the screen. "Better try another book, Rik."

"But . . ." Rik hesitated, then followed orders. Another

search through the catalog and then he chose Enning's *Composition of Space*.

The screen filled itself once more with a request to consult the librarian. Terens said, "Damn!" and deadened the screen again.

Rik said, "What's the matter?"

Terens said, "Nothing. Nothing. Now don't get panicky, Rik. I just don't quite see——"

There was a little speaker behind the grillwork on the side of the reading mechanism. The librarian's thin, dry voice emerged therefrom and froze them both.

"Room 242! Is there anyone in Room 242?"

Terens answered harshly, "What do you want?"

The voice said, "What book is it you want?"

"None at all. Thank you. We are only testing the reader."

There was a pause as though some invisible consultation was proceeding. Then the voice said with an even sharper edge to it, "The record indicates a reading request for Wrijt's *Treatise of Spatio-analytical Instrumentation*, and Enning's *Compositon of Space*. Is that correct?"

"We were punching catalog numbers at random," said Terens.

"May I ask your reason for desiring those books?" The voice was inexorable.

"I tell you we don't want them. . . . Now stop it." The last was an angry aside to Rik, who had begun whimpering.

A pause again. Then the voice said, "If you will come down to the desk you may have access to the books. They are on a reserved listing and you will have to fill out a form."

Terens held out a hand to Rik. "Let's go."

"Maybe we've broken a rule," quavered Rik.

"Nonsense, Rik. We're leaving."

"We won't fill out the form?"

"No, we'll get the books some other time."

Terens was hurrying, forcing Rik along with him. He strode down the main lobby. The librarian looked up.

"Here now," she cried, rising and circling the desk. "One moment. One moment!"

They weren't stopping for her.

That is, until a patroller stepped in front of them. "You're in an awful hurry, laddies."

The librarian, somewhat breathless, caught up to them. "You're 242, aren't you?"

"Look here," said Terens firmly, "why are we being stopped?"

"Didn't you inquire after certain books? We'd like to get them for you."

"It's too late. Another time. Don't you understand that I don't want the books? I'll be back tomorrow."

"The library," said the woman primly, "at all times endeavors to give satisfaction. The books will be made available to you in one moment." Two spots of red burned high upon her cheekbones. She turned away, hurrying through a small door that opened at her approach.

Terens said, "Officer, if you don't mind——"

But the patroller held out his moderately long, weighted neuronic whip. It could serve as an excellent club, or as a longer-range weapon of paralyzing potentialities. He said, "Now, laddy, why don't you sit down quietly and wait for the lady to come back? It would be the polite thing to do."

The patroller was no longer young, no longer slim. He looked close to retirement age and he was probably serving out his time in quiet vegetation as library guard, but he was armed and the joviality on his swarthy face had an insincere look about it.

Terens' forehead was wet and he could feel the perspiration collecting at the base of his spine. Somehow he had underestimated the situation. He had been sure of his own analysis of the matter, of everything. Yet here he was. He shouldn't have been so reckless. It was his damned desire to invade Upper City, to stalk through the library corridors as though he were a Sarkite. . . .

For a desperate moment he wanted to assault the patroller and then, unexpectedly, he didn't have to.

It was just a flash of movement at first. The patroller started to turn a little too late. The slower reactions of age betrayed him. The neuronic whip was wrenched from his grasp and before he could do more than emit the beginning of a hoarse cry it was laid along his temple. He collapsed.

Rik shrieked with delight, and Terens cried, "Valona! By all the devils of Sark, *Valona*!"

4. THE REBEL

Terens recovered almost at once. He said, "Out. Quickly!" and began walking.

For a moment he had the impulse to drag the patroller's unconscious body into the shadows behind the pillars that lined the main hall, but there was obviously no time.

They emerged onto the ramp, with the afternoon sun making the world bright and warm about them. The colors of Upper City had shifted to an orange motif.

Valona said anxiously, "Come on!" but Terens caught her elbow.

He was smiling, but his voice was hard and low. He said, "Don't run. Walk naturally and follow me. Hold on to Rik. Don't let him run."

A few steps. They seemed to be moving through glue. Were there sounds behind them from the library? Imagination? Terens did not dare look.

"In here," he said. The sign above the driveway he indicated flickered a bit in the light of afternoon. It didn't compete very well with Florina's sun. It said: Ambulance Entrance.

Up the drive, through a side entrance, and between incredibly white walls. They were blobs of foreign material against the aseptic glassiness of the corridor.

A woman in uniform was looking at them from a distance. She hesitated, frowned, began to approach. Terens did not wait for her. He turned sharply, followed a branch of the corridor, then another one. They passed others in uniform and Terens could imagine the uncertainty they aroused. It was quite unprecedented to have natives wandering about unguarded in the upper levels of a hospital. What did one do?

Eventually, of course, they would be stopped.

So Terens felt his heartbeat step up when he saw the unobtrusive door that said: To Native Levels. The elevator was at their level. He herded Rik and Valona within and the soft lurch as the elevator dropped was the most delightful sensation of the day.

There were three kinds of buildings in the City. Most were Lower Buildings, built entirely on the lower level. Workers' houses, ranging up to three stories in height. Factories, bakeries, disposal plants. Others were Upper Buildings: Sarkite homes, theaters, the library, sports arenas. But some few were Doubles, with levels and entrances both below and above; the patroller stations, for instance, and the hospitals.

One could therefore use a hospital to go from Upper City to Lower City and avoid in that manner the use of the large freight elevators with their slow movements and overattentive operators. For a native to do so was thoroughly illegal, of course, but the added crime was a pinprick to those already guilty of assaulting patrollers.

They stepped out upon the lower level. The stark aseptic walls were there still, but they had a faintly haggard appearance as though they were less often scrubbed. The upholstered benches that lined the corridors on the upper level were gone. Most of all there was the uneasy babble of a waiting room filled with wary men and frightened women. A single attendant was attempting to make sense out of the mess, and succeeding poorly.

She was snapping at a stubbled oldster who pleated and unpleated the wrinkled knee of his raveling trousers and who answered all questions in an apologetic monotone.

"Exactly what is your complaint?...How long have you had these pains?...Ever been to the hospital before? ...Now look, you people can't expect to bother us over every little thing. You sit down and the doctor will look at you and give you more medicine."

She cried shrilly, "Next!" then muttered something to herself as she looked at the large timepiece on the wall.

Terens, Valona and Rik were edging cautiously through the crowd. Valona, as though the presence of fellow Florinians had freed her tongue of paralysis, was whispering intensely.

"I had to come, Townman. I was so worried about Rik. I thought you wouldn't bring him back and——"

"How did you get to Upper City, anyway?" demanded Terens over his shoulder, as he shoved unresisting natives to either side.

"I followed you and saw you go up the freight elevator. When it came down I said I was with you and he took me up."

"Just like that."

"I shook him a little."

"Imps of Sark," groaned Terens.

"I had to," explained Valona miserably. "Then I saw the patrollers pointing out a building to you. I waited till they were gone and went there too. Only I didn't dare go inside. I didn't know what to do so I sort of hid until I saw you coming out with the patroller stopping——"

"You people there!" It was the sharp, impatient voice of the receptionist. She was standing now, and the hard rapping of her metal stylus on the cementalloy desk top dominated the gathering and reduced them to a hard-breathing silence.

"Those people trying to leave. Come here. You cannot leave without being examined. There'll be no evading work-days with pretended sick calls. Come back here!"

But the three were out in the half shadow of Lower City. There were the smells and noise of what the Sarkites called the Native Quarter about them and the upper level was once more only a roof above them. But however relieved Valona and Rik might feel at being away from the oppressive rich-ness of Sarkite surroundings, Terens felt no lifting of anx-iety. They had gone too far and henceforth there might be no safety anywhere.

The thought was still passing through his turbulent mind when Rik called, "Look!"

Terens felt salt in his throat.

It was perhaps the most frightening sight the natives of the Lower City could see. It was like a giant bird floating down through one of the openings in the Upper City. It shut off the sun and deepened the ominous gloom of that portion of the City. But it wasn't a bird. It was one of the armed ground-cars of the patrollers.

Natives yelled and began running. They might have no specific reason to fear, but they scattered anyway. One man, nearly in the path of the car, stepped aside reluctantly. He had been hurrying on his way, intent on some business of his own, when the shadow caught him. He looked about him, a rock of calm in the wildness. He was of medium height, but almost grotesquely broad across the shoulders. One of his shirt sleeves was slit down its length, revealing an arm like another man's thigh.

Terens was hesitating, and Rik and Valona could do nothing without him. The Townman's inner uncertainty had mounted to a fever. If they ran, where could they go? If they remained where they were, what would they do? There was a chance that the patrollers were after others altogether, but with a patroller unconscious on the library floor through their act, the chances of that were negligible.

The broad man was approaching at a heavy half trot. For a moment he paused in passing them, as though with uncertainty. He said in a conversational voice, "Khorov's bakery is second left, beyond the laundry."

He veered back.

Terens said, "Come on."

He was sweating freely as he ran. Through the uproar, he heard the barking orders that came naturally to patroller throats. He threw one look over his shoulder. A half dozen of them were piling out of the ground-car, fanning out. They would have no trouble, he knew. In his damned Townman's uniform, he was as conspicuous as one of the pillars supporting the Upper City.

Two of the patrollers were running in the right direction. He didn't know whether or not they had seen him, but that didn't matter. Both collided with the broad man who had just spoken to Terens. All three were close enough for Terens to hear the broad man's hoarse bellow and the patrollers' sharp cursing. Terens herded Valona and Rik around the corner.

Khorov's bakery was named as such by an almost defaced "worm" of crawling illuminated plastic, broken in half a dozen places, and was made unmistakable by the wonderful odor that filtered through its open door. There was nothing to do but enter, and they did.

An old man looked out from the inner room within which they could see the flour-obscured gleam of the radar furnaces. He had no chance to ask their business.

Terens began, "A broad man——" He was holding his arms apart in illustration, and the cries of "Patrollers! Patrollers!" began to be heard outside.

The old man said hoarsely, "This way! Quickly!"

Terens held back. "In there?"

The old man said, "This one is a dummy."

First Rik, then Valona, then Terens crawled through the furnace door. There was a faint click and the back wall of the furnace moved slightly and hung freely from the hinges above. They pushed through it and into a small room, dimly lit, beyond.

*   *   *

They waited. Ventilation was bad, and the smell of baking increased hunger without satisfying it. Valona kept smiling at Rik, patting his hand mechanically from time to time. Rik stared back at her blankly. Once in a while he put a hand to his flushed face.

Valona began, "Townman——"

He snapped back in a tight whisper, "Not now, Lona. Please!"

He passed the back of his hand across his forehead, then stared at the dampness of his knuckles.

There was a click, magnified by the close confinement of their hiding place. Terens stiffened. Without quite realizing it, he raised clenched fists.

It was the broad man, poking his immense shoulders through the opening. They scarcely fit.

He looked at Terens and was amused. "Come on, man. We're not going to be fighting."

Terens looked at his fists, and let them drop.

The broad man was in markedly poorer condition now than when they had first seen him. His shirt was all but removed from his back and a fresh weal, turning red and purple, marked one cheekbone. His eyes were little and the eyelids crowded them above and below.

He said, "They've stopped looking. If you're hungry, the fare here isn't fancy, but there's enough of it. What do you say?"

It was night in the City. There were lights in the Upper City that lit the sky for miles, but in the Lower City the darkness was clammy. The shades were drawn tightly across the front of the bakery to hide the illegal, past-curfew lights away from it.

Rik felt better with warm food inside him. His headache began to recede. He fixed his eyes on the broad man's cheek.

Timidly he asked, "Did they hurt you, mister?"

"A little," said the broad one. "It doesn't matter. It happens every day in my business." He laughed, showing large teeth. "They had to admit I hadn't done anything but

I was in their way while they were chasing someone else. The easiest way of getting a native out of the way——" His hand rose and fell, holding an invisible weapon, butt-first.

Rik flinched away and Valona reached out an anxious, protective arm.

The broad man leaned back, sucking at his teeth to get out particles of food. He said, "I'm Matt Khorov, but they just call me the Baker. Who are you people?"

Terens shrugged. "Well..."

The Baker said, "I see your point. What I don't know won't hurt anyone. Maybe. Maybe. At that, though, you might trust me. I saved you from the patrollers, didn't I?"

"Yes. Thank you." Terens couldn't squeeze cordiality into his voice. He said, "How did you know they were after us? There were quite a few people running."

The other smiled. "None of them had the faces you three were wearing. Yours could have been ground up and used for chalk."

Terens tried to smile in return. He didn't succeed well. "I'm not sure I know why you risked your life. Thank you, anyway. It isn't much, just saying 'Thank you,' but there's nothing else I can do right now."

"You don't have to do anything." The Baker's vast shoulders leaned back against the wall. "I do this as often as I can. It's nothing personal. If the patrollers are after someone I do my best for him. I hate the patrollers."

Valona gasped. "Don't you get into trouble?"

"Sure. Look at this." He put a finger gently on his bruised cheek. "But you don't think I ought to let it stop me, I hope. That's why I built the dummy oven. So the patrollers wouldn't catch me and make things too hard for me."

Valona's eyes were wide with mingled fright and fascination.

The Baker said, "Why not? You know how many Squires there are on Florina? Ten thousand. You know how many patrollers? Maybe twenty thousand. And there are five hundred million of us natives. If we all lined up against them . . ." He snapped his fingers.

Terens said, "We'd be lining up against needle-guns and blaster-cannon, Baker."

The Baker retorted, "Yeah. We'd have to get some of our own. You Townmen have been living too close to the Squires. You're scared of them."

Valona's world was being turned upside down today. This man fought with patrollers and spoke with careless self-confidence to the Townman. When Rik plucked at her sleeve she disengaged his fingers gently and told him to sleep. She scarcely looked at him. She wanted to hear what this man said.

The broad man was saying, "Even with needle-guns and blast-cannon, the only way the Squires hold Florina is with the help of a hundred thousand Townmen."

Terens looked offended, but the Baker went on, "For instance, look at you. Very nice clothes. Neat. Pretty. You've got a nice little shack, I'll bet, with book-films, a private hopper and no curfew. You can even go to Upper City if you want to. The Squires wouldn't do that for you for nothing."

Terens felt in no position to lose his temper. He said, "All right. What do you want the Townmen to do? Pick fights with the patrollers? What good would it to? I admit I keep my town quiet and up to quota, but I keep them out of trouble. I try to help them, as much as the law will allow. Isn't that something? Someday——"

"Aah, someday. Who can wait for someday? When you and I are dead, what difference will it make who runs Florina? To us, I mean."

Terens said, "In the first place, I hate the Squires more than you do. Still——" He stopped, reddening.

The Baker laughed. "Go ahead. Say it again. I won't turn you in for hating the Squires. What did you do to get the patrollers after you?"

Terens was silent.

The Baker said, "I can make a guess. When the patrollers

fell over me they were plenty sore. Sore in person, I mean, and not just because some Squire told them to be sore. I know them and I can tell. So I figure that there's only one thing that could have happened. You must've knocked down a patroller. Or killed him, maybe."

Terens was still silent.

The Baker lost none of his agreeable tone. "It's all right to keep quiet but there's such a thing as being too cautious, Townman. You're going to need help. They know who you are."

"No, they don't," said Terens hastily.

"They must have looked at your cards in the Upper City."

"Who said I was in the Upper City?"

"A guess. I'll bet you were."

"They looked at my card, but not long enough to read my name."

"Long enough to know you're a Townman. All they have to do is find a Townman missing from his town or one who can't account for his movements today. The wires all over Florina are probably scorching right now. I think you're in trouble."

"Maybe."

"You know there's no maybe. Want help?"

They were talking in whispers. Rik had curled up in the corner and gone to sleep. Valona's eyes were moving from speaker to speaker.

Terens shook his head. "No, thanks. I—I'll get out of this."

The Baker's ready laughter came. "It will be interesting to see how. Don't look down on me because I haven't got an education. I've got other things. Look, you spend the night thinking about it. Maybe you'll decide you can use help."

Valona's eyes were open in the darkness. Her bed was only a blanket thrown on the floor, but it was nearly as good as the beds she was used to. Rik slept deeply on another blanket in an opposite corner. He always slept deeply on days of excitement after his headaches passed.

The Townman had refused a bed and the Baker had laughed (he laughed at everything, it seemed), turned out the light and told him he was welcome to sit up in the darkness.

Valona's eyes remained open. Sleep was far away. Would she ever sleep again? She had knocked down a patroller!

Unaccountably, she was thinking of her father and mother.

They were very misty in her mind. She had almost made herself forget them in the years that had stretched between them and herself. But now she remembered the sound of whispered conversations during the night, when they thought her asleep. She remembered people who came in the dark.

The patrollers had awakened her one night and asked her questions she could not understand but tried to answer. She never saw her parents again after that. They had gone away, she was told, and the next day they had put her to work when other children her age still had two years of play time. People looked after her as she passed and other children weren't allowed to play with her, even when work time was over. She learned to keep to herself. She learned not to speak. So they called her "Big Lona" and laughed at her and said she was a half-wit.

Why did the conversation tonight remind her of her parents?

"Valona."

The voice was so close that its light breath stirred her hair and so low she scarcely heard it. She tensed, partly in fear, partly in embarrassment. There was only a sheet over her bare body.

It was the Townman. He said, "Don't say anything. Just listen. I am leaving. The door isn't locked. I'll be back, though. Do you hear me? Do you understand?"

She reached in the darkness, caught his hand, pressed it with her fingers. He was satisfied.

"And watch Rik. Don't let him out of your sight. And Valona." There was a long pause. Then he went on, "Don't trust this Baker too much. I don't know about him. Do you understand?"

There was a faint noise of motion, an even fainter distant creak, and he was gone. She raised herself to one elbow and, except for Rik's breathing and her own, there was only silence.

She put her eyelids together in the darkness, squeezing them, trying to think. Why did the Townman, who knew everything, say this about the Baker, who hated patrollers and had saved them? Why?

She could think of only one thing. He had been there. Just when things looked as black as they could be, the Baker had come and acted quickly. It was almost as though it had been arranged or as if the Baker had been waiting for it all to happen.

She shook her head. It seemed strange. If it weren't for what the Townman had said, she would never think this.

The silence was broken into quivering pieces by a loud and unconcerned remark. "Hello? Still here?"

She froze as a beam of light caught her full. Slowly she relaxed and bunched the sheet about her neck. The beam fell away.

She did not have to wonder about the identity of the new speaker. His squat broad form bulked in the half-light that leaked backward from the flash.

The Baker said, "You know, I thought you'd go with him."

Valona said weakly. "Who, sir?"

"The Townman. You know he left, girl. Don't waste time pretending."

"He'll be back, sir."

"Did he say he would be back? If he did, he's wrong. The patrollers will get him. He's not a very smart man, the Townman, or he'd know when a door is left open for a purpose. Are you planning to leave too?"

Valona said, "I'll wait for the Townman."

"Suit yourself. It will be a long wait. Go when you please."

His light-beam suddenly left her altogether and traveled along the floor, picking out Rik's pale, thin face. Rik's eyelids crushed together automatically, at the impact of the light, but he slept on.

The Baker's voice grew thoughtful. "But I'd just as soon you left that one behind. You understand that, I suppose. If you decide to leave, the door is open, but it isn't open for *him*."

"He's just a poor, sick fellow——" Valona began in a high, frightened voice.

"Yes? Well, I collect poor sick fellows and that one stays here. Remember!"

The light-beam did not move from Rik's sleeping face.

5. THE SCIENTIST

Dr. Selim Junz had been impatient for a year, but one does not become accustomed to impatience with time. Rather the reverse. Nevertheless the year had taught him that the Sarkite Civil Service could not be hurried; all the more so since the civil servants themselves were largely transplanted Florinians and therefore dreadfully careful of their own dignity.

He had once asked old Abel, the Trantorian Ambassador, who had lived on Sark so long that the soles of his boots had grown roots, why the Sarkites allowed their government departments to be run by the very people they despised so heartily.

Abel had wrinkled his eyes over a goblet of green wine.

"Policy, Junz," he said. "Policy. A matter of practical genetics, carried out with Sarkite logic. They're a small, no-account world, these Sarkites, in themselves, and are only important so long as they control that everlasting gold

53

mine, Florina. So each year they skim Florina's fields and villages, bringing the cream of its youth to Sark for training. The mediocre ones they set to filing their papers and filling their blanks and signing their forms and the really clever ones they send back to Florina to act as native governors for the towns. Townmen they call them."

Dr. Junz was a Spatio-analyst, primarily. He did not quite see the point of all this. He said so.

Abel pointed a blunt old forefinger at him and the green light shining through the contents of his goblet touched the ridged fingernail and subdued its yellow-grayness.

He said, "You will never make an administrator. Ask me for no recommendations. Look, the most intelligent elements of Florina are won over to the Sarkite cause whole-heartedly, since while they serve Sark they are well taken care of, whereas if they turn their backs on Sark the best they can hope for is a return to a Florinian existence, which is not good, friend, not good."

He swallowed the wine at a draught and went on. "Further, neither the Townmen nor Sark's clerical assistants may breed without losing their positions. Even with female Florinians, that is. Interbreeding with Sarkites is, of course, out of the question. In this way the best of the Florinian genes are being continually withdrawn from circulation, so that gradually Florina will be composed only of hewers of wood and drawers of water."

"They'll run out of clerks at that rate, won't they?"

"A matter for the future."

So Dr. Junz sat now in one of the outer anterooms of the Department for Florinian Affairs and waited impatiently to be allowed past the slow barriers, while Florinian underlings scurried endlessly through a bureaucratic maze.

An elderly Florinian, shriveled in service, stood before him.

"Dr. Junz?"

"Yes."

"Come with me."

A flashing number on a screen would have been as efficient in summoning him and a fluoro-channel through the air as efficient in guiding him, but where manpower is cheap, nothing need be substituted. Dr. Junz thought "manpower" advisedly. He had never seen women in any government department on Sark. Florinian women were left on their planet, except for some house servants who were likewise forbidden to breed, and Sarkite women were, as Abel said, out of the question.

He was gestured to a seat before the desk of the Clerk to the Undersecretary. He knew the man's title from the channeled glow etched upon the desk. No Florinian could, of course, be more than a clerk, regardless of how much of the actual threads of office ran through his white fingers. The Undersecretary and the Secretary of Florinian Affairs would themselves be Sarkites, but though Dr. Junz might meet them socially, he knew he would never meet them here in the department.

He sat, still impatiently, but at least nearer the goal. The Clerk was glancing carefully through the file, turning each minutely coded sheet as though it held the secrets of the universe. The man was quite young, a recent graduate perhaps, and like all Florinians, very fair of skin and light of hair.

Dr. Junz felt an atavistic thrill. He himself came from the world of Libair, and like all Libairians, he was highly pigmented and his skin was a deep, rich brown. There were few worlds in the Galaxy in which the skin color was so extreme as on either Libair or Florina. Generally, intermediate shades were the rule.

Some of the radical young anthropologists were playing with the notion that men of worlds like Libair, for instance, had arisen by independent but convergent evolution. The older men denounced bitterly any notion of an evolution that converged different species to the point where interbreeding was possible, as it certainly was among all the worlds in the Galaxy. They insisted that on the original planet, whatever it was, mankind had already been split into subgroups of varying pigmentation.

This merely placed the problem further back in time and answered nothing so that Dr. Junz found neither explanation satisfying. Yet even now he found himself thinking of the problem at times. Legends of a past of conflict had lingered, for some reason, on the dark worlds. Libairian myths, for instance, spoke of times of war between men of different pigmentation and the founding of Libair itself was held due to a party of browns fleeing from a defeat in battle.

When Dr. Junz left Libair for the Arcturian Institute of Spatial Technology and later entered his profession, the early fairy tales were forgotten. Only once since then had he really wondered. He had happened upon one of the ancient worlds of the Centaurian Sector in the course of business; one of those worlds whose history could be counted in millennia and whose language was so archaic that its dialect might almost be that lost and mythical language, English. They had a special word for a man with dark skin.

Now why should there be a special word for a man with dark skin? There was no special word for a man with blue eyes, or large ears, or curly hair. There was no——

The Clerk's precise voice broke his reverie. "You have been at this office before, according to the record."

Dr. Junz said with some asperity, "I have indeed, sir."

"But not recently."

"No, not recently."

"You are still in search of a Spatio-analyst who disappeared"—the Clerk flipped sheets—"some eleven months and thirteen days ago."

"That's right."

"In all that time," said the Clerk in his dry, crumbly voice out of which all the juice seemed carefully pressed, "there has been no sign of the man and no evidence to the effect that he ever was anywhere in Sarkite territory."

"He was last reported," said the scientist, "in space near Sark."

The Clerk looked up and his pale blue eyes focused for

a moment on Dr. Junz, then dropped quickly. "This may be so, but it is not evidence of his presence *on* Sark."

Not evidence! Dr. Junz's lips pressed tightly together. It was what the Interstellar Spatio-analytic Bureau had been telling him with increasing bluntness for months.

No evidence, Dr. Junz. We feel that your time might be better employed, Dr. Junz. The Bureau will see to it that the search is maintained, Dr. Junz.

What they really meant was, Stop wasting our dough, Junz!

It had begun, as the Clerk had carefully stated, eleven months and thirteen days ago by Interstellar Standard Time (the Clerk would, of course, not be guilty of using local time on a matter of this nature). Two days before that he had landed on Sark on what was to be a routine inspection of the Bureau's offices on that planet, but which turned out to be—well, which turned out to be what it was.

He had been met by the local representative of the I.S.B., a wispy young man who was marked in Dr. Junz's thoughts chiefly by the fact that he chewed, incessantly, some elastic product of Sark's chemical industry.

It was when the inspection was almost over and done with that the local agent had recalled something, parked his lastoplug in the space behind his molars and said, "Message from one of the field men, Dr. Junz. Probably not important. You know *them*."

It was the usual expression of dismissal: You know *them*. Dr. Junz looked up with a momentary flash of indignation. He was about to say that fifteen years ago he himself had been a "field man," then he remembered that after three months he had been able to endure it no longer. But it was that bit of anger that made him read the message with an earnest attention.

It went: *Please keep direct coded line open to I.S.B. Central HQ for detailed message involving matter of utmost importance. All Galaxy affected. Am landing by minimum trajectory.*

The agent was amused. His jaws had gone back to their rhythmic champing and he said, "Imagine, sir. 'All Galaxy affected.' That's pretty good, even for a field man. I called him after I got this to see if I could make any sense out of him, but that flopped. He just kept saying that the life of every human being on Florina was in danger. You know, half a billion lives at stake. He sounded very psychopathic. So, frankly, I don't want to try to handle him when he lands. What do you suggest?"

Dr. Junz had said, "Do you have a transcript of your talk?"

"Yes, sir." There was a few minutes searching. A sliver of film was finally found.

Dr. Junz ran it through the reader. He frowned. "This is a copy, isn't it?"

"I sent the original to the Bureau of Extra-Planetary Transportation here on Sark. I thought it would be best if they met him on the landing field with an ambulance. He's probably in a bad way."

Dr. Junz felt the impulse to agree with the young man. When the lonely analysts of the depths of space finally broke over their jobs, their psychopathies were likely to be violent.

Then he said, "But wait. You sound as though he hasn't landed yet."

The agent looked surprised. "I suppose he has, but nobody's called me about it."

"Well, call Transportation and get the details. Psychopathic or not, the details must be on our records."

The Spatio-analyst had stopped in again the next day on a last-minute check before he left the planet. He had other matters to attend to on other worlds, and he was in a moderate hurry. Almost at the doorway, he said, over his shoulder, "How's our field man doing?"

The agent said, "Oh, say—I meant to tell you. Transportation hasn't heard from him. I sent out the energy pattern of his hyperatomic motors and they say his ship is nowhere in near space. The guy must have changed his mind about landing."

Dr. Junz decided to delay his departure for twenty-four hours. The next day he was at the Bureau of Extra-Planetary Transportation in Sark City, capital of the planet. He met the Florinian bureaucracy for the first time and they shook their heads at him. They had received the message concerning the prospective landing of an analyst of the I.S.B. Oh yes, but no ship had landed.

But it was important, Dr. Junz insisted. The man was very sick. Had they not received a copy of the transcript of his talk with the local I.S.B. agent? They opened their eyes wide at him. Transcript? No one could be found who remembered receiving that. They were sorry if the man were sick, but no I.S.B. ship had landed, and no I.S.B. ship was anywhere in near space.

Dr. Junz went back to his hotel room and thought many thoughts. The new deadline for his leaving passed. He called the desk and arranged to be moved to another suite more adapted to an extended occupancy. Then he arranged an appointment with Ludigan Abel, the Trantorian Ambassador.

He spent the next day reading books on Sarkite history, and when it was time for the appointment with Abel, his heart had become a slow drumbeat of anger. He was not going to quit easily, he knew that.

The old Ambassador treated it as a social call, pumped his hand, had his mechanical bartender rolled in, and would not allow any discussion of business over the first two drinks. Junz used the opportunity for worthwhile small talk, asked about the Florinian Civil Service and received the exposition on the practical genetics of Sark. His sense of anger deepened.

Junz always remembered Abel as he had been that day. Deep-set eyes half closed under startling white eyebrows, beaky nose hovering intermittently over his goblet of wine, insunken cheeks accentuating the thinness of his face and body, and a gnarled finger slowly keeping time to some unheard music. Junz began his story, telling it with stolid economy. Abel listened carefully and without interruption.

When Junz was finished, he dabbed delicately at his lips and said, "Look now, do you know this man who has disappeared?"

"No."

"Nor met him?"

"Our field analysts are hard men to meet."

"Has he had delusions before this?"

"This is his first, according to the records at central I.S.B. offices, if it is a delusion."

"If?" The Ambassador did not follow that up. He said, "And why have you come to me?"

"For help."

"Obviously. But in what way? What can I do?"

"Let me explain. The Sarkite Bureau of Extra-Planetary Transportation has checked near space for the energy pattern of the motors of our man's ship, and there is no sign of it. They wouldn't be lying about that. I do not say that the Sarkites are above lying, but they are certainly above useless lying, and they must know that I can have the matter checked in the space of two or three hours."

"True. What then?"

"There are two times when an energy-pattern trace will fail. One, when the ship is not in near space, because it has jumped through hyperspace and is in another region of the Galaxy, and two, when it is not in space at all because it has landed on a planet. I cannot believe our man has jumped. If his statements about peril to Florina and Galactic importance are megalomanic delusions, nothing would stop him from coming to Sark to report on them. He would *not* have changed his mind and left. I've had fifteen years experience with such things. If, by any chance, his statements were sane and real, then certainly the matter would be too serious to allow him to change his mind and leave near space."

The old Trantorian lifted a finger and waved it gently. "Your conclusion then is that he is on Sark."

"Exactly. Again, there are two alternatives. First, if he *is* in the grip of a psychosis, he may have landed anywhere on the planet other than at a recognized spaceport. He may be wandering about, sick and semi-amnesiac. These things are very unusual, even for field men, but they have happened. Usually, in such a case, the fits are temporary. As they pass, the victim finds the details of his job returning first, before any personal memories at all. After all, the Spatio-analyst's job is his life. Very often the amnesiac is picked up because he wanders into a public library to look up references on Spatio-analysis."

"I see. Then you want to have me help you arrange with the Board of Librarians to have such a situation reported to you."

"No, because I don't anticipate any trouble there. I will ask that certain standard works on Spatio-analysis be placed on reserve and that any man asking for them, other than those who can prove they are native Sarkites, be held for questioning. They will agree to that because they will know, or certain of their superiors will know, that such a plan will come to nothing."

"Why?"

"Because," and Junz was speaking rapidly now, caught up in a trembling cloud of fury, "I am certain that our man landed at Sark City spaceport exactly as he planned and, sane or psychotic, was then possibly imprisoned but probably killed by the Sarkite authorities. But I'll trace that, too."

Abel put down his nearly empty glass. "Are you joking? Killed?"

"Do I look as if I were? What did you tell me just half an hour ago about Sark? Their lives, prosperity and power depend upon their control of Florina. What has all my own reading in this past twenty-four hours shown me? That the kyrt fields of Florina are the wealth of Sark. And here comes a man, sane or psychotic, it doesn't matter, who claims that something of Galactic importance has put the life of every man and woman on Florina in danger. Look at this transcript of our man's last known conversation."

Abel picked up the sliver of film that had been dashed upon his lap by Junz and accepted the reader held out to him. He ran it through slowly, his faded eyes blinking and peering at the eyepiece.

"It's not very informative."

"Of course not. It says there is a danger. It says there is horrible urgency. That's all. But it should never have been sent to the Sarkites. Even if the man were wrong, could the Sarkite government allow him to broadcast whatever madness, granting it be madness, he has in his mind and fill the Galaxy with it? Leaving out of consideration the panic it might give rise to on Florina, the interference with the production of kyrt thread, it remains a fact that the whole dirty mess of Sark-Florina political relationships would be exposed to the view of the Galaxy as a whole. Consider that they need do away with only one man to prevent all that, since I can't take action on this transcript alone and they know it. Would Sark hesitate to stop at murder in such a case? The world of such genetic experimenters as you describe would not hesitate."

"And what would you have me do? I am still, I must say, not certain." Abel seemed unmoved.

"Find out if they have killed him," said Junz grimly. "You must have an organization for espionage here. Oh, let's not quibble. I have been knocking about the Galaxy long enough to have passed my political adolescence. Get to the bottom of this while I distract their attention with my library negotiations. And when you find them out for the murderers they are, I want Trantor to see to it that no government anywhere in the Galaxy ever again has the notion it can kill an I.S.B. man and get away with it."

And there his first interview with Abel had ended.

Junz was right in one thing. The Sarkite officials were cooperative and even sympathetic as far as making library arrangements were concerned.

But he seemed right in nothing else. Months passed, and Abel's agents could find no trace of the missing field man anywhere on Sark, alive or dead.

For over eleven months that held true. Almost, Junz began to feel ready to quit. Almost, he decided to wait for the twelfth month to be done and then no more. And then the break had come and it was not from Abel at all, but from the nearly forgotten straw man he had himself set up. A report came from Sark's Public Library and Junz found himself sitting across the desk from a Florinian civil servant in the Bureau of Florinian Affairs.

The Clerk completed his mental arrangement of the case. He had turned the last sheet.

He looked up. "Now what can I do for you?"

Junz spoke with precision. "Yesterday, at 4:22 P.M., I was informed that the Florinian branch of the Public Library of Sark was holding a man for me who had attempted to consult two standard texts on Spatio-analysis and who was not a native Sarkite. I have not heard from the library since."

He continued, raising his voice to override some comment begun by the Clerk. He said, "A tele-news bulletin received over a public instrument owned by the hotel at which I maintain residence, and timed 5:05 P.M. yesterday, claimed that a member of the Florinian Patrol had been knocked unconscious in the Florinian branch of the Public Library of Sark and that three native Florinians believed responsible for the outrage were being pursued. That bulletin was not repeated in later news-broadcast summaries.

"Now I have no doubt that the two pieces of information are connected. I have no doubt that the man I want is in the custody of the Patrol. I have asked for permission to travel to Florina and been refused. I have sub-ethered Florina to send the man in question to Sark and have received no answer. I come to the Bureau of Florinian Affairs to demand action in this respect. Either I go there or he comes here."

The Clerk's lifeless voice said, "The government of Sark cannot accept ultimata from officers of the I.S.B. I have been warned by my superiors that you would probably be questioning me in these matters and I have been instructed as to the facts I am to make known to you. The man who was reported to be consulting the reserved texts, along with two companions, a Townman and a Florinian female, did indeed commit the assault you referred to, and they were pursued by the Patrol. They were not, however, apprehended."

A bitter disappointment swept over Junz. He did not bother to try to hide it. "They have escaped?"

"Not exactly. They were traced to the bakery shop of one Matt Khorov."

Junz stared. "And allowed to remain there?"

"Have you been in conference with His Excellency, Ludigan Abel, lately?"

"What has that to do with——"

"We are informed that you have been frequently seen at the Trantorian Embassy."

"I have not seen the Ambassador in a week."

"Then I suggest you see him. We allowed the criminals to remain unharmed at Khorov's shop out of respect for our delicate interstellar relationships with Trantor. I have been instructed to tell you, if it seemed necessary, that Khorov, as you probably will not be surprised to hear," and here the white face took on something uncommonly like a sneer, "is well known to our Department of Security as an agent of Trantor."

6. THE AMBASSADOR

It was ten hours before Junz had his interview with the Clerk that Terens left Khorov's bakery.

Terens kept a hand on the rough surfaces of the workers' hovels he passed, as he stepped gingerly along the alleys of the City. Except for the pale light that washed down in a periodic glimmer from the Upper City, he was in total darkness. What light might exist in Lower City would be the pearly flashes of the patrollers, marching in twos and threes.

Lower City lay like a slumbering noxious monster, its greasy coils hidden by the glittering cover of Upper City. Parts of it probably maintained a shadowy life as produce was brought in and stored for the coming day, but that was not here, not in the slums.

Terens shrank into a dusty alley (even the nightly showers of Florina could scarcely penetrate into the shadowy regions beneath the cementalloy) as the distant clank of footsteps reached him. Lights appeared, passed, and disappeared a hundred yards away.

All night long the patrollers marched back and forth. They needed only to march. The fear they inspired was strong enough to maintain order with scarcely any display of force. With no City lights, the darkness might well be cover for innumerable crawling humans, but even without patrollers as a distant threat, that danger could have been discounted. The food stores and workshops were well guarded; the luxury of Upper City was unattainable; and to steal from one another, to parasitize on one another's misery, was obviously futile.

What would be considered crime on other worlds was virtually non-existent here in the dark. The poor were at hand but had been picked clean, and the rich were strictly out of reach.

Terens flitted on, his face gleaming white when he passed under one of the openings in the cementalloy above, and he could not help but look up.

Out of reach!

Were they indeed out of reach? How many changes in attitude toward the Squires of Sark had he endured in his life? As a child, he had been but a child. Patrollers were monsters in black and silver, from whom one fled as a matter of course, whether one had done wrong or not. The Squires were misty and mystical supermen, enormously good, who lived in a paradise known as Sark and brooded watchfully and patiently over the welfare of the foolish men and women of Florina.

He would repeat every day in school: May the Spirit of the Galaxy watch over the Squires as they watch over us.

Yes, he thought now, exactly. Exactly! Let the Spirit be to them as they to us. No more and no less. His fists clenched and burned in the shadows.

When he was ten, he had written an essay for school about what he imagined life to be like on Sark. It had been a work of purely creative imagination, designed to show off his penmanship. He remembered very little, only one passage in fact. In that, he described the Squires, gathering every morning in a great hall with colors like those of the kyrt blossoms and standing about gravely in twenty-foot-high splendor, debating on the sins of the Florinians and sorrowfully somber over the necessities of winning them back to virtue.

The teacher had been very pleased, and at the end of the year, when the other boys and girls proceeded with their short sessions on reading, writing and morality, he had been promoted to a special class where he learned arithmetic, galactography, and Sarkite history. At the age of sixteen he had been taken to Sark.

He could still remember the greatness of that day, and he shuddered away from the memory. The thought of it shamed him.

Terens was approaching the outskirts of the city now. An occasional breeze brought him the heavy night odor of the kyrt blossoms. A few minutes now and he would be out in the relative safety of the open fields where there were no regular patroller beats and where, through the ragged night clouds, he would see the stars again. Even the hard, bright yellow star that was Sark's sun.

It had been *his* for half his life. When he first saw it through a spaceship's porthole as more than a star, as an unbearably bright little marble, he wanted to get on his knees. The thought that he was approaching paradise removed even the paralyzing fright of his first space flight.

He had landed on his paradise, and been delivered to an old Florinian who saw to it that he was bathed and clothed becomingly. He was brought to a large building, and on the way there his elderly guide had bowed low to a figure that passed.

"Bow!" the old one muttered angrily to the young Terens.

Terens did so and was confused. "Who was that?"

"A Squire, you ignorant farm hand."

"He! A Squire?"

He stopped dead in his tracks and had to be urged forward. It was his first sight of a Squire. Not twenty feet tall at all, but a man like men. Other Florinian youths might have recovered from the shock of such a disillusion, but not Terens. Something changed inside him, changed permanently.

In all the training he received, through all the studies in which he did so well, he never forgot that Squires were men.

For ten years he studied, and when he neither studied nor ate nor slept, he was taught to make himself useful in many small ways. He was taught to run messages and empty wastebaskets, to bow low when a Squire passed and to turn his face respectfully to the wall when a Squire's Lady passed.

For five more years he worked in the Civil Service, shifted as usual from post to post in order that his capacities might best be tested under a variety of conditions.

A plump, soft Florinian visited him once, smiling his friendship, pinching his shoulder gently, and asked what he thought of the Squires.

Terens repressed a desire to turn away and run. He wondered if his thoughts could have imprinted themselves in some obscure code upon the lines of his face. He shook his head, murmured a string of banalities on the goodness of the Squires.

But the plump one stretched his lips and said, "You don't mean that. Come to this place tonight." He gave him a small card, that crumbled and charred in a few minutes.

Terens went. He was afraid, but very curious. There he met friends of his, who looked at him with secrecy in their eyes and who met him at work later with bland glances of indifference. He listened to what they said and found that many seemed to believe what he had been hoarding in his own mind and honestly had thought to be his own creation and no one else's.

He learned that at least some Florinians thought the Squires to be vile brutes who milked Florina of its riches for their own useless good while they left the hard-working natives to wallow in ignorance and poverty. He learned that the time was coming when there would be a giant uprising against Sark and all the luxury and wealth of Florina would be appropriated by their rightful owners.

How? Terens asked. He asked it over and over again. After all, the Squires and the patrollers had the weapons.

And they told him of Trantor, of the gigantic empire that had swollen in the last few centuries until half the inhabited worlds of the Galaxy were part of it. Trantor, they said, would destroy Sark with the help of the Florinians.

But, said Terens, first to himself, then to others, if Trantor was so large and Florina so small, would not Trantor simply replace Sark as a still larger and more tyrannical master? If that were the only escape, Sark was to be endured in preference. Better the master they knew than the master they knew not.

He was derided and ejected, with threats against his life if he ever talked of what he had heard.

But some time afterward, he noted that one by one those of the conspiracy disappeared, until only the original plump one was left.

Occasionally he saw that one whisper to some newcomer here and there, but it would not have been safe to warn the young victim that he was being presented with a temptation and a test. He would have to find his own way, as had Terens.

Terens even spent some time in the Department of Security, which only a few Florinians could ever expect to accomplish. It was a short stay, for the power attached to an official in Security was such that the time spent there by any individual was even shorter than elsewhere.

But here Terens found, somewhat to his surprise, that there were real conspiracies to be countered. Somehow men and women met on Florina and plotted rebellion. Usually these were surreptitiously supported by Trantorian money. Sometimes the would-be rebels actually thought Florina would succeed unaided.

Terens meditated on the matter. His words were few, his bearing correct, but his thoughts ranged unchecked. The Squires he hated, partly because they were not twenty feet tall, partly because he might not look at their women, and partly because he had served a few, with bowed head, and had found that for all their arrogance they were foolish creatures no better educated than himself and usually far less intelligent.

Yet what alternative to this personal slavery was there? To exchange the stupid Sarkite Squire for the stupid Trantorian Imperial was useless. To expect the Florinian peasants to do something on their own was fantastically foolish. So there was no way out.

It was the problem that had been in his mind for years, as student, as petty official, and as Townman.

And then there had arisen the peculiar set of circumstances that put an undreamed-of answer in his hands in the person of this insignificant-looking man who had once been a Spatio-analyst and who now babbled of something that put the life of every man and woman on Florina in danger.

Terens was out in the fields now, where the night rain was ending and the stars gleamed wetly among the clouds. He breathed deeply of the kyrt that was Florina's treasure and her curse.

He was under no illusions. He was no longer a Townman. He was not even a free Florinian peasant. He was a criminal on the run, a fugitive who must hide.

Yet there was a burning in his mind. For the last twenty-four hours he had had in his hands the greatest weapon against Sark anyone could have dreamed of. There was no question about it. He *knew* that Rik remembered correctly, that he *had* been a Spatio-analyst once, that he *had* been psycho-probed into near brainlessness; and that what he remembered was something true and horrible and—powerful.

He was sure of it.

And now this Rik was in the thick hands of a man who pretended to be a Florinian patriot but was actually a Trantorian agent.

Terens felt the bitterness of his anger in the back of his throat. Of course this Baker was a Trantorian agent. He had

had no doubt about that from the first moment. Who else among dwellers in the Lower City would have the capital to build dummy radar ovens?

He could not allow Rik to fall into the hands of Trantor. He *would not* allow Rik to fall into the hands of Trantor. There was no limit to the risks he was prepared to run. What matter the risks? He had incurred the death penalty already.

There was a dim gleam in the corner of the sky. He would wait for dawn. The various patroller stations would have his description, of course, but it might take several minutes for his appearance to register.

And during those several minutes he would be a Townman. It would give him time to do something that even now, even now, he did not dare let his mind dwell upon.

It was ten hours after Junz had had his interview with the Clerk that he met Ludigan Abel again.

The Ambassador greeted Junz with his usual surface cordiality, yet with a definite and disturbing sensation of guilt. At their first meeting (it had been a long time ago; nearly a Standard Year had passed) he had paid no attention to the man's story *per se*. His only thought had been: Will this, or can this, help Trantor?

Trantor! It was always first in his thought, yet he was not the kind of fool who would worship a cluster of stars or the yellow emblem of Spaceship-and-Sun that the Trantorian armed forces wore. In short, he was not a patriot in the ordinary meaning of the word and Trantor as Trantor meant nothing to him.

But he did worship peace; all the more so because he was growing old and enjoyed his glass of wine, his atmosphere saturated with mild music and perfume, his afternoon nap, and his quiet wait for death. It was how he imagined all men must feel; yet all men suffered war and destruction. They died frozen in the vacuum of space, vaporized in the blast of exploding atoms, famished on a besieged and bombarded planet.

How then to enforce peace? Not by reason, certainly, nor by education. If a man could not look at the fact of peace and the fact of war and choose the former in preference to the latter, what additional argument could persuade him? What could be more eloquent as a condemnation of war than war itself? What tremendous feat of dialectic could carry with it a tenth the power of a single gutted ship with its ghastly cargo?

So then, to end the misuse of force, only one solution was left, force itself.

Abel had a map of Trantor in his study, so designed as to show the application of that force. It was a clear crystalline ovoid in which the Galactic lens was three-dimensionally laid out. Its stars were specks of white diamond dust, its nebulae, patches of light or dark fog, and near its central depths there were the few red specks that had been the Trantorian Republic.

Not "were" but "had been." The Trantorian Republic had been a mere five worlds, five hundred years earlier.

But it was a historical map, and showed the Republic at that stage only when the dial was set at zero. Advance the dial one notch and the pictured Galaxy would be as it was fifty years later and a sheaf of stars would redden about Trantor's rim.

In ten stages, half a millennium would pass and the crimson would spread like a widening bloodstain until more than half the Galaxy had fallen into the red puddle.

That red was the red of blood in more than a fanciful way. As the Trantorian Republic became the Trantorian Confederation and then the Trantorian Empire, its advance had lain through a tangled forest of gutted men, gutted ships, and gutted worlds. Yet through it all Trantor had become strong and within the red there was peace.

Now Trantor trembled at the brink of a new conversion: from Trantorian Empire to Galactic Empire and then the red would engulf all the stars and there would be universal peace—*pax Trantorica.*

Abel wanted that. Five hundred years ago, four hundred

years ago, even two hundred years ago, he would have opposed Trantor as an unpleasant nest of nasty, materialistic and aggressive people, careless of the rights of others, imperfectly democratic at home though quick to see the minor slaveries of others, and greedy without end. But the time had passed for all that.

He was not for Trantor, but for the all-embracing end that Trantor represented. So the question: How will this help Galactic peace? naturally became: How will this help Trantor?

The trouble was that in this particular instance he could not be certain. To Junz the solution was obviously a straightforward one. Trantor must uphold the I.S.B. and punish Sark.

Possibly this would be a good thing, if something could definitely be proven against Sark. Possibly not, even then. Certainly not, if nothing could be proven. But in any case Trantor could not move rashly. All the Galaxy could see that Trantor stood at the edge of Galactic dominion and there was still a chance that what yet remained of the non-Trantorian planets might unite against that. Trantor could win even such a war, but perhaps not without paying a price that would make victory only a pleasanter name for defeat.

So Trantor must never make an incautious move in this final stage of the game. Abel had therefore proceeded slowly, casting his gentle web across the labyrinth of the Civil Service and the glitter of the Sarkite Squiredom, probing with a smile and questioning without seeming to. Nor did he forget to keep the fingers of the Trantorian secret service upon Junz himself lest the angry Libairian do in a moment damage that Abel could not repair in a year.

Abel was astonished at the Libairian's persistent anger. He had asked him once, "Why does one agent concern you so?"

He had expected a speech on the integrity of the I.S.B. and the duty of all to uphold the Bureau as an instrument not of this world or that, but of all humanity. He did not get it.

Instead Junz frowned and said, "Because at the bottom of all this lies the relationship between Sark and Florina. I want to expose that relationship and destroy it."

Able felt nothing less than nausea. Always, everywhere, there was this preoccupation with single worlds that prevented, over and over again, any intelligent concentration upon the problem of Galactic unity. Certainly social injustices existed here and there. Certainly they seemed sometimes impossible to stomach. But who could imagine that such injustice could be solved on any scale less than Galactic? First, there must be an end to war and national rivalry and only then could one turn to the internal miseries that, after all, had external conflict as their chief cause.

And Junz was not even of Florina. He had not even that cause for emotionalized shortsightedness.

Abel said, "What is Florina to you?"

Junz hesitated. He said, "I feel a kinship."

"But you are a Libairian. Or at least that is my impression."

"I am, but there lies the kinship. We are both extremes in a Galaxy of the average."

"Extremes? I don't understand."

Junz said, "In skin pigmentation. They are unusually pale. We are unusually dark. It means something. It binds us together. It gives us something in common. It seems to me our ancestors must have had long histories of being different, even of being excluded from the social majority. We are unfortunate whites and darks, brothers in being different."

By that time, under Abel's astonished gaze, Junz stumbled to a halt. The subject had never been sounded again.

And now, after a year, without warning, without any previous intimations, just at the point where, perhaps, a quiet trailing end might be expected of the whole wretched matter and where even Junz showed signs of flagging zeal, it all exploded.

He faced a different Junz now, one whose anger was not

reserved for Sark, but spilled and overflowed onto Abel as well.

"It is not," the Libairian said in part, "that I resent the fact that your agents have been set upon my heels. Presumably you are cautious and must rely on nothing and nobody. Good, as far as that goes. But why was I not informed as soon as our man was located?"

Abel's hand smoothed the warm fabric of the arm of his chair. "Matters are complicated. Always complicated. I had arranged that any report on an unauthorized seeker after Spatio-analytic data be reported to certain of my own agents as well as to you. I even thought you might need protection. But on Florina——"

Junz said bitterly, "Yes. We were fools not to have considered that. We spent nearly a year proving we could find him nowhere on Sark. He *had* to be on Florina and we were blind to that. In any case, we have him now. Or you have, and presumably it will be arranged to have me see him?"

Abel did not answer directly. He said, "You say they told you this man Khorov was a Trantorian agent?"

"Isn't he? Why should they lie? Or are they misinformed?"

"They neither lie nor are they misinformed. He has been an agent of ours for a decade, and it is disturbing to me that they were aware of it. It makes me wonder what more they know of us and how shaky our structure may be altogether. But doesn't it make you wonder why they told you baldly that he was one of our men?"

"Because it was the truth, I imagine, and to keep me, once and for all, from embarrassing them by further demands that could only cause trouble between themselves and Trantor."

"Truth is a discredited commodity among diplomats and what greater trouble can they cause for themselves than to let us know the extent of their knowledge about us: to give us the opportunity before it is too late, to draw in our damaged net, mend it and put it out whole again?"

"Then answer your own question."

"I say they told you of their knowledge of Khorov's true identity as a gesture of triumph. They knew that the fact of their knowledge could no longer either help or harm them since I have known for twelve hours that they knew Khorov was one of our men."

"But how?"

"By the most unmistakable hint possible. Listen! Twelve hours ago Matt Khorov, agent for Trantor, was killed by a member of the Florinian Patrol. The two Florinians he held at the time, a woman and the man who, in all probability, is the field man you have been seeking, are gone, vanished. Presumably they are in the hands of the Squires."

Junz cried out and half rose from his seat.

Abel lifted a glass of wine to his lips calmly and said, "There is nothing I can do officially. The dead man was a Florinian and those who have vanished, for all we can prove to the contrary, are likewise Florinians. So, you see, we have been badly outplayed, and are now being mocked in addition."

7. THE PATROLLER

Rik saw the Baker killed. He saw him crumple without a sound, his chest driven in and charred into smoking ruins under the silent push of the blaster. It was a sight that drowned out for him most of what had preceded and almost all that had followed.

There was the dim memory of the patroller's first approach, of the quiet but terribly intent manner in which he had drawn his weapon. The Baker had looked up and shaped his lips for one last word that he had no time to utter. Then the deed was done, there was the rushing of blood in Rik's ears and the wild screaming scramble of the mob swirling in all directions, like a river in flood.

For a moment it negated the improvement Rik's mind had made in those last few hours of sleep. The patroller had plunged toward him, throwing himself forward upon yelling men and women as though they were a viscous sea of mud he would have to slog through. Rik and Lona turned with the current and were carried away. There were eddies and subcurrents, turning and quivering as the flying patrollers' cars began to hover overhead. Valona urged Rik forward, ever outward to the outskirts of the City. For a while he was the frightened child of yesterday, not the almost adult of that morning.

He had awakened that morning in the grayness of a dawn he could not see in the windowless room he slept in. For long minutes he lay there, inspecting his mind. Something had healed during the night; something had knit together and become whole. It had been getting ready to happen ever since the moment, two days before, when he had begun to "remember." The process had been proceeding all through yesterday. The trip to the Upper City and the library, the attack upon the patroller and the flight that followed, the encounter with Baker—it had all acted upon him like a ferment. The shriveled fibers of his mind, so long dormant, had been seized and stretched, forced into an aching activity, and now, after a sleep, there was a feeble pulsing about them.

He thought of space and the stars, of long, long, lonely stretches and great silences.

Finally he turned his head to one side and said, "Lona."

She snapped awake, lifting herself to an elbow, peering in his direction.

"Rik?"

"Here I am, Lona."

"Are you all right?"

"Sure." He couldn't hold down his excitement. "I feel fine, Lona. Listen! I remember more. I was in a ship and I know exactly——"

But she wasn't listening to him. She slipped into her dress and with her back to him smoothed the seam shut down the front and then fumbled nervously with her belt.

She tiptoed toward him. "I didn't mean to sleep, Rik. I tried to stay awake."

Rik felt the infection of her nervousness. He said, "Is something wrong?"

"Sh, don't speak so loudly. It's all right."

"Where's the Townman?"

"He's not here. He—he had to leave. Why don't you go back to sleep, Rik?"

He pushed her consoling arm aside. "I'm all right. I don't want to sleep. I wanted to tell the Townman about my ship."

But the Townman wasn't there and Valona would not listen. Rik subsided and for the first time felt actively annoyed with Valona. She treated him as though he were a child and he was beginning to feel like a man.

A light entered the room and the broad figure of the Baker entered with it. Rik blinked at him and was, for a moment, daunted. He did not entirely object when Valona's comforting arm stole about his shoulder.

The Baker's thick lips stretched in a smile. "You're early awake."

Neither answered.

The Baker said, "It's just as well. You'll be moving today."

Valona's mouth was dry. She said, "You'll not be giving us to the patrollers?"

She remembered the way he had looked at Rik after the Townman had left. He was still looking at Rik; only at Rik.

"Not to the patrollers," he said. "The proper people have been informed and you'll be safe enough."

He left, and when he returned shortly thereafter he brought food, clothes and two basins of water. The clothes were new and looked completely strange.

He watched them as they ate, saying, "I'm going to give you new names and new histories. You're to listen, and I don't want you to forget. You're not Florinians, do you understand? You're brother and sister from the planet Wotex. You've been visiting Florina——"

He went on, supplying details, asking questions, listening to their answers.

Rik was pleased to be able to demonstrate the workings

of his memory, his easy ability to learn, but Valona's eyes were dark with worry.

The Baker was not blind to that. He said to the girl, "If you give me the least trouble I'll send him on alone and leave you behind."

Valona's strong hands clenched spasmodically. "I will give you no trouble."

It was well into the morning when the Baker rose to his feet and said, "Let's go!"

His last action was to place little black sheets of limp leatherette in their breast pockets.

Once outside, Rik looked with astonishment at what he could see of himself. He did not know clothing could be so complicated. The Baker had helped him get it on, but who would help him take it off? Valona didn't look like a farm girl at all. Even her legs were covered with thin material, and her shoes were raised at the heels so that she had to balance carefully when she walked.

Passers-by gathered, staring and gawking, calling to one another. Mostly they were children, marketing women, and skulking, ragged idlers. The Baker seemed oblivious to them. He carried a thick stick which found itself occasionally, as though by accident, between the legs of any who pressed too closely.

And then, when they were still only a hundred yards from the bakery and had made but one turning, the outer reaches of the surrounding crowd swirled excitedly and Rik made out the black and silver of a patroller.

That was when it happened. The weapon, the blast, and again a wild flight. Was there ever a time when fear had not been with him, when the shadow of the patroller had not been behind him?

They found themselves in the squalor of one of the outlying districts of the City. Valona was panting harshly; her new dress bore the wet stains of perspiration.

Rik gasped, "I can't run any more."

"We've got to."

"Not like this. Listen." He pulled back firmly against the pressure of the girl's grip. "Listen to me."

The fright and panic were leaving him.

He said, "Why don't we go on and do what the Baker wanted us to do?"

She said, "How do you know what he wanted us to do?" She was anxious. She wanted to keep moving.

He said, "We were to pretend we were from another world and he gave us these." Rik was excited. He pulled the little rectangle out of his pocket, staring at both sides and trying to open it as though it were a booklet.

He couldn't. It was a single sheet. He felt about the edges and as his fingers closed at one corner he heard, or rather felt, something give, and the side toward him turned a startling milky white. The close wording on the new surface was difficult to understand though he began carefully making out the syllables.

Finally he said, "It's a passport."

"What's that?"

"Something to get us away." He was sure of it. It had popped into his head. A single word, "passport," like that. "Don't you see? He was going to have us leave Florina. On a ship. Let's go through with that."

She said, "No. They stopped him. They killed him. We couldn't, Rik, we couldn't."

He was urgent about it. He was nearly babbling. "But it would be the best thing to do. They wouldn't be expecting us to do that. And we wouldn't go on the ship he wanted us to go on. They'd be watching that. We'd go on another ship. Any other ship."

A ship. Any ship. The words rang in his ears. Whether his idea was a good one or not, he didn't care. He wanted to be on a ship. He wanted to be in space.

"*Please*, Lona!"

She said, "All right. If you really think so. I know where the spaceport is. When I was a little girl we used to go there on idle-days sometimes and watch from far away to see the ships shoot upward."

They were on their way again, and only a slight uneasiness scratched vainly at the gateway of Rik's consciousness. Some memory not of the far past but of the very near past; something he should remember and could not; could just barely not. Something.

He drowned it in the thought of the ship that waited for them.

The Florinian at the entry gate was having his fill of excitement that day, but it was excitement at long distance. There had been the wild stories of the previous evening, telling of patrollers attacked and of daring escapes. By this morning the stories had expanded and there were whispers of patrollers killed.

He dared not leave his post, but he craned his neck and watched the air-cars pass, and the grim-faced patrollers leave, as the spaceport contingent was cut and cut till it was almost nothing.

They were filling the City with patrollers, he thought, and was at once frightened and drunkenly uplifted. Why should it make him happy to think of patrollers being killed? They never bothered him. At least not much. He had a good job. It wasn't as though he was a stupid peasant.

But he was happy.

He scarcely had time for the couple before him, uncomfortable and perspiring in the outlandish clothing that marked them at once as foreigners. The woman was holding a passport through the slot.

A glance at her, a glance at the passport, a glance at the list of reservations. He pressed the appropriate button and two translucent ribbons of film sprang out at them.

"Go on," he said impatiently. "Get them on your wrists and move on."

"Which ship is ours?" asked the woman in a polite whisper.

That pleased him. Foreigners were infrequent at the Florinian spaceport. In recent years they had grown more and more infrequent. But when they did come they were neither patrollers nor Squires. They didn't seem to realize you were only a Florinian yourself and they spoke to you politely.

It made him feel two inches taller. He said, "You'll find it in Berth 17, madam. I wish you a pleasant trip to Wotex." He said it in the grand manner.

He then returned to his task of putting in surreptitious calls to friends in the City for more information and of trying, even more unobtrusively, to tap private power-beam conversations in Upper City.

It was hours before he found out that he had made a horrible mistake.

Rik said, "Lona!"

He tugged at her elbow, pointed quickly and whispered, "That one!"

Valona looked at the indicated ship doubtfully. It was much smaller than the ship in Berth 17, for which their tickets held good. It looked more burnished. Four air locks yawned open and the main port gaped, with a ramp leading from it like an outstretched tongue reaching to ground level.

Rik said, "They're airing it. They usually air passenger ships before flight to get rid of the accumulated odor of canned oxygen, used and reused."

Valona stared at him. "How do you know?"

Rik felt a sprig of vanity grow within himself. "I just know. You see, there wouldn't be anyone in it now. It isn't comfortable, with the draft on."

He looked about uneasily. "I don't know why there aren't more people about, though. Was it like this when you used to watch it?"

Valona thought not, but she could scarcely remember. Childhood memories were far away.

There was not a patroller in sight as they walked up the ramp on quivering legs. What figures they could see were civilian employees, intent on their own jobs, and small in the distance.

Moving air cut through them as they stepped into the

hold and Valona's dress bellied so that she had to bring her hands down to keep the hemline within bounds.

"Is it always like this?" she asked. She had never been on a spaceship before; never dreamed of being on one. Her lips stuck together and her heart pounded.

Rik said, "No. Just during aeration."

He walked joyfully over the hard metallite passageways, inspecting the empty rooms eagerly.

"Here," he said. It was the galley.

He spoke rapidly. "It isn't food so much. We can get along without food for quite a while. It's water."

He rummaged through the neat and compact nestings of utensils and came up with a large, capped container. He looked about for the water tap, muttered a breathless hope that they had not neglected to fill the water tanks, then grinned his relief when the soft sound of pumps came, and the steady gush of liquid.

"Now just take some of the cans. Not too many. We don't want them to take notice."

Rik tried desperately to think of ways of countering discovery. Again he groped for something he could not quite remember. Occasionally he still ran into those gaps in his thought and, cowardlike, he avoided them, denied their existence.

He found a small room devoted to fire-fighting equipment, emergency medical and surgical supplies, and welding equipment.

He said with a certain lack of confidence, "They won't be in here, except in emergencies. Are you afraid, Lona?"

"I won't be afraid with you, Rik," she said humbly. Two days before, no, twelve hours before, it had been the other way around. But on board ship, by some transmutation of personality she did not question, it was Rik who was the adult, she who was the child.

He said, "We won't be able to use lights because they would notice the power drain, and to use the toilets, we'll have to wait for rest periods and try to get out past any of the night crew."

The draft cut off suddenly. Its cold touch on their faces was no longer there and the soft, steady humming sound, that had distantly accompanied it, stopped and left a large silence to fill its place.

Rik said, "They'll be boarding soon, and then we'll be out in space."

Valona had never seen such joy in Rik's face. He was a lover going to meet his love.

If Rik had felt a man on awaking that dawn, he was a giant now, his arms stretching the length of the Galaxy. The stars were his marbles, and the nebulae were cobwebs to brush away.

He was on a ship! Memories rushed back continuously in a long flood and others left to make room. He was forgetting the kyrt fields and the mill and Valona crooning to him in the dark. They were only momentary breaks in a pattern that was now returning with its raveled ends slowly knitting.

It was the ship!

If they had put him on a ship long ago, he wouldn't have had to wait so long for his burnt-out brain cells to heal themselves.

He spoke softly to Valona in the darkness. "Now don't worry. You'll feel a vibration and hear a noise but that will be just the motors. There'll be a heavy weight on you. That's acceleration."

There was no common Florinian word for the concept and he used another word for it, one that came easily to mind. Valona did not understand.

She said, "Will it hurt?"

He said, "It will be very uncomfortable, because we don't have anti-acceleration gear to take up the pressure, but it won't last. Just stand against this wall, and when you feel yourself being pushed against it, relax. See, it's beginning."

He had picked the right wall, and as the thrumming of the thrusting hyperatomics swelled, the apparent gravity shifted, and what had been a vertical wall seemed to grow more and more diagonal.

Valona whimpered once, then lapsed into a hard-breathing silence. Their throats rasped as their chest walls, unprotected by straps and hydraulic absorbers, labored to free their lungs sufficiently for just a little air intake.

Rik managed to pant out words, any words that might let Valona know he was there and ease the terrible fear of the unknown that he knew must be filling her. It was only a ship, only a wonderful ship, but she had never been on a ship before.

He said, "There's the jump, of course, when we go through hyperspace and cut across most of the distance between the stars all at once. That won't bother you at all. You won't even know it happened. It's nothing compared to this. Just a little twitch in your insides and it's over." He got the words out syllable by grunted syllable. It took a long time.

Slowly, the weight on their chests lifted and the invisible chain holding them to the wall stretched and dropped off. They fell, panting, to the floor.

Finally Valona said, "Are you hurt, Rik?"

"I, hurt?" He managed a laugh. He had not caught his breath yet, but he laughed at the thought that he could be hurt on a ship.

He said, "I lived on a ship for years once. I didn't land on a planet for months at a time."

"Why?" she asked. She had crawled closer and put a hand to his cheek, making sure he was there.

He put his arm about her shoulder, and she rested within it quietly, accepting the reversal.

"Why?" she asked.

Rik could not remember why. He had done it; he had hated to land on a planet. For some reason it had been necessary to stay in space, but he could not remember why. Again he dodged the gap.

He said, "I had a job."

"Yes," she said. "You analyzed Nothing."

"That's right." He was pleased. "That's exactly what I did. Do you know what that means?"

"No."

He didn't expect her to understand, but he had to talk. He had to revel in memory, to delight drunkenly in the fact that he could call up past facts at the flick of a mental finger.

He said, "You see, all the material in the universe is made up of a hundred different kinds of substances. We call those substances elements. Iron and copper are elements."

"I thought they were metals."

"So they are, and elements too. Also oxygen, and nitrogen, carbon and palladium. Most important of all, hydrogen and helium. They're the simplest and most common."

"I never heard of those," Valona said wistfully.

"Ninety-five per cent of the universe is hydrogen and most of the rest is helium. Even space."

"I was once told," said Valona, "that space was a vacuum. They said that meant there was nothing there. Was that wrong?"

"Not quite. There's *almost* nothing there. But you see, I was a Spatio-analyst, which meant that I went about through space collecting the extremely small amounts of elements there and analyzing them. That is, I decided how much was hydrogen, how much helium and how much other elements."

"Why?"

"Well, that's complicated. You see, the arrangement of elements isn't the same everywhere in space. In some regions there is a little more helium than normal; in other places, more sodium than normal; and so on. These regions of special analytic make-up wind through space like currents. That's what they call them. They're the currents of space. It's important to know how these currents are arranged because that might explain how the universe was created and how it developed."

"How would it explain that?"

Rik hesitated. "Nobody knows exactly."

He hurried on, embarrassed that this immense store of knowledge in which his mind was thankfully wallowing could come so easily to an end marked "unknown" under the questioning of . . . of . . . It suddenly occurred to him that Valona, after all, was nothing but a Florinian peasant girl.

He said, "Then, again, we find out the density, you know, the thickness, of this space gas in all regions of the Galaxy. It's different in different places and we have to know exactly what it is in order to allow ships to calculate exactly how to jump through hyperspace. It's like . . ." His voice died away.

Valona stiffened and waited uneasily for him to continue, but only silence followed. Her voice sounded hoarsely in the complete darkness.

"Rik? What's wrong, Rik?"

Still silence. Her hands groped to his shoulders, shaking him. "Rik! Rik!"

And it was the voice of the old Rik, somehow, that answered. It was weak, frightened, its joy and confidence vanished.

"Lona. We did something wrong."

"What's the matter? We did what wrong?"

The memory of the scene in which the patroller had shot down the Baker was in his mind, etched hard and clear, as though called back by his exact memory of so many other things.

He said, "We shouldn't have run away. We shouldn't be here on this ship."

He was shivering uncontrollably, and Valona tried futilely to wipe the moisture from his forehead with her hand.

"Why?" she demanded. "Why?"

"Because we should have known that if the Baker were willing to take us out in daylight he expected no trouble from patrollers. Do you remember the patroller? The one who shot the Baker?"

"Yes."

"Do you remember his face?"

"I didn't dare look."

"I did, and there was something queer, but I didn't think. I didn't think. Lona, that *wasn't* a patroller. It was the Townman, Lona. It was the Townman dressed like a patroller."

8. THE LADY

Samia of Fife was five feet tall, exactly, and all sixty inches of her were in a state of quivering exasperation. She weighed one and a half pounds per inch and, at the moment, each of her ninety pounds represented sixteen ounces of solid anger.

She stepped quickly from end to end of the room, her dark hair piled in high masses, her spiked heels lending a spurious height and her narrow chin, with its pronounced cleft, trembling.

She said, "Oh no. He wouldn't do it to me. He *couldn't* do it to me. Captain!"

Her voice was sharp and carried the weight of authority. Captain Racety bowed with the storm. "My Lady?"

To any Florinian, of course, Captain Racety would have been a "Squire." Simply that. To any Florinian, all Sarkites were Squires. But to the Sarkites there were Squires and *real* Squires. The Captain was simply a Squire. Samia of

Fife was a *real* Squire; or the feminine equivalent of one, which amounted to the same thing.

"My Lady?" he asked.

She said, "I am not to be ordered about. I am of age. I am my own mistress. I choose to remain here."

The Captain said carefully, "Please to understand, my Lady, that no orders of mine are involved. My advice was not asked. I have been told plainly and flatly what I am to do."

He fumbled for the copy of his orders halfheartedly. He had tried to present her with the evidence twice before and she had refused to consider it, as though by not looking she could continue, with a clear conscience, to deny where his duty lay.

She said once again, exactly as before, "I am not interested in your orders."

She turned away with a ringing of her heels and moved rapidly away from him.

He followed and said softly, "The orders include directions to the effect that, if you are not willing to come, I am, if you will excuse my saying so, to have you carried to the ship."

She whirled. "You wouldn't dare do such a thing."

"When I consider," said the Captain, "who it is who has ordered me to do it, I would dare anything."

She tried cajolery. "Surely, Captain, there is no real danger. This is quite ridiculous, entirely mad. The City is peaceful. All that has happened is that one patroller was knocked down yesterday afternoon in the library. Really!"

"Another patroller was killed this dawn, again by Florinian attack."

That rocked her, but her olive skin grew dusky and her black eyes flashed. "What has that to do with me? I am not a patroller."

"My Lady, the ship is being prepared right now. It will leave shortly. You will have to be on it."

"And my work? My research? Do you realize——No, you wouldn't realize."

The Captain said nothing. She had turned from him. Her gleaming dress of copper kyrt, with its strands of milky silver, set off the extraordinary warm smoothness of her shoulders and upper arms. Captain Racety looked at her with something more than the bald courtesy and humble objectivity a mere Sarkite owed such a great Lady. He wondered why such an entirely desirable bite-size morsel should choose to spend her time in mimicking the scholarly pursuits of a university don.

Samia knew well that her earnest scholarship made her an object of mild derision to people who were accustomed to thinking of the aristocratic Ladies of Sark as devoted entirely to the glitter of polite society and, eventually, acting as incubators for at least, but not more than, two future Squires of Sark. She didn't care.

They would come to her and say, "Are you really writing a book, Samia?" and ask to see it, and giggle.

Those were the women. The men were even worse, with their gentle condescension and obvious conviction that it would only take a glance from themselves or a man's arm about her waist to cure her of her nonsense and turn her mind to things of real importance.

It had begun as far back, almost, as she could remember, because she had alwys been in love with kyrt, whereas most people took it for granted. Kyrt! The king, emperor, *god* of fabrics. There was no metaphor strong enough.

Chemically, it was nothing more than a variety of cellulose. The chemists swore to that. Yet with all their instruments and theories they had never yet explained why on Florina, and only on Florina in all the Galaxy, cellulose became kyrt. It was a matter of the physical state; that's what they said. But ask them exactly in what way the physical state varied from that of ordinary cellulose and they were mute.

She had learned ignorance originally from her nurse.

"Why does it shine, Nanny?"

"Because it's kyrt, Miakins."

"Why don't other things shine so, Nanny?"

"Other things aren't kyrt, Miakins."

There you had it. A two-volume monograph on the subject had been written only three years before. She had read it carefully and it could all have been boiled down to her Nanny's explanation. Kyrt was kyrt because it was kyrt. Things that weren't kyrt, weren't kyrt because they weren't kyrt.

Of course kyrt didn't really shine of itself but, properly spun, it would gleam metallically in the sun in a variety of colors or in all colors at once. Another form of treatment could impart a diamond sparkle to the thread. It could be made, with little effort, completely impervious to heat up to 600 degrees Centigrade, and quite inert to almost all chemicals. Its fibers could be spun finer than the most delicate synthetics and those same fibers had a tensile strength no steel alloy known could dupliate.

It had more uses, more versatility than any substance known to man. If it were not so expensive it could be used to replace glass, metal, or plastic in any of infinite industrial applications. As it was, it was the only material used for cross hairs on optical equipment, as molds in the casting of hydrochrons used in hyperatomic motors, and as light-weight, long-lived webbing where metal was too brittle or too heavy or both.

But this was, as said, small-scale use, since use in quantity was prohibitive. Actually the kyrt harvest of Florina went into the manufacture of cloth that was used for the most fabulous garments in Galactic history. Florina clothed the aristocracy of a million worlds, and the kyrt harvest of the one world, Florina, had to be spread thin for that. Twenty women on a world might have outfits in kyrt; two thousand more might have a holiday jacket of the material, or perhaps a pair of gloves. Twenty million more watched from a distance and wished.

The million worlds of the Galaxy shared a slang expression for the snob. It was the only idiom in the language that was easily and exactly understood everywhere. It went: "You'd think she blew her nose in kyrt!"

When Samia was older she went to her father.

"What is kyrt, Daddy?"

"It's your bread and butter, Mia."

"Mine?"

"Not just yours, Mia. It's Sark's bread and butter."

Of course! She learned the reason for that easily enough. Not a world in the Galaxy but had tried to grow kyrt on its own soil. At first Sark had applied the death penalty to anyone, native or foreign, caught smuggling kyrt seed out of the planet. That had not prevented successful smuggling, and as the centuries passed, and the truth dawned on Sark, that law had been abolished. Men from anywhere were welcome to kyrt seed at the price, of course (weight for weight), of finished kyrt cloth.

They might have it, because it turned out that kyrt grown anywhere in the Galaxy but on Florina was simply cellulose. White, flat, weak and useless. Not even honest cotton.

Was it something in the soil? Something in the characteristics of the radiation of Florina's sun? Something about the bacteria make-up of Florinian life? It had all been tried. Samples of Florinian soil had been taken. Artificial arc lights duplicating the known spectrum of Florina's sun had been constructed. Foreign soil had been infected with Florinian bacteria. And always the kyrt grew white, flat, weak and useless.

There was so much to be said about kyrt that had never been said. Material other than that contained in technical reports or in research papers or even in travel books. For five years Samia had been dreaming of writing a real book about the story of kyrt; of the land it grew on and of the people who grew it.

It was a dream surrounded by mocking laughter, but she held to it. She had insisted on traveling to Florina. She was going to spend a season in the fields and a few months in the mills. She was going to——

But what did it matter what she was going to do? She was being ordered back.

With the sudden impulsiveness that marked her every act

she made her decision. She would be able to fight this on Sark. Grimly she promised herself she would be back on Florina in a week.

She turned to the Captain and said coolly, "When do we leave, sir?"

Samia remained at the observation port for as long as Florina was a visible globe. It was a green, springlike world, much pleasanter than Sark in climate. She had looked forward to studying the natives. She didn't like the Florinians on Sark, sapless men who dared not look at her but turned away when she passed, in accordance with the law. On their own world, however, the natives, by universal report, were happy and carefree. Irresponsible, of course, and like children, but they had charm.

Captain Racety interrupted her thoughts. He said, "My Lady, would you retire to your room?"

She looked up, a tiny vertical crease between her eyes. "What new orders have you received, Captain? Am I a prisoner?"

"Of course not. Merely a precaution. The space field was unusually empty before the take-off. It seems that another killing had taken place, again by a Florinian, and the field's patroller contingent had joined the rest on a man hunt through the City."

"And the connection of that with myself?"

"It is only that under the circumstances, which I ought to have reacted to by placing a guard of my own (I do not minimize my own offense), unauthorized persons may have boarded the ship."

"For what reason?"

"I could not say, but scarcely to do our pleasure."

"You are romancing, Captain."

"I am afraid not, my Lady. Our energometrics were, of course, useless within planetary distance of Florina's sun, but that is not the case now and I am afraid there is definite excess heat radiation from Emergency Stores."

"Are you serious?"

The Captain's lean, expressionless face regarded her aloofly for a moment. He said, "The radiation is equivalent to that which would be given off by two ordinary people."

"Or a heating unit someone forgot to turn off."

"There is no drain on our power supply, my Lady. We are ready to investigate, my Lady, and ask only that you first retire to your room."

She nodded silently and left the room. Two minutes later his calm voice spoke unhurriedly into the communi-tube. "Break into Emergency Stores."

Myrlyn Terens, had he released his taut nerves the slightest, might easily, and even thankfully, have gone into hysteria. He had been a trifle too late in returning to the bakery. They had already left it and it was only by good fortune that he met them in the street. His next action had been dictated; it was in no way a matter of free choice; and the Baker lay quite horribly dead before him.

Afterward, with the crowd swirling, Rik and Valona melting into the crowd, and the air-cars of the patrollers, the *real* patrollers, beginning to put in their vulture appearance, what could he do?

His first impulse to race after Rik he quickly fought down. It would do no good. He would never find them, and there was too great a chance that the patrollers would not miss him. He scurried in another direction, toward the bakery.

His only chance lay in the patroller organization itself. There had been generations of a quiet life. At least there had been no Florinian revolts to speak of in two centuries. The institution of the Townman (he grinned savagely at the thought) had worked wonders and the patrollers had only perfunctory police duties since. They lacked the fine-pointed teamwork that would have developed under more strenuous conditions.

It had been possible for him to walk into a patroller station at dawn, where his description must have already been sent, though obviously it had not been much regarded. The lone patroller on duty was a mixture of indifference and sulkiness. Terens had been asked to state his business, but his business included a plastic two-by-four he had wrenched from the side of a crazy hovel at the outskirts of town.

He had brought it down upon the patroller's skull, changed clothing and weapons. The list of his crimes was already so formidable that it did not bother him in the least to discover that the patroller had been killed, not stunned.

Yet he was still at large and the rusty machinery of patroller justice had so far creaked after him in vain.

He was at the bakery. The Baker's elderly helper, standing in the doorway in a vain attempt to peer knowledge of the disturbance into himself, squeaked thinly at the sight of the dread black and silver of patrollerhood and oozed back into his shop.

The Townman lunged after him, crumpling the man's loose, floury collar into his pudgy fist and twisting. "Where was the Baker going?"

The old man's lips yawned open, but no sound came.

The Townman said, "I killed a man two minutes ago. I don't care if I kill another."

"Please. Please. I do not know, sir."

"You will die for not knowing."

"But he did not tell me. He made some sort of reservations."

"You have overheard so much, have you? What else did you overhear?"

"He mentioned Wotex once. I think the reservations were on a spaceship."

Terens thrust him away.

He would have to wait. He would have to let the worst of the excitement outside die. He would have to risk the arrival of real patrollers at the bakery.

But not for long. Not for long. He could guess what his erstwhile companions would do. Rik was unpredictable, of course, but Valona was an intelligent girl. From the way they ran, they must have taken him for a patroller indeed and Valona was sure to decide that their only safety lay in continuing the flight that the Baker had begun for them.

The Baker had made reservations for them. A spaceship would be waiting. They would be there.

And he would have to be there first.

There was this about the desperation of the situation. Nothing more mattered. If he lost Rik, if he lost that potential weapon against the tyrants of Sark, his life was a small additional loss.

So when he left, it was without a qualm, though it was broad daylight, though the patrollers must know by now it was a man in patroller uniform they sought, and though two air-cars were in easy sight.

Terens knew the spaceport that would be involved. There was only one of its type on the planet. There were a dozen tiny ones in Upper City for the private use of space-yachts and there were hundreds all over the planet for the exclusive use of the ungainly freighters that carried gigantic bolts of kyrt cloth to Sark, and machinery and simple consumer goods back. But among all those there was only one spaceport for the use of ordinary travelers, for the poorer Sarkites, Florinian civil servants and the few foreigners who managed to obtain permission to visit Florina.

The Florinian at the port's entry gate observed Terens' approach with every symptom of lively interest. The vacuum that surrounded him had grown insupportable.

"Greetings, sir," he said. There was a slyly eager tone in his voice. After all, patrollers were being killed. "Considerable excitement in the City, isn't there?"

Terens did not rise to the bait. He had drawn the arced visor of his hat low and buttoned the uppermost button of the tunic.

Gruffly he snapped, "Did two persons, a man and a woman, enter the port recently en route to Wotex?"

The gatekeeper looked startled. For a moment he gulped and then, in a considerably subdued tone, said, "Yes, Officer. About half an hour ago. Maybe less." He reddened suddenly. "Is there any connection between them and—Officer, they had reservations which were entirely in order. I wouldn't let foreigners through without proper authority."

Terens ignored that. Proper authority! The Baker had managed to establish that in the course of a night. Galaxy, he wondered, how deeply into the Sarkite administration did the Trantorian espionage organization go?

"What names did they give?"

"Gareth and Hansa Barne."

"Has their ship left? Quickly!"

"N-no, sir."

"What berth?"

"Seventeen."

Terens forced himself to refrain from running, but his walk was little short of that. Had there been a real patroller in sight that rapid, undignified half run of his would have been his last trip in freedom.

A spaceman in officer's uniform stood at the ship's main air lock.

Terens panted a little. He said, "Have Gareth and Hansa Barne boarded ship?"

"No, they haven't," said the spaceman phlegmatically. He was a Sarkite and a patroller was only another man in uniform to him. "Do you have a message from them?"

With cracking patience Terens said, "They *haven't* boarded!"

"That's what I've said. And we're not waiting for them. We leave on schedule, with or without them."

Terens turned away.

He was at the gatekeeper's booth again. "Have they left?"

"Left? Who, sir?"

"The Barnes. The ones for Wotex. They're not on board ship. Did they leave?"

"No, sir. Not to my knowledge."

"What about the other gates?"

"They're not exits, sir. This is the only exit."

"Check them, you miserable idiot."

The gatekeeper lifted the communi-tube in a state of

panic. No patroller had ever spoken to him so in anger and he dreaded the results. In two minutes he put it down.

He said, "No one has left, sir."

Terens stared at him. Under his black hat his sandy hair was damping against his skull and down each cheek there was the gleaming mark of perspiration.

He said, "Has any ship left the port since they entered?"

The gatekeeper consulted the schedule. "One," he said, "the liner *Endeavor*."

Volubly he went on, eager to gain favor with the angry patroller by volunteering information. "The *Endeavor* is making a special trip to Sark to carry the Lady Samia of Fife back from Florina."

He did not bother to describe exactly by what refined manner of eavesdropping he had managed to acquaint himself with the "confidential report."

But to Terens now, nothing mattered.

He backed slowly away. Eliminate the impossible and whatever remained, however improbable, was the truth. Rik and Valona had entered the spaceport. They had not been captured or the gatekeeper would certainly have known about it. They were not simply wandering about the port, or they would by now have been captured. They were not on the ship for which they had tickets. They had not left the field. The only object that had left the field was the *Endeavor*. Therefore, on it, possibly as captives, possibly as stowaways, were Rik and Valona.

And the two were equivalent. If they were stowaways they would soon be captives. Only a Florinian peasant girl and a mindwrecked creature would fail to realize that one could not stow away on a modern spaceship.

And of all spaceships to choose, they chose that which carried the daughter of the Squire of Fife.

The Squire of Fife!

9. THE SQUIRE

The Squire of Fife was the most important individual on Sark and for that reason did not like to be seen standing. Like his daughter, he was short, but unlike her, he was not perfectly proportioned, since most of the shortness lay in his legs. His torso was even beefy, and his head was undoubtedly majestic, but his body was fixed upon stubby legs that were forced into a ponderous waddle to carry their load.

So he sat behind a desk and except for his daughter and personal servants and, when she had been alive, his wife, none saw him in any other position.

There he looked the man he was. His large head, with its wide, nearly lipless mouth, broad, large-nostriled nose, and pointed, cleft chin, could look benign and inflexible in turn, with equal ease. His hair, brushed rigidly back and, in careless disregard for fashion, falling nearly to his shoulders, was blue-black, untouched by gray. A shadowy blue marked the regions of his cheeks, lips and chin where his

Florinian barber twice daily battled the stubborn growth of facial hair.

The Squire was posing and he knew it. He had schooled expression out of his face and allowed his hands, broad, strong and short-fingered, to remain loosely clasped on a desk whose smooth, polished surface was completely bare. There wasn't a paper on it, no communi-tube, no ornament. By its very simplicity the Squire's own presence was emphasized.

He spoke to his pale, fish-white secretary with the special lifeless tone he reserved for mechanical appliances and Florinian civil servants. "I presume all have accepted?"

He had no real doubt as to the answer.

His secretary replied in a tone as lifeless, "The Squire of Bort stated that the press of previous business arrangements prevented his attending earlier than three."

"And you told him?"

"I stated that the nature of the present business made any delay inadvisable."

"The result?"

"He will be here, sir. The rest have agreed without reservation."

Fife smiled. Half an hour this way or that would have made no difference. There was a new principle involved, that was all. The Great Squires were too touchy with regard to their own independence, and such touchiness would have to go.

He was waiting, now. The room was large, the places for the others were prepared. The large chronometer, whose tiny powering spark of radioactivity had not failed or faltered in a thousand years, said two twenty-one.

What an explosion in the last two days! The old chronometer might yet witness events equal to any in the past.

Yet that chronometer had seen many in its millennium. When it counted its first minutes Sark had been a new world of hand-hewn cities with doubtful contacts among the other, older worlds. The timepiece had been in the wall of an old brick building then, the very bricks of which had since become dust. It had counted its even tenor through three short-lived Sarkite "empires" when the undisciplined soldiers of Sark managed to govern, for a longer or shorter interval, some half a dozen surrounding worlds. Its radio-active atoms had exploded in strict statistical sequence through two periods when the fleets of neighboring worlds dictated policy on Sark.

Five hundred years ago it had marked cool time as Sark discovered that the world nearest to it, Florina, had a treasure in its soil past counting. It had moved evenly through two victorious wars and recorded solemnly the establishment of a conqueror's peace. Sark had abandoned its empires, absorbed Florina tightly, and become powerful in a way that Trantor itself could not duplicate.

Trantor wanted Florina and other powers had wanted it. The centuries had marked Florina as a world for which hands stretched out through space, groping and reaching eagerly. But it was Sark whose hand clasped it and Sark, sooner than release that grasp, would allow Galactic war.

Trantor knew that! Trantor knew that!

It was as though the silent rhythm of the chronometer set up the little singsong in the Squire's brain.

It was two twenty-three.

Nearly a year before, the five Great Squires of Sark had met. Then, as now, it had been here, in his own hall. Then, as now, the Squires, scattered over the face of the planet, each on his own continent, had met in trimensic personification.

In a bald sense, it amounted to three-dimensional television in life size with sound and color. The duplicate could be found in any moderately well-to-do private home on Sark. Where it went beyond the ordinary was in the lack of any visible receiver. Except for Fife, the Squires present were present in every possible way but reality. The wall could not be seen behind them, they did not shimmer, yet a hand could have passed through their bodies.

The true body of the Squire of Rune was sitting in the

antipodes, his continent the only one upon which, at the moment, night prevailed. The cubic area immediately surrounding his image in Fife's office had the cold, white gleam of artificial light, dimmed by the brighter daylight about it.

Gathered in the one room, in body or in image, was Sark itself. It was a queer and not altogether heroic personification of the planet. Rune was bald and pinkly fat, while Balle was gray and dryly wrinkled. Steen was powdered and rouged, wearing the desperate smile of a worn-out man pretending to a life force he no longer had, and Bort carried indifference to creature comforts to the unpleasant point of a two-day growth of beard and dirty fingernails.

Yet they were the five Great Squires.

They were the topmost of the three rungs of ruling powers on Sark. The lowest rung was, of course, the Florinian Civil Service, which remained steady through all the vicissitudes that marked the rise and fall of the individual noble houses of Sark. It was they who actually greased the axles and turned the wheels of government. Above them were the ministers and department heads appointed by the hereditary (and harmless) Chief of State. Their names and that of the Chief himself were needed on state papers to make them legally binding, but their only duties consisted of signing their names.

The highest rung was occupied by these five, each tacitly allowed a continent by the remaining four. They were the heads of the families that controlled the major volume of the kyrt trade, and the revenues therefrom derived. It was money that gave power and eventually dictated policy on Sark, and these had it. And of the five, it was Fife who had the most.

The Squire of Fife had faced them that day, nearly a year ago, and said to the other masters of the Galaxy's second richest single planet (second richest after Trantor, which, after all, had half a million worlds to draw upon, rather than two):

"I have received a curious message."

They said nothing. They waited.

Fife handed a slip of metallite film to his secretary, who stepped from one seated figure to another, holding it well up for each to see, lingering just long enough for each to read.

To each of the four who attended the conference in Fife's office, he, himself, was real, and the others, including Fife, only shadows. The metallite film was a shadow as well. They could only sit and observe the light rays that focused across vast world-sectors from the Continent of Fife to those of Balle, Bort, Steen, and the island Continent of Rune. The words they read were shadows on shadow.

Only Bort, direct and ungiven to subtleties, forgot that fact and reached for the message.

His hand extended to the edge of the rectangular image-receptor and was cut off. His arm ended in a featureless stump. In his own chambers, Fife knew, Bort's arm had succeeded merely in closing upon nothingness and passing through the filmed message. He smiled, and so did the others. Steen giggled.

Bort reddened. He drew back his arm and his hand reappeared.

Fife said, "Well, you have each seen it. If you don't mind, I will now read it aloud so that you may consider its significance."

He reached upward, and his secretary, by hastening his steps, managed to hold the film in the proper position for Fife's grasp to close upon it without an instant's groping.

Fife read mellowly, imparting drama to the words as though the message were his own and he enjoyed delivering it.

He said, "This is the message: 'You are a Great Squire of Sark and there is none to compete with you in power and wealth. Yet that power and wealth rest on a slender foundation. You may think that a planetary supply of kyrt, such as exists on Florina, is by no means a slender foundation, but ask yourself, how long will Florina exist? Forever?

"'No! Florina may be destroyed tomorrow. It may exist for a thousand years. Of the two, it is more likely to be destroyed tomorrow. Not by myself, to be sure, but in a way you cannot predict or foresee. Consider that destruction. Consider, too, that your power and wealth are already gone, for I demand the greater part of them. You will have time to consider, but not too much time.

"'Attempt to take too much time and I shall announce to all the Galaxy and particularly to Florina the truth about the waiting destruction. After that there will be no more kyrt, no more wealth, no more power. None for me, but then I am used to that. None for you, and that would be extremely serious, since you were born to great wealth.

"'Turn over most of your estates to myself in the amount and in the manner which I shall dictate in the near future and you will remain in secure possession of what remains. Not a great deal will be left by your present standards, to be sure, but it will be more than the nothing that will otherwise be left you. Do not sneer at the fragment you will retain, either. Florina *may* last your lifetime and you will live, if not lavishly, at least comfortably.'"

Fife had finished. He turned the film over and over in his hand, then folded it gently into a silvery translucent cylinder through which the stenciled letters merged into a reddish blur.

He said in his natural voice, "It is an amusing letter. There is no signature and the tone of the letter, as you heard, is stilted and pompous. What do you think of it, Squires?"

Rune's ruddy face was set in displeasure. He said, "It's obviously the work of a man not far removed from the psychotic. He writes like a historical novel. Frankly, Fife, I don't see that such rubbish is a decent excuse to disrupt our traditions of continental autonomy by calling us together. And I don't like all this going on in the presence of your secretary."

"My secretary? Because he is a Florinian? Are you afraid his mind will be unsettled by such things as this letter? Nonsense." His tone shifted from one of mild amusement to the unmodulated syllables of command. "Turn to the Squire of Rune."

The secretary did so. His eyes were discreetly lowered and his white face was uncreased by lines and unmarred by expression. It almost seemed untouched by life.

"This Florinian," said Fife, careless of the man's presence, "is my personal servant. He is never away from me, never with others of his kind. But it is not for that reason that he is absolutely trustworthy. Look at him. Look at his eyes. Isn't it obvious to you that he has been under the psychic probe? He is incapable of any thought which is disloyal to myself in the slightest degree. With no offense intended, I can say that I would sooner trust him than any of you."

Bort chuckled. "I don't blame you. None of us owes you the loyalty of a probed Florinian servant."

Steen giggled again and writhed in his seat as though it were growing gently warm.

Not one of them made any comment on Fife's use of a psychic probe for personal servants. Fife would have been tremendously astonished had they done so. The use of the psychic probe for any reason other than the correction of mental disorders or the removal of criminal impulses was forbidden. Strictly speaking, it was forbidden even to the Great Squires.

Yet Fife probed whenever he felt it necessary, particularly when the subject was a Florinian. The probing of a Sarkite was a much more delicate matter. The Squire of Steen, whose writhings at the mention of the probing Fife did not miss, was well reputed to make use of probed Florinians of both sexes for purposes far removed from the secretarial.

"Now." Fife put his blunt fingers together. "I did not bring you all together for the reading of a crackpot letter. That, I hope, is understood. Actually I am afraid we have an important problem on our hands. First of all, I ask myself, why bother only with me? To be sure, I am the wealthiest of the Squires, but alone, I control only a third of the kyrt trade. Together the five of us control it all. It is easy to make five cello-copies of a letter, as easy as it is to make one."

"You use too many words," muttered Bort. "What do you want?"

Balle's withered and colorless lips moved in a dull gray face. "He wants to know, my Lord of Bort, if we have received copies of this letter."

"Then let him say so."

"I thought I was saying so," said Fife evenly. "Well?"

They looked at one another, doubtfully or defiantly, as the personality of each dictated.

Rune spoke first. His pink forehead was moist with discrete drops of perspiration and he lifted a soft square of kyrt to mop the dampness out of the creases between the folds of fat that ran semicircles from ear to ear.

He said, "I wouldn't know, Fife. I can ask my secretaries, who are all Sarkites, by the way. After all, even if such a letter had reached my office, it would have been considered a—what is it we say?—a crank letter. It would never have come to me. That's certain. It's only your own peculiar secretarial system that kept you from being spared this trash yourself."

He looked about and smiled, his gums gleaming wetly between his lips above and below artificial teeth of chrome-steel. Each individual tooth was buried deeply, knit to the jawbone, and stronger than any tooth of mere enamel could ever be. His smile was more frightening than his frown could possibly be.

Balle shrugged. "I imagine that what Rune has just said can hold for all of us."

Steen tittered. "I never read mail. Really, I never do. It's such a bore and such loads come in that I just wouldn't have any *time*." He looked about him earnestly, as though it were really necessary to convince the company of this important fact.

Bort said, "Nuts. What's wrong with you all? Afraid of Fife? Look here, Fife, I don't keep any secretary because I don't need anyone between myself and my business. I got a copy of that letter and I'm sure these three did too. Want to know what I did with mine? I threw it into the disposal chute. I'd advise you to do the same with yours. Let's stop this. I'm tired."

His hand reached upward for the toggle switch that would cut contact and release his image from its presence in Fife.

"Wait, Bort." Fife's voice rang out harshly. "Don't do that. I'm not done. You wouldn't want us to take measures and come to decisions in your absence. Surely you wouldn't."

"Let us linger, Squire Bort," urged Rune in his softer tones, though his little fat-buried eyes were not particularly amiable. "I wonder why Squire Fife seems to worry so about a trifle."

"Well," said Balle, his dry voice scratching at their ears, "perhaps Fife thinks our letter-writing friend has information about a Trantorian attack on Florina."

"Pooh," said Fife with scorn. "How would he know, whoever he is? Our secret service is adequate, I assure you. And how would he stop the attack if he received our properties as bribe? No, no. He speaks of the destruction of Florina as though he meant physical destruction and not political destruction."

"It's just too *insane*," said Steen.

"Yes?" said Fife. "Then you don't see the significance of the events of the last two weeks?"

"Which particular events?" asked Bort.

"It seems a Spatio-analyst has disappeared. Surely you've heard of that."

Bort looked annoyed and in no way soothed. "I've heard from Abel of Trantor about it. What of it? I know nothing of Spatio-analysts."

"At least you've read a copy of the last message to his base on Sark before he turned up missing."

"Able showed it to me. I paid no attention to it."

"What about the rest of you?" Fife's eyes challenged them one by one. "Your memory goes back a week?"

"I read it," said Rune. "I remember it too. Of course! It spoke of destruction also. Is that what you're getting at?"

"Look here," Steen said shrilly, "it was full of nasty hints that made no sense. Really, I do hope we're not going to discuss it now. I could scarcely get rid of Abel, and it was just before dinner, too. Most distressing. Really."

"There's no help for it, Steen," said Fife with more than a trace of impatience. (What could one do with a thing like Steen?) "We must speak of it again. The Spatio-analyst spoke of the destruction of Florina. Coincident with his disappearance, we receive messages also threatening the destruction of Florina. *Is* that coincidence?"

"You are saying that the Spatio-analyst sent the blackmailing message?" whispered old Balle.

"Not likely. Why say it first in his own name, then anonymously?"

"When he spoke of it at first," said Balle, "he was communicating with his district office, not with us."

"Even so. A blackmailer deals with no one but his victim if he can help it."

"Well then?"

"He has disappeared. Call the Spatio-analyst honest. But he broadcast dangerous information. He is now in the hands of others who are *not* honest and they are blackmailers."

"What others?"

Fife sat grimly back in his chair, his lips scarcely moving. "You ask me seriously? Trantor."

Steen shivered. "Trantor!" His highpitched voice broke.

"Why not? What better way to gain control of Florina? It's one of the prime aims of their foreign policy. And if they can do it without war, so much the better for them. Look here, if we accede to this impossible ultimatum, Florina is theirs. They offer us a little"—he brought two fingers close together before his face—"but how long shall we keep even that?

"On the other hand, suppose we ignore this, and, really, we have no choice. What would Trantor do then? Why, they will spread rumors of an imminent end of the world to the Florinian peasants. As their rumors spread the peasants will panic, and what can follow but disaster? What force can make a man work if he thinks the end of the world will come tomorrow? The harvest will rot. The warehouses will empty."

Steen lifted a finger to smooth the coloring on one cheek, as he glanced at a mirror in his own apartments, out of range of the receptor-cube.

He said, "I don't think that would harm us much. If the supply goes down, wouldn't the price go up? Then after a while it would turn out that Florina was still there and the peasants would go back to work. Besides, we could always threaten to clamp down on exports. Really, I don't see how any cultured world could be expected to live without kyrt. Oh, it's King Kyrt all right. I think this is a fuss about nothing."

He threw himself into an attitude of boredom, one finger placed delicately upon his cheek.

Balle's old eyes had been closed through all of this last. He said, "There can be no price increases now. We've got them at absolute ceiling height."

"Exactly," said Fife. "It won't come to serious disruption anyway. Trantor waits for any sign of disorder on Florina. If they could present the Galaxy with the prospect of a Sark that was unable to guarantee kyrt shipments, it would be the most natural thing in the universe for them to move in to maintain what they call order and to keep the kyrt coming. And the danger would be that the free worlds of the Galaxy would probably play along with them for the sake of the kyrt. Especially if Trantor agreed to break the monopoly, increase production and lower prices. Afterward it would be another story, but meanwhile, they would get their support.

"It's the only logical way that Trantor could possibly grip Florina. If it were simple force, the free Galaxy outside the Trantorian sphere of influence would join us in sheer self-protection."

Rune said, "How does the Spatio-analyst fit in this? Is he necessary? If your theory is adequate it should explain that."

"I think it does. These Spatio-analysts are unbalanced for the most part, and this one has developed some"—Fife's fingers moved, as though building a vague structure—"some crazy theory. It doesn't matter what. Trantor can't let it come out, or the Spatio-analytic Bureau would quash it. To seize the man and learn the details would, however, give them something that would probably possess a surface validity to non-specialists. They could use it, make it sound real. The Bureau is a Trantorian puppet, and their denials, once the story is spread by way of scientific rumormongering, would never be forceful enough to overtake the lie."

"It sounds too complicated," said Bort. "Nuts. They can't let it come out, but then again they will let it come out."

"They can't let it come out as a serious scientific announcement, or even reach the Bureau as such," said Fife patiently. "They can let it leak out as a rumor. Don't you see that?"

"What's old Abel doing wasting his time looking for the Spatio-analyst then?"

"You expect him to advertise the fact that he's got him? What Abel does and what Abel seems to be doing are two different things."

"Well," said Rune, "if you're right, what are we to do?"

Fife said, "We have learned the danger, and that is the important thing. We'll find the Spatio-analyst if we can. We must keep all known agents of Trantor under strict scrutiny without really interfering with them. From their actions we may learn the course of coming events. We must suppress thoroughly any propaganda on Florina to the effect of the planet's destruction. The first faint whisper must meet with instant counteraction of the most violent sort.

"Most of all, we must remain united. That is the whole purpose of this meeting, in my eyes; the forming of a common front. We all know about continental autonomy and I'm sure there is no one more insistent upon it than I am. That is, under ordinary circumstances. These are not ordinary circumstances. You see that?"

More or less reluctantly, for continental autonomy was not a thing to be abandoned lightly, they saw that.

"Then," said Fife, "we will wait for the second move."

That had been a year ago. They had left and there had followed the strangest and most complete fiasco ever to have fallen to the lot of the Squire of Fife in a moderately long and a more than moderately audacious career.

No second move followed. There were no further letters to any of them. The Spatio-analyst remained unfound, while Trantor maintained a desultory search. There was no trace of apocalyptic rumors on Florina, and the harvesting and processing of kyrt continued its smooth pace.

The Squire of Rune took to calling Fife at weekly intervals.

"Fife," he would call. "Anything new?" His fatness would quiver with delight and thick chuckles would force their way out of his gullet.

Fife took it bleakly and stolidly. What could he do? Over and over again he sifted the facts. It was no use. Something was missing. Some vital factor was missing.

And then it all began exploding at once, and he had the answer. He *knew* he had the answer, and it was what he had *not* expected.

He had called a meeting once again. The chronometer now said two twenty-nine.

They were beginning to appear now. Bort first, lips compressed and a rough hangnailed finger rasping against the grain of his grizzly-stubbled cheek. Then Steen, his face freshly washed clear of its paint and presenting a pallid, unhealthy appearance. Balle, indifferent and tired, his cheeks sunken, his armchair well cushioned, a glass of warm milk at his side. Lastly Rune, two minutes late, wet-lipped and sulky, sitting in the night once again. This time his lights were dimmed to the point where he was a hazy bulk sitting in a cube of shadow which Fife's lights could not have illuminated though they had had the power of Sark's sun.

Fife began. "Squires! Last year I speculated on a distant

and complicated danger. In so doing I fell into a trap. The danger exists, but it is not distant. It is near us, very near. One of you already knows what I mean. The others will find out shortly."

"What *do* you mean?" asked Bort shortly.

"High treason!" shot back Fife.

10. THE FUGITIVE

Merlyn Terens was not a man of action. He told himself that as an excuse, since now, leaving the spaceport, he found his mind paralyzed.

He had to pick his pace carefully. Not too slowly, or he would seem to be dawdling. Not too quickly, or he would seem to be running. Just briskly, as a patroller would walk, a patroller who was about his business and ready to enter his ground-car.

If only he could enter a ground-car! Driving one, unfortunately, did not come within the education of a Florinian, not even a Florinian Townman, so he tried to think as he walked and could not. He needed silence and leisure.

And he felt almost too weak to walk. He might not be a man of action but he *had* acted quickly now for a day and a night and part of another day. It had used up his lifetime's supply of nerve.

Yet he dared not stop.

If it were night he might have had a few hours to think. But it was early afternoon.

If he could drive a ground-car he could put the miles between himself and the City. Just long enough to think a bit before deciding on the next step. But he had only his legs.

If he could think. That was it. If he could think. If he could suspend all motion, all action. If he could catch the universe between instants of time, order it to halt, while he thought things through. There must be some way.

He plunged into the welcome shade of Lower City. He walked stiffly, as he had seen the patrollers walk. He swung his shock-stick in a firm grip. The streets were bare. The natives were huddling in their shacks. So much the better.

The Townman chose his house carefully. It would be best to choose one of the better ones, one with patches of colored plastic briquets and polarized glass in the windows. The lower orders were sullen. They had less to lose. An "upper man" would be falling over himself to help.

He walked up a short path to such a house. It was set back from the street, another sign of affluence. He knew he would have no need of pounding the door or breaking it in. There had been a noticeable movement at one window as he walked up the ramp. (How generations of necessity enabled a Florinian to smell the approach of a patroller.) The door would open.

It did open.

A young girl opened it, her eyes white-rimmed circles. She was gawky in a dress whose frills showed a determined effort on the part of her parents to uphold their status as something more than the ordinary run of "Florinian trash." She stood aside to let him pass, her breath coming quickly between parted lips.

The Townman motioned to her to shut the door. "Is your father here, girl?"

She screamed, "Pa!" then gasped, "Yes, sir!"

"Pa" was moving in apologetically from another room. He came slowly. It was no news to him that a patroller was at the door. It was simply safer to let a young girl admit him. She was less apt to be knocked down out of hand than he himself was, if the patroller happened to be angry.

"Your name?" asked the Townman.

"Jacof, if it please you, sir."

The Townman's uniform had a thin-sheeted notebook in one of its pockets. The Townman opened it, studied it briefly, made a crisp check mark and said, "Jacof! Yes! I want to see every member of the household. Quickly!"

If he could have found room for any emotion but one of hopeless oppression, Terens would almost have enjoyed himself. He was not immune to the seductive pleasures of authority.

They filed in. A thin woman, worried, a child of about two years wriggling in her arms. Then the girl who had admitted him and a younger brother.

"That's all?"

"Everyone, sir," said Jacof humbly.

"Can I tend the baby?" asked the woman anxiously. "It's her nap time. I was putting her to bed." She held the young child out as though the sight of young innocence might melt a patroller's heart.

The Townman did not look at her. A patroller, he imagined, would not have, and he was a patroller. He said, "Put it down and give it a sugar sucker to keep it quiet. Now, you! Jacof!"

"Yes, sir."

"You're a responsible boy, aren't you?" A native of whatever age was, of course, a "boy."

"Yes, sir." Jacof's eyes brightened and his shoulders lifted a trifle. "I'm a clerk in the food-processing center. I've had mathematics, long division. I can do logarithms."

Yes, the Townman thought, they've shown you how to use a table of logarithms and taught you how to pronounce the word.

He knew the type. The man would be prouder of his logarithms than a Squireling of his yacht. The polaroid in his windows was the consequence of his logarithms and the tinted briquets advertised his long division. His contempt for the uneducated native would be equal to that of the average Squire for all natives and his hatred would be more intense since he had to live among them and was taken for one of them by his betters.

"You believe in the law, don't you, boy, and in the good Squires?" The Townman maintained the impressive fiction of consulting his notebook.

"My husband is a good man," burst in the woman volubly. "He hasn't ever been in trouble. He doesn't associate with trash. And I don't. No more do the children. We always——"

Terens waved her down. "Yes. Yes. Now look, boy, I want you to sit right here and do what I say. I want a list of everyone you know about on this block. Names, addresses, what they do, and what kind of boys they are. Especially the last. If there's one of these troublemakers, I want to know. We're going to clean up. Understand?"

"Yes, sir. Yes, sir. There's Husting first of all. He's down the block a way. He——"

"Not like that, boy. Get him a piece of paper, you. Now you sit there and write it all down. Every bit. Write it slowly because I can't read native chicken tracks."

"I have a trained writing hand, sir."

"Let's see it, then."

Jacof bent to his task, hand moving slowly. His wife looked over his shoulder.

Terens spoke to the girl who had let him in. "Go to the window and let me know if any other patrollers come this way. I'll want to speak to them. Don't *you* call them. Just tell me."

And then, finally, he could relax. He had made a momentarily secure niche for himself in the midst of danger.

Except for the noisy sucking of the baby in the corner, there was reasonable silence. He would be warned of the enemy's approach in time for a fighting chance at escape.

Now he could think.

In the first place, his role as patroller was about over.

There were undoubtedly road blocks at all possible exits from the town, and they knew he could use no means of transportation more complicated than a diamagnetic scooter. It would not be long before it would dawn on the search-rusty patrollers that only by a systematic quartering of the town, block by block and house by house, could they be sure of their man.

When they finally decided that, they would undoubtedly start at the outskirts and work inward. If so, this house would be among the first to be entered, so his time was particularly limited.

Until now, despite its black and silver conspicuousness, the patroller uniform had been useful. The natives themselves had not questioned it. They had not stopped to see his pale Florinian face; they had not studied his appearance. The uniform had been enough.

Before long the pursuing hounds would find that fact dawning upon them. It would occur to them to broadcast instructions to all natives to hold any patroller unable to show proper identification, particularly one with a white skin and sandy hair. Temporary identifications would be passed out to all legitimate patrollers. Rewards would be offered. Perhaps only one native in a hundred would be courageous enough to tackle the uniform no matter how patently false the occupant was. One in a hundred would be enough.

So he would have to stop being a patroller.

That was one thing. Now another. He would be safe nowhere on Florina from now on. Killing a patroller was the ultimate crime and in fifty years, if he could elude capture so long, the chase would remain hot. So he would have to leave Florina.

How?

Well, he gave himself one more day of life. This was a generous estimate. It assumed the patrollers to be at maximum stupidity and himself in a state of maximum luck.

In one way this was an advantage. A mere twenty-four

hours of life was not much to risk. It meant he could take chances no sane man could possibly take.

He stood up.

Jacof looked up from his paper. "I'm not quite done, sir. I'm writing very carefully."

"Let me see what you have written."

He looked at the paper handed him and said, "It is enough. If other patrollers should come, don't waste their time saying that you have already made a list. They are in a hurry and may have other tasks for you. Just do as they say. Are there any coming now?"

The girl at the window said, "No, sir. Shall I go out in the street and look?"

"It's not necessary. Let's see now. Where is the nearest elevator?"

"It's about a quarter of a mile to the left, sir, as you leave the house. You can——"

"Yes, yes. Let me out."

A squad of patrollers turned into the street just as the door of the elevator ground into place behind the Townman. He could feel his heart pound. The systematic search was probably starting, and they were at his heels.

A minute later, heartbeat still drumming, he stepped out of the elevator into Upper City. There would be no cover here. No pillars. No cementalloy hiding him from above.

He felt like a moving black dot among the glare of the garish buildings. He felt visible for two miles on every side and for five miles up in the sky. There seemed to be large arrows pointing to him.

There were no patrollers in view. The Squires who passed looked through him. If a patroller was an object of fear to a Florinian, he was an object of nothing-at-all to a Squire. If anything would save him, that would.

He had a vague notion of the geography of Upper City. Somewhere in this section was City Park. The most logical step would have been to ask directions, the next most logical to enter any moderately tall building and look out from several of the upper-story terraces. The first alternative was impossible. No patroller could possibly need directions. The second was too risky. Inside a building, a patroller would be more conspicuous. Too conspicuous.

He simply struck out in the direction indicated by his memory of the maps of Upper City he had seen on occasion. It served well enough. It was unmistakably City Park that he came across in five minutes' time.

City Park was an artificial patch of greenery about one hundred acres in area. On Sark itself, City Park had an exaggerated reputation for many things from bucolic peace to nightly orgies. On Florina, those who had vaguely heard of it imagined it ten to a hundred times its actual size and a hundred to a thousand times its actual luxuriance.

The reality was pleasant enough. In Florina's mild climate it was green all year round. It had its patches of lawn, wooded areas and stony grottoes. It had a little pool with decorative fish in it and a larger pool for children to paddle in. At night it was aflame with colored illumination till the light rain started. It was between twilight and the rain that it was most alive. There was dancing, trimensional shows, and couples losing themselves along the winding walks.

Terens had never actually been inside it. He found its artificiality repellent when he entered the Park. He knew that the soil and rocks he stepped on, the water and trees around him, all rested on a dead-flat cementalloy bottom and it annoyed him. He thought of the kyrt fields, long and level, and the mountain ranges of the south. He despised the aliens who had to build toys for themselves in the midst of magnificence.

For half an hour Terens tramped the walks aimlessly. What he had to do would have to be done in City Park. Even here it might be impossible. Elsewhere it *was* impossible.

No one saw him. No one was conscious of him. He was sure of that. Let them ask the Squires and Squirettes who passed him, "Did you see a patroller in the Park yesterday?"

They could only stare. They might as well be asked whether they had seen a tree midge skitter across the path.

The Park was *too* tame. He felt panic begin to grow. He made his way up a staircase between boulders and began descending into the cuplike hollow circled by small caves designed to shelter couples caught in the nightly rainfall. (More were caught than could be accounted for by chance alone.)

And then he saw what he was looking for.

A man! A Squire, rather. Stepping back and forth quickly. Smoking the stub of a cigarette with sharp drags, cramming it into an ash recess, where it lay quietly for a moment, then vanished with a quick flash. Consulting a pendant watch.

There was no one else in the hollow. It was a place made for the evening and night.

The Squire was waiting for someone. So much was obvious. Terens looked about him. No one was following him up the stairs.

There might be other stairs. There were sure to be. No matter. He could not let the chance go.

He stepped down toward the Squire. The Squire did not see him, of course, until Terens said, "If you'll pardon me?"

It was respectful enough, but a Squire is not accustomed to having a patroller touch the crook of his elbow in however respectful a fashion.

"What the hell?" he said.

Terens abandoned neither the respect nor the urgency in his tone. (Keep him talking. Keep his eyes on yours for just half a minute!) He said, "This way, sir. It is in connection with the City-wide search for the native murderer."

"What are you talking about?"

"It will take just a moment."

Unobtrusively Terens had drawn his neuronic whip. The Squire never saw it. It buzzed a little and the Squire strained into rigor and toppled.

The Townman had never raised a hand against a Squire before. He was surprised at how sick and guilty he felt.

There was still no one in sight. He dragged the wooden

body, with its glazed and staring eyes, into the nearest cave. He dragged it to the cave's shallow end.

He stripped the Squire, yanking clothing off the stiffened arms and legs with difficulty. He stepped out of his own dusty, sweat-stained patroller uniform and climbed into the Squire's underclothing. For the first time he felt kyrt fabric with some part of himself beside his fingers.

Then the rest of the clothing, and the Squire's skullcap. The last was necessary. Skullcaps were not entirely fashionable among the younger set but some wore them, this Squire luckily among them. To Terens it was a necessity as otherwise his light hair would make the masquerade impossible. He pulled the cap down tightly, covering his ears.

Then he did what had to be done. The killing of a patroller was, he suddenly realized, not the ultimate crime after all.

He adjusted his blaster to maximum dispersion and turned it on the unconscious Squire. In ten seconds only a charred mass was left. It would delay identification, confuse the pursuers.

He reduced the patroller's uniform to a powdery white ash with the blaster and clawed out of the heap blackened silver buttons and buckles. That, too, would make the chase harder. Perhaps he was buying only an additional hour, but that, too, was worth it.

And now he would have to leave without delay. He paused a moment just outside the mouth of the cave to sniff. The blaster worked cleanly. There was only the slightest odor of burned flesh and the light breeze would clear it in a few moments.

He was walking down the steps when a young girl passed him on the way up. For a moment he dropped his eyes out of habit. She was a Lady. He lifted them in time to see that she was young and quite good-looking, and in a hurry.

His jaws set. She wouldn't find him, of course. But she was late, or he wouldn't have been staring at his watch so. She might think he had grown tired of waiting and had left. He walked a trifle faster. He didn't want her returning, pursuing him breathlessly, asking if he had seen a young man.

He left the Park, walking aimlessly. Another half hour passed.

What now? He was no longer a patroller, he was a Squire. But what now?

He stopped at a small square in which a fountain was centered in a plot of lawn. To the water a small quantity of detergent had been added so that it frothed and foamed in gaudy iridescence.

He leaned against the railing, back to the western sun, and, bit by bit, slowly, he dropped blackened silver into the fountain.

He thought of the girl who had passed him on the steps as he did so. She had been very young. Then he thought of Lower City and the momentary spasm of remorse left him.

The silver remnants were gone and his hands were empty. Slowly he began searching his pockets, doing his best to make it seem casual.

The contents of the pockets were not particularly unusual. A booklet of key slivers, a few coins, an identification card. (Holy Sark! Even the Squires carried them. But then, they didn't have to produce them for every patroller that came along.)

His new name, apparently, was Alstare Deamone. He hoped he wouldn't have to use it. There were only ten thousand men, women and children in Upper City. The chance of his meeting one among them who knew Deamone personally was not large, but it wasn't insignificant either.

He was twenty-nine. Again, he felt a rising nausea as he thought of what he had left in the cave, and fought it. A Squire was a Squire. How many twenty-nine-year-old Florinians had been done to death at their hands or by their directions? How many nine-year-old Florinians?

He had an address, too, but it meant nothing to him. His knowledge of Upper City geography was rudimentary.

Say!

A color portrait of a young boy, perhaps three, in pseudo-trimension. The colors flashed as he drew it out of its container, faded progressively as he returned it. A young son? A nephew? There had been the girl in the Park so it couldn't be a son, could it?

Or was he married? Was the meeting one of those they called "clandestine?" Would such a meeting take place in daylight? Why not, under certain circumstances?

Terens hoped so. If the girl were meeting a married man she would not quickly report his absence. She would assume he had not been able to evade his wife. That would give him time.

No, it wouldn't. Instant depression seized him. Children playing hide-and-seek would stumble on the remains and run screaming. It was bound to happen within twenty-four hours.

He turned to the pocket's contents once more. A pocket-copy license as yacht pilot. He passed it by. All the richer Sarkites owned yachts and piloted them. It was this century's fad. Finally, a few strips of Sarkite credit vouchers. Now those might be temporarily useful.

It occurred to him that he hadn't eaten since the night before at the Baker's place. How quickly one could grow conscious of hunger.

Suddenly he turned back to the yacht license. Wait, now, the yacht wasn't in use now, not with the owner dead. And it was *his* yacht. Its hangar number was 26, at Port 9. Well . . .

Where was Port 9? He hadn't the slightest notion.

He leaned his forehead against the coolness of the smooth railing around the fountain. What now? What now?

The voice startled him.

"Hello," it said. "Not sick?"

Terens looked up. It was an older Squire. He was smoking a long cigarette containing some aromatic leaf while a green stone of some sort hung suspended from a gold wristband. His expression was one of kindly interest that astonished Terens into a moment of speechlessness, until he remembered. He was one of the clan himself now. Among themselves, Squires might well be decent human beings.

The Townman said, "Just resting. Decided to take a walk and lost track of time. I'm afraid I'm late for an appointment now."

He waved his hand in a wry gesture. He could imitate the Sarkite accent fairly well from long association but he didn't make the mistake of trying to exaggerate it. Exaggeration was easier to detect than insufficiency.

The other said, "Stuck without a skeeter, hey?" He was the older man, amused by the folly of youth.

"No skeeter," admitted Terens.

"Use mine," came the instant offer. "It's parked right outside. You can set the controls and send it back here when you're through. I won't be needing it for the next hour or so."

To Terens, that was almost ideal. The skeeters were fast and skittery as chain lightning, could outspeed and out-maneuver any patroller ground-car. It fell short of ideal only in that Terens could no more drive the skeeter than he could fly without it.

"From here to Sark," he said. He knew that piece of Squire slang for "thanks," and threw it in. "I think I'll walk. It isn't far to Port 9."

"No, it isn't far," agreed the other.

That left Terens no better off than before. He tried again. "Of course, I wish I were closer. The walk to Kyrt Highway is healthy enough by itself."

"Kyrt Highway? What's that got to do with it?"

Was he looking queerly at Terens? It occurred to the Townman, suddenly, that his clothing probably lacked the proper fitting. He said quickly, "Wait! I'm twisted at that. I've got myself crossed up walking. Let's see now." He looked about vaguely.

"Look. You're on Recket Road. All you have to do is go down to Triffis and turn left, then follow it into the port." He had pointed automatically.

Terens smiled. "You're right. I'm going to have to stop dreaming and start thinking. From here to Sark, sir."

"You can still use my skeeter."

"Kind of you, but..."

Terens was walking away, a bit too quickly, waving his hand. The Squire stared after him.

Perhaps tomorrow, when they found the corpse in the rocks and began searching, the Squire might think of this interview again. He would probably say, "There was something queer about him, if you know what I mean. He had an odd turn of phrase and didn't seem to know where he was. I'll swear he'd never heard of Triffis Avenue."

But that would be tomorrow.

He walked in the direction that the Squire had pointed out. He came to the glittering sign "Triffis Avenue," almost drab against the iridescent orange structure that was its background. He turned left.

Port 9 was alive with youth in yachting costume, which seemed to feature high-peaked hats and hip-bellying breeches. Terens felt conspicuous but no one paid attention to him. The air was full of conversation spiced with terms he did not understand.

He found Booth 26 but waited for minutes before approaching it. He wanted no Squire remaining persistently in its vicinity, no Squire who happened to own a yacht in a nearby booth who would know the real Alstare Deamone by sight and would wonder what a stranger was doing about his ship.

Finally, with the booth's neighborhood apparently safe, he walked over. The yacht's snout peered out from its hangar into the open field about which the booths were placed. He craned his neck to stare at it.

Now what?

He had killed three men in the last twelve hours. He had risen from Florinian Townman to patroller, from patroller to Squire. He had come from Lower City to Upper City and from Upper City to a spaceport. To all intents and purposes he owned a yacht, a vessel sufficiently spaceworthy to take him to safety on any inhabited world in this sector of the Galaxy.

There was only one catch.

He could not pilot a yacht.

He was tired to the bone, and hungry to boot. He had come this far, and now he could go no further. He was on the edge of space but there was no way of crossing the edge.

By now the patrollers must have decided he was nowhere in Lower City. They would turn the search to Upper City as soon as they could get it through their thick skulls that a Florinian would *dare*. Then the body would be found and a new direction would be taken. They would look for an impostor Squire.

And here he was. He had climbed to the farthest niche of the blind alley and with his back to the closed end he could only wait for the faint sounds of pursuit to grow louder and louder until eventually the bloodhounds would be on him.

Thirty-six hours ago the greatest opportunity of his life had been in his hands. Now the opportunity was gone and his life would soon follow.

11. THE CAPTAIN

It was the first time, really, that Captain Racety had found himself unable to impose his will upon a passenger. Had that passenger been one of the Great Squires themselves, he might still have counted on co-operation. A Great Squire might be all-powerful on his own continent, but on a ship he would recognize that there could be only one master, the Captain.

A woman was different. Any woman. And a woman who was daughter of a Great Squire was completely impossible.

He said, "My Lady, how can I allow you to interview them in private?"

Samia of Fife, her dark eyes snapping, said, "Why not? Are they armed, Captain?"

"Of course not. That's not the point."

"Anyone can see they're only a pair of very frightened creatures. They're half scared to death."

129

"Frightened people can be very dangerous, my Lady. They can't be counted on to act sensibly."

"Then why do you keep them frightened?" She had the tiniest stammer when she was angry. "You've got three tremendous sailors standing over them with blasters, poor things. Captain, I'll not forget this."

No, she wouldn't, the Captain thought. He could feel himself beginning to give way.

"If Your Ladyship pleases, will you tell me exactly what it is that you want?"

"It's simple. I've told you. I want to speak to them. If they're Florinians, as you say they are, I can get tremendously valuable information from them for my book. I can't do that, though, if they're too frightened to speak. If I could be with them alone it would be fine. Alone, Captain! Can you understand a simple word? *Alone!*"

"And what would I say to your father, my Lady, if he discovers that I allowed you to remain unguarded in the presence of two desperate criminals?"

"Desperate criminals! Oh, Great Space! Two poor fools that tried to escape their planet and had no more sense than to board a ship going to Sark! Besides, how would my father know?"

"If they hurt you he would know."

"Why should they hurt me?" Her small fist lifted and vibrated, while she put every atom of force she could find into her voice. "I *demand* it, Captain."

Captain Racety said, "How about this then, my Lady? I will be present. I shall not be three sailors with blasters. I shall be one man with no blaster in view. Otherwise"—and in his turn he put all his resolution into his voice—"I must refuse your demand."

"Very well, then." She was breathless. "Very well. But if I can't get them to speak because of you I will personally see to it that you captain no more ships."

Valona put her hand hastily over Rik's eyes as Samia entered the brig.

"What's the matter, girl?" asked Samia sharply, before she could remember that she was going to speak to them comfortingly.

Valona spoke with difficulty. She said, "He is not bright, Lady. He wouldn't know you were a Lady. He might have looked at you. I mean without intending any harm, Lady."

"Oh, goodness," said Samia. "Let him look." She went on, "Must they stay here, Captain?"

"Would you prefer a stateroom, my Lady?"

Samia said, "Surely you could manage a cell not quite so grim."

"It is grim to you, my Lady. To them, I am sure this is luxury. There is running water here. Ask them if there was any in their hut on Florina."

"Well, tell those men to leave."

The Captain motioned to them. They turned, stepping out nimbly.

The Captain set down the light aluminum folding chair he had brought with him. Samia took it.

He said brusquely to Rik and Valona, "Stand up."

Samia broke in instantly. "No! Let them sit. You're not to interfere, Captain."

She turned to them. "So you are a Florinian, girl."

Valona shook her head. "We're from Wotex."

"You needn't be frightened. It doesn't matter that you're from Florina. No one will hurt you."

"We're from Wotex."

"But don't you see that you've practically admitted you're from Florina, girl? Why did you cover the boy's eyes?"

"He's not allowed to look at a Lady."

"Even if he's from Wotex?"

Valona was silent.

Samia let her think about it. She tried to smile in a friendly way. Then she said, "Only Florinians aren't allowed to look at Ladies. So you see you've admitted that you're a Florinian."

Valona burst out, "*He's* not."

"Are *you*?"

"Yes, I am. But he's not. Don't do anything to him. He *really* isn't a Florinian. He was just found one day. I don't know where he comes from, but it's not Florina." Suddenly she was almost voluble.

Samia looked at her with some surprise. "Well, I'll speak to him. What's your name, boy?"

Rik was staring. Was that how women Squires looked? So small, and friendly-looking. And she smelled so nice. He was very glad she had let him look at her.

Samia said again, "What's your name, boy?"

Rik came to life but stumbled badly in the attempt to shape a monosyllable.

"Rik," he said. Then he thought, Why, that's not my name. He said, "I think it's Rik."

"Don't you know?"

Valona, looking woebegone, tried to speak, but Samia held up a sharply restraining hand.

Rik shook his head. "I don't know."

"Are you a Florinian?"

Rik was positive here. "No. I was on a ship. I came here from somewhere else." He could not bear to look away from Samia but he seemed to see the ship co-existing with her. A small and very friendly and homelike ship.

He said, "It was on a ship that I came to Florina and before that I lived on a planet."

"What planet?"

It was as though the thought were forcing its way painfully through mental channels too small for it. Then Rik remembered and was delighted at the sound his voice made, a sound so long forgotten.

"Earth! I come from Earth!"

"Earth?"

Rik nodded.

Samia turned to the Captain. "Where is this planet Earth?"

Captain Racety smiled briefly. "I never heard of it. Don't take the boy seriously, my Lady. A native lies the way he breathes. It comes naturally to him. He says whatever comes first into his mind."

"He doesn't *talk* like a native." She turned to Rik again. "Where is Earth, Rik?"

"I—" He put a shaking hand to his forehead. Then he said, "It's in the Sirius Sector." The intonation of the statement made it half a question.

Samia said to the Captain, "There is a Sirius Sector, isn't there?"

"Yes, there is. I'm amazed he has that right. Still, that doesn't make Earth any more real."

Rik said vehemently, "But it is. I remember, I tell you. It's been so long since I remembered. I can't be wrong now. I can't."

He turned, gripping Valona's elbows and clawing at her sleeve. "Lona, tell them I come from Earth. I do. I do."

Valona's eyes were wide with anxiety. "We found him one day, Lady, and he had no mind at all. He couldn't dress himself or talk or walk. He was nothing. Ever since then he's been remembering little by little. So far everything he's remembered has been so." She cast a quick, fearful glance at the bored face of the Captain. "He may really have come from Earth, Squire. No contradiction intended."

The last was a long-established conventional phrase that went with any statement that seemed in contradiction to a previous statement by a superior.

Captain Racety grunted. "He may have come from the center of Sark for all that story proves, my Lady."

"Maybe, but there's something queer about all this," insisted Samia, making up her mind flatly, woman-wise, on the side of romance. "I'm sure of it. . . . What made him so helpless when you found him, girl? Had he been hurt?"

Valona said nothing at first. Her eyes darted helplessly back and forth. First to Rik, whose fingers clutched at his hair, then to the Captain, who was smiling without humor, finally to Samia, who waited.

"Answer me, girl," said Samia.

It was a hard decision for Valona to make, but no conceivable lie could substitute for the truth in this place and at this time. She said, "A doctor once looked at him. He said m—my Rik was psycho-probed."

"Psycho-probed!" Samia felt a slight wash of repulsion well over her. She pushed her chair away. It squeaked against the metal floor. "You mean he was psychotic?"

"I don't know what that means, Lady," said Valona humbly.

"Not in the sense you're thinking of, my Lady," said the Captain almost simultaneously. "Natives aren't psychotic. Their needs and desires are too simple. I've never heard of a psychotic native in my life."

"But then——"

"It's simple, my Lady. If we accept this fantastic story the girl tells, we can only conclude that the boy had been a criminal, which is a way of being psychotic, I suppose. If so, he must have been treated by one of those quacks who practice among the natives, been nearly killed and was then dumped in a deserted section to avoid detection and prosecution."

"But it would have to be someone with a psycho-probe," protested Samia. "Surely you wouldn't expect natives to be able to use them."

"Perhaps not. But then you wouldn't expect an authorized medical man to use one so inexpertly. The fact that we arrive at a contradiction proves the story to be a lie throughout. If you will accept my suggestion, my Lady, you will leave these creatures to our handling. You see that it's useless to expect anything out of them."

Samia hesitated. "Perhaps you're right."

She rose and looked uncertainly at Rik. The Captain stepped behind her, lifted the little chair and folded it with a snap.

Rik jumped to his feet. "Wait!"

"If you please, my Lady," said the Captain, holding the door open for her. "My men will quiet him."

Samia stopped at the threshold. "They won't hurt him?"

"I doubt if he'll make us go to extremes. He will be easy handling."

"Lady! Lady!" Rik called. "I can prove it. I'm from Earth."

Samia stood irresolute for a moment. "Let's hear what he has to say."

The Captain said coldly, "As you wish, my Lady."

She returned, but not very far. She remained a step from the door.

Rik was flushed. With the effort of remembering, his lips drew back into the caricature of a smile. He said, "I remember Earth. It was radioactive. I remember the Forbidden Areas and the blue horizon at night. The soil glowed and nothing would grow in it. There were just a few spots men could live on. That's why I was a Spatio-analyst. That's why I didn't mind staying in space. My world was a dead world."

Samia shrugged. "Come along, Captain. He's simply raving."

But this time it was Captain Racety who stood there, open-mouthed. He muttered, "A radioactive world!"

She said, "You mean there *is* such a thing?"

"Yes." He turned wondering eyes on her. "Now where could he have picked *that* up?"

"How could a world be radioactive and inhabited?"

"But there *is* one. And it *is* in the Sirius Sector. I don't remember its name. It might even be Earth."

"It *is* Earth," said Rik, proudly and with confidence. "It is the oldest planet of the Galaxy. It is the planet on which the whole human race originated."

The Captain said softly, "That's so!"

Samia said, mind whirling, "You mean the human race originated on this Earth?"

"No, no," said the Captain abstractedly. "That's superstition. It's just that that's how I came to hear about the radioactive planet. It claims to be Man's home planet."

"I didn't know we were supposed to have a home planet."

"I suppose we started somewhere, my Lady, but I doubt that anyone can possibly know on what planet it happened."

With sudden decision he walked toward Rik. "What else do you remember?"

He almost added "boy," but held it back.

"The ship mostly," said Rik, "and Spatio-analysis."

Samia joined the Captain. They stood there, directly before Rik, and Samia felt the excitement returning. "Then it's all true? But then how did he come to be psycho-probed?"

"Psycho-probed!" said Captain Racety thoughtfully. "Suppose we ask him. Here, you, native or outworlder or whatever you are. How did you come to be psycho-probed?"

Rik looked doubtful. "You all say that. Even Lona. But I don't know what the word means."

"When did you stop remembering, then?"

"I'm not sure." He began again, desperately. "I was on a ship."

"We know that. Go on."

Samia said, "It's no use barking, Captain. You'll drive out what few wits are left him."

Rik was entirely absorbed in wrenching at the dimness within his mind. The effort left no room for any emotion. It was to his own astonishment that he said, "I'm not afraid of him, Lady. I'm trying to remember. There was danger. I'm sure of that. Great danger to Florina, but I can't remember the details about it."

"Danger to the whole planet?" Samia cast a swift glance at the Captain.

"Yes. It was in the currents."

"What currents?" asked the Captain.

"The currents of space."

The Captain spread his hands and let them drop. "This is madness."

"No, no. Let him go on." The tide of belief had shifted to Samia again. Her lips were parted, her dark eyes gleamed and little dimples between cheek and chin made their appearance as she smiled. "What are the currents of space?"

"The different elements," said Rik vaguely. He had explained that before. He didn't want to go through that again.

He went on rapidly, nearly incoherently, speaking as the

thoughts came to him, driven by them. "I sent a message to the local office on Sark. I remember that very clearly. I had to be careful. It was a danger that went beyond Florina. Yes. Beyond Florina. It was as wide as the Milky Way. It had to be handled carefully."

He seemed to have lost all real contact with those who listened to him, to be living in a world of the past before which a curtain was tearing away in places. Valona placed a soothing hand upon his shoulder and said, "Don't!" but he was unresponsive even to that.

"Somehow," he went on breathlessly, "my message was intercepted by some official on Sark. It was a mistake. I don't know how it happened."

He frowned. "I'm sure I sent it to the local office on the Bureau's own wave length. Do you suppose the sub-ether could have been tapped?" He did not even wonder that the word "sub-ether" came so easily to him.

He might have been waiting for an answer, but his eyes were still unseeing. "Anyway, when I landed on Sark they were waiting for me."

Again a pause, this time long and meditative. The Captain did nothing to break it; he seemed to be meditating himself.

Samia, however, said, "Who was waiting for you? Who?"

Rik said, "I—I don't know. I can't remember. It wasn't the office. It was someone of Sark. I remember speaking to him. He knew about the danger. He spoke of it. I'm sure he spoke of it. We sat at a table together. I remember the table. He sat opposite me. It's as clear as space. We spoke for quite a while. It seems to me I wasn't anxious to give details. I'm sure of that. I would have had to speak to the office first. And then he..."

"Yes?" prompted Samia.

"He did something. He——No, nothing more will come. *Nothing will come!*"

He screamed the words and then there was silence, a silence that was anticlimatically broken by the prosaic buzz of the Captain's wrist communo.

He said, "What is it?"

The answering voice was reedy and precisely respectful. "A message to the Captain from Sark. It is requested that he accept it personally."

"Very well. I will be at the sub-etherics presently."

He turned to Samia. "My Lady, may I suggest that it is, in any case, dinnertime."

He saw that the girl was about to protest her lack of appetite, to urge him to leave and not to bother about her. He continued, more diplomatically, "It is also time to feed these creatures. They are probably tired and hungry."

Samia could say nothing against that. "I must see them again, Captain."

The Captain bowed silently. It might have been acquiescence. It might not.

Samia of Fife was thrilled. Her studies of Florina satisfied a certain aspiration to intellect within her. But the Mysterious Case of the Psycho-probed Earthman (she thought of the matter in capitals) appealed to something much more primitive and much more demanding. It roused the sheer animal curiosity in her.

It was a mystery!

There were three points that fascinated her. Among these was not the perhaps reasonable question (under the circumstances) of whether the man's story was a delusion or a deliberate lie, rather than the truth. To believe it anything other than truth would spoil the mystery and Samia could not allow that.

The three points were therefore these. (1) What was the danger that threatened Florina, or, rather, the entire Galaxy? (2) Who was the person who had psycho-probed the Earthman? (3) Why had the person used the psycho-probe?

She was determined to sift the matter to her own thorough satisfaction. No one is so modest as not to believe himself a competent amateur sleuth, and Samia was far from modest.

As soon after dinner as she could politely manage, she hurried down to the brig.

She said to the guard, "Open the door!"

The sailor remained perfectly erect, staring blankly and respectfully ahead. He said, "If Your Ladyship pleases, the door is not to be opened."

Samia gasped. "How dare you say so? If you do not open the door instantly, the Captain shall be informed."

"If Your Ladyship pleases, the door is not to be opened. That is by the strict order of the Captain."

She stormed up the levels once more, bursting into the Captain's stateroom like a tornado compressed into sixty inches.

"Captain!"

"My Lady?"

"Have you ordered the Earthman and the native woman to be kept from me?"

"I believe, my Lady, it was agreed that you were to interview them only in my presence."

"Before dinner, yes. But you saw they were harmless?"

"I saw that they *seemed* harmless."

Samia simmered. "In that case I order you to come with me now."

"I cannot, my Lady. The situation has changed."

"In what way?"

"They must be questioned by the proper authorities on Sark and until then I think they should be left alone."

Samia's lower jaw dropped, but she rescued it from its undignified position almost immediately. "Surely you are not going to deliver them to the Bureau of Florinian Affairs."

"Well," temporized the Captain, "that was certainly the original intention. They have left their village without permission. In fact they have left their planet without permission. In addition, they have taken secret passage on a Sarkite vessel."

"The last was a mistake."

"Was it?"

"In any case, you knew all their crimes before our last interview."

"But it was only at the interview that I heard what the so-called Earthman had to say."

"So-called. You said yourself that the planet Earth existed."

"I said it might exist. But, my Lady, may I be so bold as to ask what you would like to see done with these people?"

"I think the Earthman's story should be investigated. He speaks of a danger to Florina and of someone on Sark who has deliberately attempted to keep knowledge of that danger from the proper authorities. I think it is even a case for my father. In fact I would take him to my father, when the proper time came."

The Captain said, "The cleverness of it all!"

"Are you being sarcastic, Captain?"

The Captain flushed. "Your pardon, my Lady. I was referring to our prisoners. May I be allowed to speak at some length?"

"I don't know what you mean by 'some length,'" she retorted angrily, "but I suppose you may begin."

"Thank you. In the first place, my Lady, I hope you will not minimize the importance of the disturbances on Florina."

"What disturbances?"

"You cannot have forgotten the incident in the library."

"A patroller killed! Really, Captain!"

"And a second patroller killed this morning, my Lady, and a native as well. It is not very usual for natives to kill patrollers and here is one who has done it twice, and yet remains uncaught. Is he a lone hand? Is it an accident? Or is it all part of a carefully laid scheme?"

"Apparently you believe the last."

"Yes, I do. The murdering native had two accomplices. Their description is rather like that of our two stowaways."

"You never said so!"

"I did not wish to alarm Your Ladyship. You'll remember, however, that I told you repeatedly that they could be dangerous."

"Very well. What follows from all this?"

"What if the murders on Florina were simply side shows intended to distract the attention of the patroller squadrons while these two sneaked aboard our ship?"

"That sounds so silly."

"Does it? Why are they running away from Florina? We haven't asked them. Let us suppose they are running away from the patrollers since that is certainly the most reasonable assumption. Would they be running to Sark of all places? And on a ship that carries Your Ladyship? And then he claims to be a Spatio-analyst."

Samia frowned. "What of that?"

"A year ago a Spatio-analyst was reported missing. The story was never given wide publicity. I knew, of course, because my ship was one of those that searched near space for signs of his ship. Whoever is backing these Florinian disorders has undoubtedly seized on that fact, and just knowing that the matter of the missing Spatio-analyst is known to them shows what a tight and unexpectedly efficient organization they have."

"It might be that the Earthman and the missing Spatio-analyst have no connection."

"No real connection, my Lady, undoubtedly. But to expect no connection at all is to expect too much of coincidence. It is an impostor we are dealing with. That is why he claims to have been psycho-probed."

"Oh?"

"How can we prove he *isn't* a Spatio-analyst? He knows no details of the planet Earth beyond the bare fact that it is radioactive. He cannot pilot a ship. He knows nothing of Spatio-analysis. And he covers up by insisting he was psycho-probed. Do you see, my Lady?"

Samia could make no direct answer. "But to what purpose?" she demanded.

"So that you might do exactly what you said you intended to do, my Lady."

"Investigate the mystery?"

"No, my Lady. Take the man to your father."

"I still see no point."

"There are several possibilities. At the best, he could be a spy upon your father, either for Florina or possibly for Trantor. I imagine old Abel of Trantor would certainly come

forward to identify him as an Earthman, if for no other
reason than to embarrass Sark by demanding the truth concerning this fictitious psycho-probing. At the worst, he will
be your father's assassin."

"Captain!"

"My Lady?"

"This is ridiculous!"

"Perhaps, my Lady. But if so, the Department of Security
is also ridiculous. You will recall that just before dinner I
was called away to receive a message from Sark."

"Yes."

"This is it."

Samia received the thin translucent foil with its red lettering. It said: "Two Florinians are reported to have taken
secret, illegal passage on your ship. Secure them immediately. One of them may claim to be a Spatio-analyst and
not a Florinian native. You are to take no action in this
matter. You will be held strictly responsible for the safety
of these people. They are to be held for delivery to Depsec.
Extreme secrecy. Extreme urgency."

Samia felt stunned. "Depsec," she said. "The Department
of Security."

"Extreme secrecy," said the Captain. "I stretch a point
to tell you this, but you have left me no choice, my Lady."

She said, "What will they do to him?"

"I cannot say for certain," said the Captain. "Certainly
a suspected spy and assassin cannot expect gentle treatment.
Probably his pretense will become partly a reality and he
will learn what a psycho-probe is really like."

12. THE DETECTIVE

The Four Great Squires regarded the Squire of Fife each in his own way. Bort was angry, Rune was amused, Balle was annoyed, and Steen was frightened.

Rune spoke first. He said, "High treason? Are you trying to frighten us with a phrase? What does it mean? Treason against you? Against Bort? Against myself? By whom and how? And for Sark's sake, Fife, these conferences interfere with my normal sleeping hours."

"The results," said Fife, "may interfere with many sets of sleeping hours. I don't refer to treason against any of us, Rune. I mean treason against Sark."

Bort said, "Sark? What's that, anyway, if not us?"

"Call it a myth. Call it something ordinary Sarkites believe in."

"I don't understand," moaned Steen. "You men always seem so interested in talking each other down. Really! I wish you'd get all this over with."

Balle said, "I agree with Steen." Steen looked gratified.

Fife said, "I'm perfectly willing to explain immediately. You have heard, I suppose, of the recent disturbances on Florina."

Rune said, "The Depsec dispatches speak of several patrollers killed. Is that what you mean?"

Bort broke in angrily. "By Sark, if we must have a conference, let's talk about that. Patrollers killed! They deserve to be killed! Do you mean to say a native can simply come up to a patroller and bash his head in with a two-by-four? Why should any patroller let any native with a two-by-four in his hand come close enough to use it? Why wasn't the native burned down at twenty paces?

"By Sark, I'd rattle the Patrol Corps from captain to recruit and send every dunderhead out on ship duty. The entire Corps is just an accumulation of fat. It's too easy a life for them down there. I say that every five years we should put Florina under martial law and scrape out the troublemakers. It would keep the natives quiet and our own men on their toes."

"Are you through?" asked Fife.

"For now, yes. But I'll take it up again. It's my investment down there, too, you know. It may not be as big as yours, Fife, but it's big enough for me to worry about."

Fife shrugged. He turned suddenly to Steen. "And have *you* heard of the disturbances?"

Steen jumped. "I have. I mean, I've heard you just saying——"

"You haven't read the Depsec announcements?"

"Well, really!" Steen became intensely interested in his long, pointed fingernails with their exquisitely applied coppery coating. "I don't always have time to read *all* the announcements. I didn't know it was required of me. In fact," and he gathered his courage in both hands and looked full at Fife, "I didn't know you were making rules for me. Really!"

"I haven't," said Fife. "Just the same since you, at least,

know none of the details, let me summarize it for you. The rest may find it interesting as well."

It was surprising into how few words the events of forty-eight hours could be put and how flat they could sound. First, there had been an unexpected reference to Spatio-analysis texts. Then a blow on the head of a superannuated patroller who died of a fractured skull two hours later. Then a pursuit that ended with untouchability in the lair of a Trantorian agent. Then a second patroller dead at dawn with the murderer tricked out in the patroller's uniform and the Trantorian agent dead in his turn some hours later.

"If you wish the very latest nugget of news," Fife concluded, "you might add this to this catalog of apparent trivia. Some hours ago a body, or, rather, the bony remnants of one, was found in City Park on Florina."

"Whose body?" asked Rune.

"Just a moment, please. Lying next to it was a pile of ash that seemed to be the charred remnants of clothing. Anything of metal had been carefully removed from it, but the ash analysis proved it to be what was left of a patroller uniform."

"Our impostoring friend?" asked Balle.

"Not likely," said Fife. "Who would kill him in secret?"

"Suicide," said Bort viciously. "How long did the bloody bastard expect to keep out of our hands? I imagine he had a better death this way. Personally, I'd find out who in the corps were responsible for letting him reach the suicide stage and put a one-charge blaster in *their* hands."

"Not likely," said Fife again. "If the man committed suicide he either killed himself first, then took off his uniform, blasted it to ash, removed the buckles and braid, and then got rid of them. Or else he first removed his uniform, ashed it, removed the buckles and braid, left the cave naked, or perhaps in his underwear, discarded them, came back and killed himself."

"The body was in a cave?" asked Bort.

"In one of the ornamental caves of the Park. Yes."

"Then he had plenty of time and plenty of privacy," said

Bort belligerently. He hated to give up a theory. "He could have taken off the buckles and braid first, then——"

"Ever try to remove braid from a patroller uniform that hasn't been ashed first?" asked Fife sarcastically. "And can you suggest a motive, if the body were that of the impostor after suicide? Besides, I have a report from the medical examiners who studied the bone structure. The skeleton is that of neither a patroller nor a Florinian. It is of a Sarkite."

Steen cried, "Really!"; Balle's old eyes opened wide; Rune's metal teeth, which, by catching a gleam of light now and then, added a bit of life to the cube of dusk in which he sat, vanished as he closed his mouth. Even Bort was dumbfounded.

"Do you follow?" asked Fife. "Now you see why the metal was removed from the uniform. Whoever killed the Sarkite wanted the ash to be taken for that of the Sarkite's own clothing, removed and ashed before the killing, which we might then take for suicide or for the result of a private feud in no way connected with our patroller-impostor friend. What he did not know was that ash analysis could distinguish between the kyrt of Sarkite clothing and the cellulite of a patroller uniform even with the buckles and braid removed.

"Now given a dead Sarkite and the ash of a patroller uniform, we can only assume that somewhere in Upper City there is a live Townman in Sarkite clothing. Our Florinian, having posed as a patroller long enough, and finding the danger too great and growing greater, decided to become a Squire. And he did that in the only way he could."

"Has he been caught?" inquired Bort thickly.

"No, he hasn't."

"Why not? By Sark, why not?"

"He will be caught," said Fife indifferently. "At the moment we have more important things to wonder about. This last atrocity is a trifle in comparison."

"Get to the point!" demanded Rune instantly.

"Patience! First, let me ask you if you remember the missing Spatio-analyst of last year."

Steen giggled.

Bort said with infinite contempt, "That again?"

Steen asked, "Is there a connection? Or are we just going to talk about that horrible affair of last year all over again? I'm tired."

Fife was unmoved. He said, "This explosion of yesterday and day before yesterday began with a request at the Florinian library for reference books on Spatio-analysis. That is connection enough for me. Let's see if I can't make it connection for the rest of you as well. I will begin by describing the three people involved in the library incident, and please, let me have no interruptions for a few moments.

"First, there is a Townman. He is the dangerous one of the three. On Sark he had an excellent record as an intelligent and faithful piece of material. Unfortunately he has now turned his abilities against us. He is undoubtedly the one responsible for four killings now. Quite a record for anyone. Considering that the four include two patrollers and a Sarkite, it is unbelievably remarkable for a native. And he is still uncaught.

"The second person involved is a native woman. She is uneducated and completely insignificant. However, the last couple of days have seen an extensive search into every facet of this affair and we know her history. Her parents were members of the 'Soul of Kyrt' if any of your remember that rather ridiculous peasant conspiracy that was wiped out without trouble some twenty years ago.

"This brings us to the third person, the most unusual one of the three. This third person was a common mill hand and an idiot."

There was an expulsion of breath from Bort and another high-pitched giggle from Steen. Balle's eyes remained closed and Rune was motionless in the dark.

Fife said, "The word 'idiot' is not used figuratively. Depsec has driven itself mercilessly but his history could not be traced back more than ten and a half months. At that time he was found in a village just outside Florina's main metropolis in a state of complete mindlessness. He could neither walk nor talk. He could not even feed himself.

"Now note that he made this first appearance some few weeks after the disappearance of the Spatio-analyst. Note in addition that, in a matter of months, he learned how to talk and even how to fill a job at a kyrt mill. What kind of an idiot could learn so quickly?"

Steen began, almost eagerly, "Oh, really, if he were psycho-probed properly, it could be arranged so . . ." His voice trailed off.

Fife said sardonically, "I can think of no greater authority on the subject. Even without Steen's expert opinion, however, the same thought occurred to me. It was the only possible explanation.

"Now the psycho-probing could have taken place only on Sark or in Upper City on Florina. As a matter of simple thoroughness, doctors' offices in Upper City were checked. There was no trace of any unauthorized psycho-probing. It was then the notion of one of our agents to check the records of doctors who had died since the idiot first made his appearance. I shall see to it that he is promoted for that idea.

"We found a record of our idiot in just one of those offices. He had been brought in for a physical checkup about six months ago by the peasant woman who is the second of our trio. Apparently this was done secretly since she was absent that day from her job on quite another pretext. The doctor examined the idiot and recorded definite evidence of psycho-probic tampering.

"Now here is the interesting point. The doctor was one of those who kept double-deck offices in Upper City and Lower City. He was one of those idealists who thought the natives deserved first-rate medical care. He was a methodical man and kept duplicate records in full in both his offices to avoid unnecessary elevator travel. Also it pleased his idealism, I imagine, to practice no segregation between Sarkite and Florinian in his files. But the record of the idiot in question was not duplicated, and it was the *only* record not duplicated.

"Why should that be? If, for some reason, he had decided of his own accord not to duplicate that particular record, why should it have appeared only in the Upper City records, which is where it did appear? Why not only in the Lower City records, which is where it did not appear? After all, the man was a Florinian. He had been brought in by a Florinian. He had been examined in the Lower City office. All that was plainly recorded in the copy we found.

"There is only one answer to that particular puzzle. The record *was* duly entered in both files, but it was destroyed in the Lower City files by somebody who did not realize there would remain another record in the Upper office. Now let's pass on.

"Included with the idiot's examination record was the definite notation to include the findings of this case with the doctor's next routine report to Depsec. That was entirely proper. Any case of psycho-probing could involve a criminal or even a subversive. But no such report was ever made. Within the week he was dead in a traffic accident.

"The coincidences pile up past endurance, don't they?"

Balle opened his eyes. He said, "This is a detective thriller you are telling us."

"Yes," cried Fife with satisfaction, "a detective thriller. And for the moment I am the detective."

"And who are the accused?" asked Balle in a tired whisper.

"Not yet. Let me play the detective for a moment longer."

In the middle of what Fife considered to be the most dangerous crisis that had ever confronted Sark, he suddenly found that he was enjoying himself hugely.

He said, "Let's approach the story from the other end. We will, for the moment, forget the idiot and remember the Spatio-analyst. The first we hear of him is the notification to the Bureau of Transportation that his ship will soon land. A message received from him earlier accompanies the notification.

"The Spatio-analyst never arrives. He is located nowhere in near space. Furthermore, the message sent by the Spatio-analyst, which had been forwarded to BuTrans, disappeared. The I.S.B. claimed that we were deliberately concealing the message. Depsec believed that they were inventing a fictitious message for propaganda purposes. It now occurs to me that we were both wrong. The message *had* been delivered but it had *not* been concealed by the government of Sark.

"Let us invent someone and, for the moment, call him X. X has access to the records of BuTrans. He learns of this Spatio-analyst and his message and has the brains and ability to act quickly. He arranges that a secret sub-ethergram be sent out to the Spatio-analyst's ship, directing the man's landing on some small, private field. The Spatio-analyst does so and X meets him there.

"X has taken the Spatio-analyst's message of doom with him. There may be two reasons for that. First, it would confuse possible attempts at detection by eliminating a piece of evidence. Second, it would serve, perhaps, to win the confidence of the mad Spatio-analyst. If the Spatio-analyst felt he could talk only to his own superiors, and he might feel that, X might persuade him to grow confidential by proving that he was already in possession of the essentials of the story.

"Undoubtedly the Spatio-analyst talked. However incoherent, mad, and generally impossible that talk might have been, X recognized it as an excellent handle for propaganda. He sent out his blackmailing letter to the Great Squires, to us. His procedure, as then planned, was probably precisely that which I attributed to Trantor at the time. If we didn't come to terms with him, he intended to disrupt Florinian production by rumors of destruction until he forced surrender.

"But then came his first miscalculation. Something frightened him. We'll consider exactly what that was later. In any case, he decided he would have to wait before continuing. Waiting, however, involved one complication. X didn't believe the Spatio-analyst's story, but there is no question that the Spatio-analyst himself was madly sincere. X would have to arrange affairs so that the Spatio-analyst would be willing to allow his 'doom' to wait.

"The Spatio-analyst could not do that unless his warped mind was put out of action. X might have killed him, but I am of the opinion that the Spatio-analyst was necessary to him as a source of further information (after all, he knew nothing of Spatio-analysis himself and he couldn't conduct successful blackmail on total bluff), and, perhaps, as ransom in case of ultimate failure. In any case, he used a psycho-probe. After treatment, he had on his hands, not a Spatio-analyst, but a mindless idiot who would, for a time, cause him no trouble. And after a time his senses would be recovered.

"The next step? That was to make certain that during the year's wait the Spatio-analyst would not be located, that no one of importance would see him even in his role as idiot. So he proceeded with a masterly simplicity. He carried his man to Florina and for nearly a year the Spatio-analyst was simply a half-wit native, working in the kyrt mills.

"I imagine that during that year he, or some trusted subordinate, visited the town where he had 'planted' the creature, to see that he was safe and in reasonable health. On one of these visits he learned, somehow, that the creature had been taken to a doctor who knew a psycho-probing when he saw one. The doctor died and his report disappeared, at least from his Lower City office. That was X's first miscalculation. He never thought a duplicate might be in the office above.

"And then came his second miscalculation. The idiot began regaining his senses a little too quickly and the village Townman had brains enough to see that there was something more to it than simple raving. Perhaps the girl who took care of the idiot told the Townman about the psycho-probing. That's a guess.

"There you have the story."

Fife clasped his strong hands and waited for the reaction.

Rune supplied it first. The light had turned on in his cubicle some moments earlier and he sat there, blinking and smiling. He said, "And a moderately dull story it was, Fife. Another moment in the dark and I would have been asleep."

"As nearly as I can see," said Balle slowly, "you have created a structure as insubstantial as the one of last year. It is nine tenths guesswork."

"Hogwash!" said Bort.

"Who is X, anyway?" asked Steen. "If you don't know who X is, it just doesn't make any sense." And he yawned delicately, covering his small white teeth with a bent forefinger.

Fife said, "At least one of you sees the essential point. The identity of X is the nub of the affair. Consider the characteristics that X must possess if my analysis is accurate.

"In the first place, X is a man with contacts in the Civil Service. He is a man who can order a psycho-probing. He is a man who thinks he can arrange a powerful blackmailing campaign. He is a man who can take the Spatio-analyst from Sark to Florina without trouble. He is a man who can arrange the death of a doctor on Florina. He isn't a nobody, certainly.

"In fact he is a very definite somebody. He must be a Great Squire. Wouldn't you say so?"

Bort rose from his seat. His head disappeared and he sat down again. Steen burst into high, hysterical laughter. Rune's eyes, half buried in the pulpy fat that surrounded them, glittered feverishly. Balle slowly shook his head.

Bort yelled, "Who in Space is being accused, Fife?"

"No one yet." Fife remained even-tempered. "No one specifically. Look at it this way. There are five of us. Not another man on Sark could have done what X did. Only we five. That can be taken as settled. Now which of the five is it? To begin with, it isn't myself."

"We can take your word for it, can we?" sneered Rune.

"You don't have to take my word for it," retorted Fife. "I'm the only one without a motive. X's motive is to gain control of the kyrt industry. I *have* control of it. I own a third of Florina's land outright. My mills, machine plants and shipping fleets are sufficiently predominant to force any or all of you out of business if I wish. I wouldn't have to resort to complicated blackmail."

He was shouting over their united voices. "Listen to me! The rest of you have every motive. Rune has the smallest continent and the smallest holdings. I know he doesn't like that. He can't pretend he likes it. Balle has the oldest lineage. There was a time when his family ruled all of Sark. He probably hasn't forgotten that. Bort resents the fact that he is always outvoted in council and cannot therefore conduct business in his territories in quite the whip-and-blaster fashion he would like. Steen has expensive tastes and his finances are in a bad way. The necessity of recouping is a hard-driving one. We have it there. All the possible motives. Envy. Greed for power. Greed for money. Questions of prestige. Now which of you is it?"

There was a gleam of sudden malice in Balle's old eyes. "You don't know?"

"It doesn't matter. Now hear this. I said that something frightened X (let's still call him X) after his first letters to us. Do you know what it was? It was our first conference when I preached the necessity of united action. X was here. X was, and is, one of us. He knew united action meant failure. He had counted on winning over us because he knew that our rigid ideal of continental autonomy would keep us at odds to the last moment and beyond. He saw that he was wrong and he decided to wait until the sense of urgency vanished and he could proceed again.

"But he is still wrong. We will still take united action and there is only one way we can do it safely, considering that X is one of us. Continental autonomy is at an end. It is a luxury we can no longer afford, for X's schemes will end only with the economic defeat of the rest of us or the intervention of Trantor. I, myself, am the only one I can trust, so from now on I head a united Sark. Are you with me?"

They were out of their seats, shouting. Bort was waving his fist. There was a light froth at the corner of his lips.

Physically, there was nothing they could do. Fife smiled. Each was a continent away. He could sit behind his desk and watch them foam.

He said, "You have no choice. In the year since our first conference I, too, have made my preparations. While you four have been quietly in conference, listening to me, officers loyal to myself have taken charge of the Navy."

"Treason!" they howled.

"Treason to continental autonomy," retorted Fife. "Loyalty to Sark."

Steen's fingers intertwined nervously, their ruddy, copper tips the only splash of color upon his skin. "But it's X. Even if X is one of us, there are three innocent. I'm not X." He cast a poisonous glance about him. "It's one of the others."

"Those of you who are innocent will form part of my government if they wish. They have nothing to lose."

"But you won't say who is innocent," bawled Bort. "You will keep us all out on the story of X, on the—on the——" Breathlessness brought him to a halt.

"I will not. In twenty-four hours I will know who X is. I have not told you. The Spatio-analyst we have all been discussing is now in my hands."

They fell silent. They looked at one another with reserve and suspicion.

Fife chuckled. "You are wondering which of you can be X. One of you knows, be sure of that. And in twenty-four hours we shall all know. Now keep in mind, gentlemen, that you are all quite helpless. The ships of war are mine. Good day!"

His gesture was one of dismissal.

One by one they went out, like stars in the depths of the vacuum being blotted out on the visiplate by the passing and unseen bulk of a wrecked spaceship.

Steen was the last to leave. "Fife," he said tremulously.

Fife looked up. "Yes? You wish to confess now that we two are alone? You are X?"

Steen's face twisted in wild alarm. "No, no. Really. I just wanted to ask if you're really serious. I mean, continental autonomy and all that. Really?"

Fife stared at the old chronometer in the wall. "Good day."

Steen whimpered. His hand went up to the contact switch and he, too, disappeared.

Fife sat there, stony and unmoving. With the conference over, the heat of the crisis gone, depression seized him. His lipless mouth was a severe gash in his large face.

All calculations began with this fact: that the Spatio-analyst was mad, there was no doom. But over a madman, so much had taken place. Would Junz of the I.S.B. have spent a year searching for a madman? Would he be so unyielding in his chase after fairy stories?

Fife had told no one this. He scarcely dared share it with his own soul. What if the Spatio-analyst had never been mad? What if destruction dangled over the world of kyrt?

The Florinian secretary glided before the Great Squire, his voice pallid and dry.

"Sir!"

"What is it?"

"The ship with your daughter has landed."

"The Spatio-analyst and the native woman are safe?"

"Yes, sir."

"Let there be no questioning in my absence. They are to be held incommunicado until I arrive. . . . Is there news from Florina?"

"Yes, sir. The Townman is in custody and is being brought to Sark."

13. THE YACHTSMAN

The port's lights brightened evenly as the twilight deepened. At no time did the over-all illumination vary from that to be expected of a somewhat subdued late afternoon. At Port 9, as at the other yacht ports of Upper City, it was daylight throughout Florina's rotation. The brightness might grow unusually pronounced under the midday sun, but that was the only deviation.

Markis Genro could tell that the day proper had passed only because, in passing into the port, he had left the colored night lights of the City behind him. Those were bright against the blackening sky but they made no pretense of substituting for day.

Genro paused just inside the main entrance and seemed in no way impressed by the gigantic horseshoe with its three dozen hangars and five take-off pits. It was part of him, as it was part of any experienced yachtsman.

He took a long cigarette, violet in color and tipped with

the filmiest touch of silvery kyrt, and put it to his lips. He cupped his palms about the exposed tip and watched it glow to greenish life as he inhaled. It burned slowly and left no ash. An emerald smoke filtered out his nostrils.

He murmured, "Business as usual!"

A member of the yacht committee, in yachting costume, with only a discreet and tasteful lettering above one tunic button to indicate that he was a member of the committee, had moved up quickly to meet Genro, carefully avoiding any appearance of hurry.

"Ah, Genro! And why not business as usual?"

"Hello, Doty. I only thought that with all this fume and fuss going on it might occur to some bright boy to close the ports. Thank Sark it hasn't."

The committeeman sobered. "You know, it may come to that. Have you heard the latest?"

Genro grinned. "How you can tell the latest from the next-to-the-latest?"

"Well, have you herd that it's definite now about the native? The killer?

"You mean they've caught him? I hadn't heard that."

"No, they haven't caught him. But they know he's not in Lower City!"

"No? Where is he then?"

"Why, in Upper City. Here."

"Go on." Genro's eyes widened, then narrowed in disbelief.

"No, really," said the committeeman, a little hurt, "I have it for a fact. The patrollers are swooping up and down Kyrt Highway. They've got City Park surrounded and they're using Central Arena as a coordination point. This is all authentic."

"Well, maybe." Genro's eyes roved carelessly over the hangared ships. "I haven't been at 9 for two months, I think. Are there any new ships in the place?"

"No. Well, yes, there's Hjordesse's *Flame Arrow*."

Genro shook his head. "I've seen that. It's all chromium

and nothing else. I hate to think I'll have to end by designing my own."

"Are you selling *Comet V?*"

"Selling it or junking it. I'm tired of these late models. They're too automatic. With their automatic relays and trajectory computers, they're killing the sport."

"You know, I've heard others say the same thing," agreed the committeeman. "Tell you what. If I hear of an old model in good condition on the market, I'll let you know."

"Thanks. Mind if I wander about the place?"

"Of course not. Go ahead." The committeeman grinned, waved, trotted away.

Genro made his slow rounds, his cigarette, half gone, drooping from one side of his mouth. He stopped at each occupied hangar, appraising its contents shrewdly.

At Hangar 26 he displayed a heightened interest. He looked over the low barrier and said, "Squire?"

The call was one of polite inquiry, but after a pause of several moments he had to call again, a little more peremptorily, a little less politely.

The Squire who emerged to view was not an impressive sight. For one thing, he was not in yachting costume. Secondly, he needed a shave, and his rather repellent-looking skull cap was yanked down in a most unfashionable manner. It seemed to cover half his face. Lastly, his attitude was one of peculiarly suspicious overcaution.

Genro said, "I'm Markis Genro. Is this your craft, sir?"

"Yes, it is." The words were slow and tense.

Genro disregarded that. He tilted his head back and looked over the yacht's lines carefully. He removed what was left of his cigarette from between his lips and flicked it high in the air. It had not yet reached the high point of its arc when, with a little flash, it vanished.

Genro said, "I wonder if you'd mind my coming in?" The other hesitated, then stepped aside. Genro entered.

He said, "What kind of motor does the craft carry, sir?"

"Why do you ask?"

Genro was tall, skin and eyes were dark, hair crisp and

cut short. He topped the other by half a head, and his smile showed white, evenly spaced teeth. He said, "To be very frank, I'm in the market for a new ship."

"You mean you're interested in this one?"

"I don't know. Something like it, maybe, if the price is right. But anyway, I wonder if you'd mind my looking at the controls and engines?"

The Squire stood there silently.

Genro's voice grew a trifle colder. "As you please, of course." He turned away.

The Squire said, "I might sell." He fumbled in his pockets. "Here's the license!"

Genro looked at each side with a quick, experienced glance. He handed it back. "You're Deamone?"

The Squire nodded. "You can come in if you wish."

Genro looked briefly at the large port-chronometer, the luminescent hands, sparking brightly even in the daylight illumination, indicating the beginning of the second hour after sunset.

"Thank you. Won't you lead the way?"

The Squire rummaged his pockets again and held out a booklet of key slivers. "After you, sir."

Genro took the booklet. He leafed through the slivers, looking at the small code marks for the "ship stamp." The other man made no attempt to help him.

Finally he said, "This one, I suppose?"

He walked up the short ramp to the air-lock balcony and considered the fine seam at the right of the lock carefully. "I don't see——Oh, here it is," and he stepped to the other side of the lock.

Slowly, noiselessly, the lock yawned and Genro moved into the blackness. The red air-lock went on automatically as the door closed behind them. The inner door opened and as they stepped into the ship proper white lights flickered on over all the length of the ship.

Myrlyn Terens had no choice. He no longer remembered the time, long since, when such a thing as "choice" had existed. For three long, wretched hours, now, he had remained near Deamone's ship, waiting and helpless to do anything else. It had led to nothing till now. He did not see that it could lead to anything but capture.

And then this fellow had come with an eye to the ship. To deal with him at all was madness. He could not possibly maintain his imposture at such close quarters. But then he could not possibly remain where he was, either.

At least within the ship there might be food. Strange that that had not occurred to him before.

There was.

Terens said, "It's close to dinnertime. Would you like to have something?"

The other had scarcely looked over his shoulder. "Why, later, perhaps. Thank you."

Terens did not urge him. He let him roam the ship and applied himself thankfully to the potted meat and cellulite-wrapped fruit. He drank thirstily. There was a shower across the corridor from the kitchen. He locked its door and bathed. It was a pleasure to be able to remove the tight skullcap, at least temporarily. He even found a shallow closet from which he could choose a change of clothing.

He was far more master of himself when Genro returned.

Genro said, "Say, would you mind if I tried to fly this ship?"

"I have no objection. Can you handle this model?" asked Terens with an excellent imitation of nonchalance.

"I think so," said the other with a little smile. "I flatter myself I can handle any of the regular models. Anyway, I've taken the liberty of calling the control tower, and there's a take-off pit available. Here's my yachtsman's license if you'd like to see it before I take over."

Terens gave it as cursory a glance as Genro had given his. "The controls are yours," he said.

The ship rolled out of the hangar like an air-borne whale, moving slowly, its diamagnetized hull clearing the smooth-packed clay of the field by three inches.

Terens watched Genro handling the controls with finger-tip precision. The ship was a live thing under his touch. The small replica of the field that was upon the visiplate shifted and changed with each tiny motion of every contact.

The ship came to a halt, pinpointed at the tip of a take-off pit. The diamagnetic field strengthened progressively towards the ship's prow and it began tipping upward. Terens was mercifully unaware of this as the pilot room turned on its universal gimbals to meet the shifting gravity. Majestically, the ship's rear flanges fitted into the appropriate grooves of the pit. It stood upright, pointing to the sky.

The duralite cover of the take-off pit slipped into its recess, revealing the neutralized lining, a hundred yards deep, that received the first energy thrusts of the hypera-tomic motors.

Genro kept up a cryptic exchange of information with the control tower. Finally, "Ten seconds to take-off," he said.

A rising red thread in a quartz tube marked off the dis-appearing seconds. It made contact and the first surge of power tore backward.

Terens grew heavier, felt himself pressing against the seat. Panic tore at him.

He grunted, "How does it handle?"

Genro seemed impervious to acceleration. His voice had almost its natural timbre as he said, "Moderately well."

Terens leaned back in his chair, trying to relax with the pressure, watching the stars in the visiplate turn hard and bright as the atmosphere vanished from between himself and them. The kyrt next to his skin felt cold and damp.

They were out in space now. Genro was putting the ship through its paces. Terens had no way of telling that first hand but he could see the stars march steadily across the visiplate as the yachtsman's long, slim fingers played with the controls as though they were the keys of a musical instrument. Finally a bulky orange segment of a globe filled the visiplate's clear surface.

"Not bad," said Genro. "You keep your craft in good condition, Deamone. It's small but it has its points."

Terens said carefully, "I suppose you'd like to test its speed and its jumping capacity. You may, if you like. I have no objection."

Genro nodded. "Very well. Where do you suggest we take ourselves? What about——" He hesitated, then went on, "Well, why not to Sark?"

Terens breathed a little more quickly. He had expected that. He was on the point of believing himself to be living in a world of magic. How things forced his moves, even without his connivance. It would not have been difficult to convince him that it was not "things" but design that prompted the moves. His childhood had been steeped in the superstitions that the Squires fostered among the natives and such things are hard to outgrow. On Sark was Rik with his returning memories. The game was not over.

He said wildly, "Why not, Genro?"

Genro said, "Sark it is then."

With gathering speed, the globe of Florina slanted out beyond the visiplate's view and the stars returned.

"What's your best time on the Sark-Florina run?" asked Genro.

"Nothing record-breaking," said Terens. "About average."

"Then you've done it in better than six hours, I suppose?"

"On occasion, yes."

"Do you object to my trying to shave five?"

"Not at all," said Terens.

It took hours to reach a point far enough from star-mass distortion of the space fabric to make a jump possible.

Terens found wakefulness a torture. This was his third night with little or no sleep and the tension of the days had exaggerated that lack.

Genro looked at him askance. "Why don't you turn in?"

Terens forced an expression of liveliness onto his sagging facial muscles. He said, "It's nothing. Nothing."

He yawned prodigiously and smiled in apology. The yachtsman turned back to his instruments and Terens' eyes glazed over once again.

Seats in a space-yacht are comfortable by very necessity. They must cushion the person against accelerations. A man not particularly tired can easily and sweetly fall asleep upon them. Terens, who could, at the moment, have slept on broken glass, never knew when he passed the border line.

He slept for hours; he slept as deeply and as dreamlessly as ever in his life.

He did not stir; he showed no single sign of life other than his even breathing when the skullcap was removed from his head.

Terens woke blearily, slowly. For long minutes he had not the slightest notion of his whereabouts. He thought he was back in his Townman's cottage. The true state of affairs seeped back in stages. Eventually he could smile at Genro, who was still at the controls, and say, "I guess I fell asleep."

"I guess you did. There's Sark." Genro nodded toward the large white crescent in the visiplate.

"When do we land?"

"About an hour."

Terens was awake enough now to sense a subtle change in the other's attitude. It was an icy shock to him that the steel-gray object in Genro's hand turned out to be the graceful barrel of a needle-gun.

"What in Space——" began Terens, rising to his feet.

"Sit down," said Genro carefully. There was a skullcap in his other hand.

Terens raised a hand to his head and his fingers found themselves clutching sandy hair.

"Yes," said Genro, "it's quite obvious. You're a native."

Terens stared and said nothing.

Genro said, "I knew you were a native before I ever got on poor Deamone's ship."

Terens' mouth was cotton-dry and his eyes burned. He watched the tiny, deadly muzzle of the gun and waited for a sudden, noiseless flash. He had carried it so far, so far, and had lost the gamble after all.

Genro seemed in no hurry. He held the needle-gun steady and his words were even and slow.

"Your basic mistake, Townman, was the thought that you could really outwit an organized police force indefinitely. Even so, you would have done better if you hadn't made the unfortunate choice of Deamone as your victim."

"I didn't choose him," croaked Terens.

"Then call it luck. Alstare Deamone, some twelve hours ago, was standing in City Park, waiting for his wife. There was no reason, other than sentiment, for him to meet her there of all places. They had met in that very spot originally, and they met there again on every anniversary of that meeting. There's nothing particularly original about that sort of ceremony between young husbands and wives, but it seems important to them. Of course Deamone did not realize that the comparative isolation of the spot made him an appropriate victim for a murderer. Who would have thought that in Upper City?

"In the ordinary course of events the murder might not have been discovered for days. Deamone's wife, however, was on the scene within half an hour of the crime. The fact that her husband was not there astonished her. He was not the type, she explained, to leave in a fury because she herself was a trifle late. She was often late. He would more or less have expected that. It occurred to her that her husband might be waiting for her inside 'their' cave.

"Deamone had been waiting outside 'their' cave, naturally. It was the nearest one to the scene of the assault, consequently, and the one into which he was dragged. His wife entered that cave and found—well, you know what she found. She managed to relay the news to the Patrol Corps through our own Depsec offices, although she was almost incoherent with shock and hysteria.

"How does it feel, Townman, to kill a man in cold blood, leaving him to be found by his wife at the one spot most steeped with happy memories for them both?"

Terens was choking. He gasped out, through a red mist of anger and frustration, "You Sarkites have killed millions of Florinians. Women. Children. You've grown rich out of us. This yacht——" It was all he could manage.

"Deamone wasn't responsible for the state of affairs he found at birth," said Genro. "If you had been born a Sarkite, what would you have done? Resigned your estates, if any, and gone to work in the kyrt fields?"

"Well then, shoot," cried Terens, writhing. "What are you waiting for?"

"There's no hurry. There is plenty of time to finish my story. We weren't certain as to the identity of either the corpse or the murderer, but it was a very good guess that they were Deamone and yourself respectively. It seemed obvious to us from the fact that the ashes next to the body were of a patroller uniform that you were masquerading as a Sarkite. It seemed further probable that you would make for Deamone's yacht. Don't overestimate our stupidity, Townman.

"Matters were still rather complex. You were a desperate man. It was insufficient to track you down. You were armed and would undoubtedly commit suicide if trapped. Suicide was something we did not wish. They wanted you on Sark and they wanted you in working order.

"It was a particularly delicate affair for myself and it was quite necessary to convince Depsec that I could handle it alone, that I could get you to Sark without noise or difficulty. You'll have to admit that is just what I'm doing.

"To tell you the truth, I wondered at first if you were really our man. You were dressed in ordinary business costume on the yacht-port grounds. It was in incredibly bad taste. No one, it seemed to me, would dream of impersonating a yachtsman without the proper costume. I thought you were being deliberately sent in as a decoy, that you were *trying* to be arrested while the man we wanted escaped in another direction.

"I hesitated and tested you in other ways. I fumbled with the ship's key in the wrong place. No ship ever invented opened at the right side of the air lock. It opens always and invariably at the left side. You never showed any surprise at my mistake. None at all. Then I asked you if your ship had ever made the Sark-Florina run in less than six hours. You said you had—occasionally. That is quite remarkable. The record time for the run is over 9 hours.

"I decided you couldn't be a decoy. The ignorance was too supreme. You had to be naturally ignorant and probably the right man. It was only a question of your falling asleep (and it was obvious from your face that you needed sleep desperately), disarming you and covering you quietly with an adequate weapon. I removed your hat more out of curiosity than anything else. I wanted to see what a Sarkite costume looked like with a red-haired head sticking out of it."

Terens kept his eyes on the whip. Perhaps Genro saw his jaw muscles bunch. Perhaps he simply guessed at what Terens was thinking.

He said, "Of course I must not kill you, even if you jump me. I can't kill you even in self-defense. Don't think that gives you an advantage. Begin to move and I'll shoot your leg off."

The fight went out of Terens. He put the heels of his palms to his forehead and sat rigid.

Genro said softly, "Do you know why I tell you all this?"

Terens did not answer.

"First," said Genro, "I rather enjoy seeing you suffer. I don't like murderers and I particularly don't like natives who kill Sarkites. I've been ordered to deliver you alive but nothing in my orders says I have to make the trip pleasant for you. Secondly, it is necessary for you to be fully aware of the situation since, after we land on Sark, the next steps will be up to you."

Terens looked up. "What!"

"Depsec knows you're coming in. The Florinian regional office sent the word as soon as this craft cleared Florina's atmosphere. You can be sure of that. But I said it was quite necessary for me to convince Depsec that I could handle this alone and the fact that I have makes all the difference."

"I don't understand you," said Terens desperately.

With composure, Genro answered, "I said 'they' wanted you on Sark, 'they' wanted you in working order. By 'they' I don't mean Depsec, I mean Trantor!"

14. THE RENEGADE

Selim Junz had never been the phlegmatic type. A year of frustration had done nothing to improve that. He could not sip wine carefully while his mental orientation sat upon suddenly trembling foundations. In short, he was not Ludigan Abel.

And when Junz had done with his angry shouting that on no account was Sark to be allowed freedom to kidnap and imprison a member of the I.S.B. regardless of the condition of Trantor's espionage network, Abel merely said, "I think you had better spend the night here, Doctor."

Junz said freezingly, "I have better things to do."

Abel said, "No doubt, man, no doubt. Just the same, if my men are being blasted to death, Sark must be bold indeed. There is a great possibility that some accident may happen to you before the night is over. Let us wait a night then and see what comes of a new day."

Junz's protests against inaction came to nothing. Abel,

without ever losing his cool, almost negligent air of indifference, was suddenly hard of hearing. Junz was escorted with firm courtesy to a chamber.

In bed, he stared at the faintly luminous, frescoed ceiling (on which glowed a moderately skillful copy of Lenhaden's "Battle of the Arcturian Moons") and knew he would not sleep. Then he caught one whiff, a faint one, of the gas, somnin, and was asleep before he could catch another. Five minutes later, when a forced draft swept the room clean of the anesthetic, enough had been administered to assure a healthful eight hours.

He was awakened in the cold half-light of dawn. He blinked up at Abel.

"What time is it?" he asked.

"Six."

"Great Space." He looked about and thrust his bony legs out from under the sheet. "You're up early."

"I haven't slept."

"What?"

"I feel the lack, believe me. I don't respond to antisomnin as I did when I was younger."

Junz murmured, "If you will allow me a moment."

This once his morning preparations for the day took scarcely more than that. He reentered the room, drawing the belt about his tunic and adjusting the magneto-seam.

"Well?" he asked. "Surely you don't wake through the night and rouse me at six unless you have something to tell me."

"You're right. You're right." Abel sat down on the bed vacated by Junz and threw his head back in a laugh. It was high-pitched and rather subdued. His teeth showed, their strong, faintly yellow plastic incongruous against his shrunken gums.

"I beg your pardon, Junz," he said. "I am not quite myself. This drugged wakefulness has me a little lightheaded. I almost think I will advise Trantor to replace me with a younger man."

Junz said, with a flavor of sarcasm not entirely unmixed with sudden hope, "You find they haven't got the Spatio-analyst after all?"

"No, they do. I'm sorry but they do. I'm afraid that my amusement is due entirely to the fact that our nets are intact."

Junz would have liked to say, "Damn your nets," but refrained.

Abel went on, "There is no doubt they know Khorov was one of our agents. They may know of others on Florina. Those are small fry. The Sarkites knew that and never felt it worth while to do more than hold them under observation."

"They killed one," Junz pointed out.

"They did not," retorted Abel. "It was one of the Spatio-analyst's own companions in a patroller disguise who used the blaster."

Junz stared. "I don't understand."

"It's a rather complicated story. Won't you join me at breakfast? I need food badly."

Over the coffee, Abel told the story of the last thirty-six hours.

Junz was stunned. He put down his own coffee cup, half full, and returned to it no more. "Even allowing them to have stowed away on that ship of all ships, the fact still remains they might not have been detected. If you send men to meet that ship as it lands——"

"Bah. You know better than that. No modern ship could fail to detect the presence of excess body heat."

"It might have been overlooked. Instruments may be infallible but men are not."

"Wishful thinking. Look here. At the very time that the ship with the Spatio-analyst aboard is approaching Sark, there are reports of excellent reliability that the Squire of Fife is in conference with the other great Squires. These intercontinental conferences are spaced as widely as the stars of the Galaxy. Coincidence?"

"An intercontinental conference over a Spatio-analyst?"

"An unimportant subject in itself, yes. But we have made it important. The I.S.B. has been searching for him for nearly a year with remarkable pertinacity."

"Not the I.S.B.," insisted Junz. "Myself. I've been working in almost an unofficial manner."

"The Squires don't know that and wouldn't believe it if you told them. Then, too, Trantor has been interested."

"At my request."

"Again they don't know that and wouldn't believe it."

Junz stood up and his chair moved automatically away from the table. Hands firmly interlocked behind his back, he strode the carpet. Up and back. Up and back. At intervals he glanced harshly at Abel.

Abel turned unemotionally to a second cup of coffee.

Junz said, "How do you know all this?"

"All what?"

"Everything. How and when the Spatio-analyst stowed away. How and in what manner the Townman has been eluding capture. Is it your purpose to deceive me?"

"My dear Dr. Junz."

"You admitted you had your men watching for the Spatio-analyst independently of myself. You saw to it that I was safely out of the way last night, leaving nothing to chance." Junz remembered, suddenly, that whiff of somnin.

"I spent a night, Doctor, in constant communication with certain of my agents. What I did and what I learned comes under the heading of, shall we say, classified material. You had to be out of the way, and yet safe. What I have told you just now I learned from my agents last night."

"To learn what you did you would need spies in the Sarkite government itself."

"Well, naturally."

Junz whirled on the ambassador. "Come, now."

"You find that surprising? To be sure, Sark is proverbial for the stability of its government and the loyalty of its people. The reason is simple enough since even the poorest Sarkite is an aristocrat in comparison with Florinians and can consider himself, however fallaciously, to be a member of a ruling class.

"Consider, though, that Sark is not the world of billionaires most of the Galaxy thinks it is. A year's residence must have well convinced you of that. Eighty per cent of its population has its living standard at a par with that of other worlds and not much higher than the standard of Florina itself. There will always be a certain number of Sarkites who, in their hunger, will be sufficiently annoyed with the small fraction of the population obviously drenched in luxury to lend themselves to my uses.

"It is the great weakness of the Sarkite government that for centuries they have associated rebellion only with Florina. They have forgotten to watch over themselves."

Junz said, "These small Sarkites, assuming they exist, can't do you much good."

"Individually, no. Collectively, they form useful tools for our more important men. There are members even of the real ruling class who have taken the lessons of the last two centuries to heart. They are convinced that in the end Trantor will have established its rule over all the Galaxy, and, I believe, rightly convinced. They even suspect that the final dominion may take place within their lifetimes, and they prefer to establish themselves, in advance, on the winning side."

Junz grimaced. "You make interstellar politics sound a very dirty game."

"It is, but disapproving of dirt doesn't remove it. Nor are all its facets unrelieved dirt. Consider the idealist. Consider the few men in Sark's government who serve Trantor neither for money nor for promises of power but only because they honestly believe that a unified Galactic government is best for humanity and that only Trantor can bring such a government about. I have one such man, my best one, in Sark's Department of Security, and at this moment he is bringing in the Townman."

Junz said, "You said he had been captured."

"By Depsec, yes. But my man is Depsec *and my man*."

For a moment Abel frowned and turned pettish. "His usefulness will be sharply reduced after this. Once he lets the Townman get away, it will mean demotion at the best and imprisonment at the worst. Oh well!"

"What are you planning now?"

"I scarcely know. First, we must have our Townman. I am sure of him only to the point of arrival at the spaceport. What happens thereafter..." Abel shrugged, and his old, yellowish skin stretched parchmentlike over his cheekbones.

Then he added, "The Squires will be waiting for the Townman as well. They are under the impression they have him, and until one or the other of us has him in our fists, nothing more can happen."

But that statement was wrong.

Strictly speaking, all foreign embassies throughout the Galaxy maintained extraterritorial rights over the immediate area of their location. Generally this amounted to nothing more than a pious wish, except where the strength of the home planet enforced respect. In actual practice it meant that only Trantor could truly maintain the independence of its envoys.

The grounds of the Trantorian Embassy covered nearly a square mile and within it armed men in Trantorian costume and insignia maintained patrol. No Sarkite might enter but on invitation, and no armed Sarkite on any account. To be sure, the sum of Trantorian men and arms could withstand the determined attack of a single Sarkite armored regiment for not more than two or three hours, but behind the small band was the power of reprisal from the organized might of a million worlds.

It remained inviolate.

It could even maintain direct material communication with Trantor, without the need of passing through Sarkite ports of entry or debarkation. From the hold of a Trantorian mothership, hovering just outside the hundred-mile limit that marked off the boundary between "planetary space" and "free space," small gyro-ships, vane-equipped for atmospheric travel with minimum power expenditure, might emerge and needle down (half coasting, half driven) to the small port maintained within the embassy grounds.

The gyro-ship which now appeared over the embassy port, however, was neither scheduled nor Trantorian. The mosquito-might of the embassy was brought quickly and truculently into play. A needle-cannon lifted its puckered muzzle into the air. Force screens went up.

Radioed messages whipped back and forth. Stubborn words rode the impulses upward, agitated ones slipped down.

Lieutenant Camrum turned away from the instrument and said, "I don't know. He claims he'll be shot out of the sky in two minutes if we don't let him down. He claims sanctuary."

Captain Elyut had just entered. He said, "Sure. Then Sark will claim we're interfering in politics and if Trantor decides to let things ride, you and I are broken as a gesture. Who is he?"

"Won't say," said the lieutenant with more than a little exasperation. "Says he must speak to the Ambassador. Suppose you tell me what to do, Captain."

The short-wave receiver sputtered and a voice, half hysterical, said, "Is anyone *there*? I'm just coming down, that's all. Really! I can't wait another moment, I tell you." It ended in a squeak.

The captain said, "Great Space, I know that voice. Let him down! My responsibility!"

The orders went out. The gyro-ship sank vertically, more quickly than it should have, the result of a hand at the controls that was both inexperienced and panicky. The needle-cannon maintained focus.

The captain established a through line to Abel and the embassy was thrown into full emergency. The flight of Sarkite ships that hovered overhead not ten minutes after the first vessel had landed maintained a threatening vigil for two hours, then departed.

* * *

They sat at dinner, Abel, Junz and the newcomer. With admirable aplomb, considering the circumstances, Abel had acted the unconcerned host. For hours he had refrained from asking why a Great Squire needed sanctuary.

Junz was far less patient. He hissed at Abel, "Space! What are you going to do with him?"

And Abel smiled back. "Nothing. At least until I find out whether I have my Townman or not. I like to know what my hand is before tossing chips onto the table. And since he's come to me, waiting will rattle him more than it will us."

He was right. Twice the Squire launched into rapid monolog and twice Abel said, "My dear Squire! Surely serious conversation is unpleasant on an empty stomach." He smiled gently and ordered dinner.

Over the wine, the Squire tried again. He said, "You'll want to know why I have left Steen Continent."

"I cannot conceive of any reason," admitted Abel, "for the Squire of Steen ever to have run from Sarkite vessels."

Steen watched them carefully. His slight figure and thin, pale face were tense with calculation. His long hair was bound into carefully arranged tufts held by tiny clips that rubbed against one another with a rustling sound whenever he moved his head, as though to call attention to his disregard for the current Sarkite clipped-hair fashion. A faint fragrance came from his skin and clothing.

Abel, who did not miss the slight tightening of Junz's lips and the quick way in which the Spatio-analyst patted his own short, woolly hair, thought how amusing Junz's reaction might have been if Steen had appeared more typically, with rouged cheeks and coppered fingernails.

Steen said, "There was an intercontinental conference today."

"Really?" said Abel.

Abel listened to the tale of the conference without a quiver of countenance.

"And we have twenty-four hours," Steen said indignantly. "It's sixteen hours now. Really!"

"And you're X," cried Junz, who had been growing increasingly restless during the recitation. "You're X. You've come here because he's caught you. Well now, that's fine. Abel, here's our proof as to the identity of the Spatio-analyst. We can use him to force a surrender of the man."

Steen's thin voice had difficulty making itself heard over Junz's staunch baritone.

"Now really. I say, now really. You're mad. Stop it! Let me speak, I tell you. . . . Your Excellency, I can't remember this man's name."

"Dr. Selim Junz, Squire."

"Well then, Dr. Selim Junz, I have never in my life seen this idiot or Spatio-analyst or whatever in the world he may be. Really! I never heard such nonsense. I am certainly not X. Really! I'll thank you not even to use the silly letter. Imagine believing Fife's ridiculous melodrama! Really!"

Junz clung to his notion. "Why did you run then?"

"Good Sark, isn't it clear? Oh, I could choke. Really! Look here, don't you see what Fife was doing?"

Abel interrupted quietly. "If you'll explain, Squire, there will be no interruptions."

"Well, thank *you* at least." He continued, with an air of wounded dignity. "The others don't think much of me because I don't see the point of bothering with documents and statistics and all those boring details. But, really, what is the Civil Service for, I'd like to know, if a Great Squire can't *be* a Great Squire?

"Still that doesn't mean I'm a ninny, you know, just because I like my comfort. Really! Maybe the others are blind, but I can see that Fife doesn't give a darn for the Spatio-analyst. I don't even think he exists. Fife just got the idea a year ago and he's been manipulating it ever since.

"He's been playing us for fools and idiots. Really! And so the others are. Disgusting fools! He's *arranged* all this perfectly awful nonsense about idiots and Spatio-analysis. I wouldn't be surprised if the native who's supposed to be killing patrollers by the dozen isn't just one of Fife's spies in a red wig. Or if he's a real native, I suppose Fife has hired him.

"I wouldn't put it past Fife. Really! He would use natives against his own kind. That's how low he is.

"Anyway, it's obvious that he's using it just as an excuse to ruin the rest of us and to make himself dictator of Sark. Isn't it obvious to you?

"There isn't any X at all, but tomorrow, unless he's stopped, he'll spread the sub-etherics full of conspiracies and declarations of emergencies and he'll have himself declared Leader. We haven't had a leader on Sark in five hundred years but that won't stop Fife. He'd just let the constitution go hang. Really!

"Only I mean to stop him. That's why I had to leave. If I were still in Steen, I'd be under house arrest.

"As soon as the conference was over I had my own personal port checked, and, you know, his men had taken over. It was in clear disregard of continental autonomy. It was the act of a cad. Really! But nasty as he is, he isn't so bright. He thought some of us might try to leave the planet so he had the spaceports watched, but"—here he smiled in vulpine fashion and emitted the ghost of a giggle—"it didn't occur to him to watch the gyro-ports.

"Probably he thought there wasn't a place on the planet that would be safe for us. But I thought of the Trantorian Embassy. It's more than the others did. They make me tired. Especially Bort. Do you know Bort? He's terribly uncouth. Actually *dirty*. Talks at me as though there were something wrong with being clean and smelling pleasant."

He put his finger tips to his nose and inhaled gently.

Abel put a light hand on Junz's wrist as the latter moved restlessly in his seat. Abel said, "You have left a family behind. Have you thought that Fife can still hold a weapon over you?"

"I couldn't very well pile all my pretty ones in my gyroplane." He reddened a trifle. "Fife wouldn't dare touch them. Besides, I'll be back in Steen tomorrow."

"How?" asked Abel.

Steen looked at him in astonishment. His thin lips parted. "I'm offering alliance, Your Excellency. You can't pretend Trantor isn't *interested* in Sark. Surely you'll tell Fife that any attempt to change Sark's constitution would necessitate Trantor's intervention."

"I scarcely see how that can be done, even if I felt my government would back me," said Abel.

"How can it *not* be done?" asked Steen indignantly. "If he controls the entire kyrt trade he'll raise the price, ask concessions for rapid delivery and all sorts of things."

"Don't the five of you control the price as is?"

Steen threw himself back in the seat. "Well, really! I don't know all the details. Next you'll be asking me for figures. Goodness, you're as bad as Bort." Then he recovered and giggled. "I'm just teasing, of course. What I mean is that, with Fife out of the way, Trantor *might* make an arrangement with the rest of us. In return for your help, it would only be right that Trantor get preferential treatment, or even maybe a small interest in the trade."

"And how would we keep intervention from developing into a Galaxy-wide war?"

"Oh, but really, don't you see? It's plain as day. You wouldn't be *aggressors*. You would just be preventing civil war to keep the kyrt trade from disruption. I'd announce that I'd appealed to you for help. It would be worlds removed from aggression. The whole Galaxy would be on your side. Of course, if Trantor benefits from it afterward, why, that's nobody's business at all. Really!"

Abel put his gnarled fingers together and regarded them. "I can't believe you really mean to join forces with Trantor."

An intense look of hatred passed momentarily over Steen's weakly smiling face. He said, "Rather Trantor than Fife."

Abel said, "I don't like threatening force. Can't we wait and let matters develop a bit——"

"No, no," cried Steen. "Not a day. Really! If you're not firm now, right now, it will be too late. Once the deadline is past, he'll have gone too far to retreat without losing face. If you'll help me now, the people of Steen will back me, the other Great Squires will join me. If you wait even a day, Fife's propaganda mill will begin to grind. I'll be smeared as a renegade. Really! I! *I!* A renegade! He'll use all the anti-Trantor prejudice he can whip up and you know, meaning no offense, that's quite a bit."

"Suppose we ask him to allow us to interview the Spatio-analyst?"

"What good will that do? He'll play both ends. He'll tell us the Florinian idiot is a Spatio-analyst, but he'll tell you the Spatio-analyst is a Florinian idiot. You don't know the man. He's *awful!*"

Abel considered that. He hummed to himself, his forefinger keeping gentle time. Then he said, "We have the Townman, you know."

"What Townman?"

"The one who killed the patrollers and the Sarkite."

"Oh! Well, really! Do you suppose Fife will care about that if it's a question of taking all Sark?"

"I think so. You see, it isn't that we have the Townman. It's the circumstances of his capture. I think, Squire, that Fife will listen to me and listen very humbly, too."

For the first time in his acquaintance with Abel, Junz sensed a lessening of coolness in the old man's voice, a substitution for it of satisfaction, almost of triumph.

15. THE CAPTIVE

It was not very usual for the Lady Samia of Fife to feel frustrated. It was unprecedented, even inconceivable, that she had felt frustrated for hours now.

The commander of the spaceport was Captain Racety all over again. He was polite, almost obsequious, looked unhappy, expressed his regrets, denied the least willingness to contradict her, and stood like iron against her plainly stated wishes.

She was finally forced from stating her desires to demanding her rights as though she were a common Sarkite. She said, "I suppose that as a citizen I have the right to meet any incoming vessel if I wish."

She was poisonous about it.

The commander cleared his throat and the expression of pain on his lined face grew, if anything, clearer and more definite. Finally he said, "As a matter of fact, my Lady, we have no wish at all to exclude you. It is only that we have received specific orders from the Squire, your father, to forbid your meeting the ship."

Samia said frozenly, "Are you ordering me to leave the port, then?"

"No, my Lady." The commander was glad to compromise. "We were not ordered to exclude you from the port. If you wish to remain here you may do so. But, with all due respect, we will have to stop you from approaching closer to the pits."

He was gone and Samia sat in the futile luxury of her private ground-car, a hundred feet inside the outermost entrance of the port. They had been waiting and watching for her. They would probably keep on watching her. If she as much as rolled a wheel onward, she thought indignantly, they would probably cut her power-drive.

She gritted her teeth. It was unfair of her father to do this. It was all of a piece. They always treated her as though she understood nothing. Yet she had thought he understood.

He had risen from his seat to greet her, a thing he never did for anyone else now that Mother was dead. He had clasped her, squeezed her tightly, abandoned all his work for her. He had even sent his secretary out of the room because he knew she was repelled by the native's still, white countenance.

It was almost like the old days before Grandfather died when Father had not yet become Great Squire.

He said, "Mia, child, I've counted the hours. I never knew it was such a long way from Florina. When I heard that those natives had hidden on your ship, the one I had sent just to insure your safety, I was nearly wild."

"Daddy! There was nothing to worry about."

"Wasn't there? I almost sent out the entire fleet to take you off and bring you in with full military security."

They laughed together at the thought. Minutes passed before Samia could bring the conversation back to the subject that filled her.

She said casually, "What are you going to do with the stowaways, Dad?"

"Why do you want to know, Mia?"

"You don't think they've plans to assassinate you, or anything like that?"

Fife smiled. "You shouldn't think morbid thoughts."

"You don't think so, do you?" she insisted.

"Of course not."

"Good! Because I've talked to them, Dad, and I just don't believe they're anything more than poor harmless people. I don't care what Captain Racety says."

"They've broken a considerable number of laws for 'poor harmless people,' Mia."

"You can't treat them as common criminals, Dad." Her voice rose in alarm.

"How else?"

"The man isn't a native. He's from a planet called Earth and he's been psycho-probed and he's not responsible."

"Well then, dear, Depsec will realize that. Suppose you leave it to them."

"No, it's too important to just leave to them. They won't understand. Nobody understands. Except me!"

"Only you in the whole world, Mia?" he asked indulgently, and put out a finger to stroke a lock of hair that had fallen over her forehead.

Samia said with energy, "Only I! Only I! Everyone else is going to think he's crazy, but I'm *sure* he isn't. He says there is some great danger to Florina and to all the Galaxy. He's a Spatio-analyst and you know they specialize in cosmology. He would *know*!"

"How do you know he's a Spatio-analyst, Mia?"

"He says so."

"And what are the details of the danger?"

"He doesn't know. He's been psycho-probed. Don't you see that that's the best evidence of all? He knew too much. Someone was interested in keeping it dark." Her voice instinctively fell and grew huskily confidential. She restrained an impulse to look over her shoulder. She said, "If his theories were false, don't you see, there wouldn't have been any need to psycho-probe him."

"Why didn't they kill him, if that's the case?" asked Fife and instantly regretted the question. There was no use in teasing the girl.

Samia thought awhile, fruitlessly, then said, "If you'll order Depsec to let me speak to him, I'll find out. He trusts me. I know he does. I'll get more out of him then Depsec can. Please tell Depsec to let me see him, Dad. It's *very* important."

Fife squeezed her clenched fists gently and smiled at her. "Not yet, Mia. Not yet. In a few hours we'll have the third person in our hands. After that, perhaps."

"The third person? The native who did all the killings?"

"Exactly. The ship carrying him will land in about an hour."

"And you won't do anything with the native girl and the Spatio-analyst till then?"

"Not a thing."

"Good! I'll meet the ship." She rose.

"Where are you going, Mia?"

"To the port, Father. I have a great deal to ask of this other native." She laughed. "I'll show you that your daughter can be quite a detective."

But Fife did not respond to her laughter. He said, "I'd rather you didn't."

"Why not?"

"It's essential that there be nothing out of the way about this man's arrival. You'd be too conspicuous at the port."

"What of it?"

"I can't explain statecraft to you, Mia."

"Statecraft, pooh." She leaned toward him, pecked a quick kiss at the center of his forehead and was gone.

Now she sat helplessly car-bound in the port while far overhead there was a growing speck in the sky, dark against the brightness of the late afternoon.

She pressed the button that opened the utility compartment and took out her polo-glasses. Ordinarily they were used to follow the gyrating antics of the one-man speedsters which took part in stratospheric polo. They could be put to more serious use too. She put them to her eyes and the descending dot became a ship in miniature, the ruddy glow of its stern drive plainly visible.

She would at least see the men as they left, learn as much as she could by the one sense of sight, arrange an interview somehow, *somehow* thereafter.

Sark filled the visiplate. A continent and half an ocean, obscured in part by the dead cotton-white of clouds, lay below.

Genro said, his words a trifle uneven as the only indication that the better part of his mind was perforce on the controls before him, "The spaceport will not be heavily guarded. That was at my suggestion too. I said that any unusual treatment of the arrival of the ship might warn Trantor that something was up. I said that success depended upon Trantor being at no time aware of the true state of affairs until it was too late. Well, never mind that."

Terens shrugged his shoulders glumly. "What's the difference?"

"Plenty, to you. I will use the landing pit nearest the East Gate. You will get out the safety exit in the rear as soon as I land. Walk quickly but not too quickly toward that gate. I have some papers that may get you through without trouble and may not. I'll leave it to you to take necessary action if there is trouble. From past history, I judge I can trust you that far. Outside the gate there will be a car waiting to take you to the embassy. That's all."

"What about you?"

Slowly Sark was changing from a huge featureless sphere of blinding browns and greens and blues and cloud-white into something more alive, into a surface broken by rivers and wrinkled by mountains.

Genro's smile was cool and humorless. "Your worries may end with yourself. When they find you gone, I may be shot as a traitor. If they find me completely helpless and physically unable to stop you, they may merely demote me as a fool. The latter, I suppose, is preferable, so I will ask you, before you leave, to use a neuronic whip on me."

The Townman said, "Do you know what a neuronic whip is like?"

"Quite." There were small drops of perspiration at his temples.

"How do you know I won't kill you afterward? I'm a Squire-killer, you know."

"I know. But killing me won't help you. It will just waste your time. I've taken worse chances."

The surface of Sark as viewed in the visiplate was expanding, its edge rushed out past the border of visibility, its center grew and the new edges rushed out in turn. Something like the rainbow of a Sarkite city could be made out.

"I hope," said Genro, "you have no ideas of striking out on your own. Sark is no place for that. It's either Trantor or the Squires. Remember."

The view was definitely that of a city now and a green-brown patch on its outskirts expanded and became a spaceport below them. It floated up toward them at a slowing pace.

Genro said, "If Trantor doesn't have you in the next hour the Squires will have you before the day is out. I don't guarantee what Trantor will do to you, but I can guarantee what Sark will do to you."

Terens had been in the Civil Service. He knew what Sark would do with a Squire-killer.

The port held steady in the visiplate, but Genro no longer regarded it. He was switching to instruments, riding the pulsebeam downward. The ship turned slowly in air, a mile high, and settled, tail down.

A hundred yards above the pit, the engines thundered high. Over the hydraulic springs, Terens could feel their shuddering. He grew giddy in his seat.

Genro said, "Take the whip. Quickly now. Every second is important. The emergency lock will close behind you. It will take them five minutes to wonder why I don't open the main lock, another five minutes to break in, another five minutes to find you. You have fifteen minutes to get out of the port and into the car."

The shuddering ceased and in the thick silence Terens knew they had made contact with Sark.

The shifting diamagnetic fields took over. The yacht tipped majestically and slowly moved down upon its side.

Genro said, "Now!" His uniform was wet with perspiration.

Terens, with swimming head, and eyes that all but refused to focus, raised his neuronic whip....

Terens felt the nip of a Sarkite autumn. He had spent years in its harsh seasons until he had almost forgotten the soft eternal June of Florina. Now his days in Civil Service rushed back upon him as though he had never left this world of Squires.

Except that now he was a fugitive and branded upon him was the ultimate crime, the murder of a Squire.

He was walking in time to the pounding of his heart. Behind him was the ship and in it was Genro, frozen in the agony of the whip. The lock had closed softly behind him, and he was walking down a broad, paved path. There were workmen and mechanics in plenty about him. Each had his own job and his own troubles. They didn't stop to stare a man in the face. They had no reason to.

Had anyone actually seen him emerge from the ship?

He told himself no one had, or by now there would have been the clamor of pursuit.

He touched his hat briefly. It was still down over his ears, and the little medallion it now carried was smooth to the touch. Genro had said that it would act as identification. The men from Trantor would be watching for just that medallion, glinting in the sun.

He could remove it, wander away on his own, find his way to another ship—somehow. He would get away from Sark—somehow. He would escape—somehow.

Too many somehows! In his heart he knew he had come to the final end, and as Genro had said, it was either Trantor or Sark. He hated and feared Trantor, but he knew that in any choice it could not and must not be Sark.

"You! You there!"

Terens froze. He looked up in cold panic. The gate was a hundred feet away. If he ran . . . But they wouldn't allow a running man to get out. It was a thing he dared not do. He must not run.

The young woman was looking out the open window of a car such as Terens had never seen, not even during fifteen years on Sark. It gleamed with metal and sparkled with translucent gemmite.

She said, "Come here."

Terens' legs carried him slowly to the car. Genro had said Trantor's car would be waiting outside the port. Or had he? And would they send a woman on such an errand? A girl, in fact. A girl with a dark, beautiful face.

She said, "You arrived on the ship that just landed, didn't you?"

He was silent.

She became impatient. "Come, I saw you leave the ship!" She tapped her polo-glasses. He had seen such glasses before.

Terens mumbled, "Yes. Yes."

"Get in then."

She held the door open for him. The car was even more luxurious inside. The seat was soft and it all smelled new and fragrant and the girl was beautiful.

She said, "Are you a member of the crew?"

She was testing him, Terens imagined. He said, "You know who I am." He raised his fingers momentarily to the medallion.

Without any sound of motive power the car backed and turned.

At the gate, Terens shrank back into the soft, cool, kyrt-covered upholstery, but there was no need for caution. The girl spoke peremptorily and they passed through.

She said, "This man is with me. I am Samia of Fife."

It took seconds for the tired Terens to hear and understand that. When he lurched tensely forward in his seat the car was traveling along the express lanes at a hundred per.

A laborer within the port looked up from where he stood and muttered briefly into his lapel. He entered the building then and returned to his work. His superintendent frowned and made a mental note to talk to Tip about this habit of lingering outside to smoke cigarettes for half an hour at a time.

Outside the port one of two men in a ground-car said with annoyance, "Got into a car with a girl? What car? What girl?" For all his Sarkite costume, his accent belonged definitely to the Arcturian worlds of the Trantorian Empire.

His companion was a Sarkite, well versed in the visicast news releases. When the car in question rolled through the gate and picked up speed as it began to veer off and upward to the express level, he half rose in his seat and cried, "It's the Lady Samia's car. There isn't another like it. Good Galaxy, what do we do?"

"Follow," said the other briefly.

"But the Lady Samia——"

"She's nothing to me. She shouldn't be anything to you either. Or what are you doing here?"

Their own car was making the turn, climbing upward onto the broad, nearly empty stretches on which only the speediest of ground travel was permitted.

The Sarkite groaned, "We can't catch that car. As soon as she spots us she'll kick out resistance. That car can make two-fifty."

"She's staying at a hundred so far," said the Arcturian.

After a while he said, "She's not going to Depsec. That's for sure."

And after another while he said, "She's not going to the Palace of Fife."

Still another interval and he said, "I'll be spun in space if I know *where* she's going. She'll be leaving the city again."

The Sarkite said, "How do we know it's the Squire-killer that's in there? Suppose it's a game to get us away from the post. She's not trying to shake us and she wouldn't use a car like that if she didn't *want* to be followed. You can't miss it at two miles."

"I know, but Fife wouldn't send his girl to get us out of the way. A squad of patrollers would have done the job better."

"Maybe it isn't really the Lady in it."

"We're going to find out, man. She's slowing. Flash past and stop around a curve!"

"I want to speak to you," said the girl.

Terens decided it was not the ordinary kind of trap he had first considered it. She *was* the Lady of Fife. She must be. It did not seem to occur to her that anyone could or ought to interfere with her.

She had never looked back to see if she were followed. Three times as they turned he had noted the same car to the rear, keeping its distance, neither closing the gap nor falling behind.

It was not just a car. That was certain. It might be Trantor, which would be well. It might be Sark, in which case the Lady would be a decent sort of hostage.

He said, "I'm ready to speak."

She said, "You were on the ship that brought the native from Florina? The one wanted for all those killings?"

"I said I was."

"Very well. Now I've brought you out here so that there'll be no interference. Was the native questioned during the trip to Sark?"

Such naïveté, Terens thought, could not be assumed. She really did not know who he was. He said guardedly, "Yes."

"Were you present at the questioning?"

"Yes."

"Good. I thought so. Why did you leave the ship, by the way?"

That, thought Terens, was the question she should have asked first of all.

He said, "I was to bring a special report to——" He hesitated.

She seized on the hesitation eagerly. "To my father? Don't worry about that. I'll protect you completely. I'll say you came with me at my orders."

He said, "Very well, my Lady."

The words "my Lady" struck deeply into his own consciousness. She was a Lady, the greatest in the land, and he was a Florinian. A man who could kill patrollers could learn easily how to kill Squires, and a Squire-killer might, by the same token, look a Lady in the face.

He looked at her, his eyes hard and searching. He lifted his head and stared down at her.

She was very beautiful.

And because she was the greatest Lady in the land, she was unconscious of his regard. She said, "I want you to tell me everything that you heard at the questioning. I want to know all that was told to you by the native. It's very important."

"May I ask why you are interested in the native, my Lady?"

"You may not," she said flatly.

"As you wish, my Lady."

He didn't know what he was going to say. With half his consciousness he was waiting for the pursuing car to catch up. With the other half he was growing more aware of the face and body of the beautiful girl sitting near him.

Florinians in the Civil Service and those acting as Townmen were, theoretically, celibates. In actual practice, most evaded that restriction when they could. Terens had done what he dared and what was expedient in that direction. At best, his experiences had never been satisfactory.

So it was all the more important that he had never been so near a beautiful girl in a car of such luxuriance under conditions of such isolation.

She was waiting for him to speak, dark eyes (such dark

eyes) aflame with interest, full red lips parted in anticipation, a figure more beautiful for being set off in kyrt. She was completely unaware that anyone, *anyone*, could possibly dare harbor dangerous thought with regard to the Lady of Fife.

The half of his consciousness that waited for the pursuers faded out.

He suddenly knew that the killing of a Squire was not the ultimate crime after all.

He wasn't quite aware that he moved. He knew only that her small body was in his arms, that it stiffened, that for an instant she cried out, and then he smothered the cry with his lips....

There were hands on his shoulder and the drift of cool air on his back through the opened door of the car. His fingers groped for his weapon, too late. It was ripped from his hand.

Samia gasped wordlessly.

The Sarkite said with horror, "Did you see what he did?"

The Arcturian said, "Never mind!"

He put a small black object into his pocket and smoothed the seam shut. "Get him," he said.

The Sarkite dragged Terens out of the car with the energy of fury. "And she let him," he muttered. "She let him."

"Who *are* you?" cried Samia with sudden energy. "Did my father send you?"

The Arcturian said, "No questions, please."

"You're a foreigner," said Samia angrily.

The Sarkite said, "By Sark, I ought to bust his head in." He cocked his fist.

"Stop it!" said the Arcturian. He seized the Sarkite's wrist and forced it back.

The Sarkite growled sullenly, "There are limits. I can take the Squire-killing. I'd like to kill a few myself, but standing by and watching a native do what he did is just about too much for me."

Samia said in an unnaturally high-pitched voice, "Native?"

The Sarkite leaned forward, snatched viciously at Terens' cap. The Townman paled but did not move. He kept his gaze steadily upon the girl and his sandy hair moved slightly in the breeze.

Samia moved helplessly back along the car seat as far as she could and then, with a quick movement, she covered her face with both hands, her skin turning white under the pressure of her fingers.

The Sarkite said, "What are we going to do with her?"

"Nothing."

"She saw us. She'll have the whole planet after us before we've gone a mile."

"Are you going to kill the Lady of Fife?" asked the Arcturian sarcastically.

"Well, no. But we can wreck her car. By the time she gets to a radio-phone, we'll be all right."

"Not necessary." The Arcturian leaned into the car. "My Lady, I have only a moment. Can you hear me?"

She did not move.

The Arcturian said, "You had better hear me. I am sorry I interrupted you at a tender moment but luckily I have put that moment to use. I acted quickly and was able to record the scene by tri-camera. This is no bluff. I will transmit the negative to a safe place minutes after I leave you and thereafter any interference on your part will force me to be rather nasty. I'm sure you understand me."

He turned away. "She won't say anything about this. Not a thing. Come along with me, Townman."

Terens followed. He could not look back at the white, pinched face in the car.

Whatever might now follow, he had accomplished a miracle. For one moment he had kissed the proudest Lady on Sark, had felt the fleeting touch of her soft, fragrant lips.

16. THE ACCUSED

Diplomacy has a language and a set of attitudes all its own. Relationships between the representatives of sovereign states, if conducted strictly according to protocol, are stylized and stultifying. The phrase "unpleasant consequences" becomes synonymous with war and "suitable adjustment" with surrender.

When on his own, Abel preferred to abandon diplomatic double-talk. With a tight personal beam connecting himself and Fife, he might merely have been an elderly man talking amiably over a glass of wine.

He said, "You have been hard to reach, Fife."

Fife smiled. He seemed at ease and undisturbed. "A busy day, Abel."

"Yes. I've heard a bit about it."

"Steen?" Fife was casual.

"Partly. Steen's been with us about seven hours."

"I know. My own fault, too. Are you considering turning him over to us?"

"I'm afraid not."

"He's a criminal."

Abel chuckled and turned the goblet in his hand, watching the lazy bubbles. "I think we can make out a case for his being a political refugee. Interstellar law will protect him on Trantorian territory."

"Will your government back you?"

"I think it will, Fife. I haven't been in the foreign service for thirty-seven years without knowing what Trantor will back and what it won't."

"I can have Sark ask for your recall."

"What good would that do? I'm a peaceable man with whom you are well acquainted. My successor might be anybody."

There was a pause. Fife's leonine countenance puckered. "I think you have a suggestion."

"I do. You have a man of ours."

"What man of yours?"

"A Spatio-analyst. A native of the planet Earth, which, by the way, is part of the Trantorian domain."

"Steen told you this?"

"Among other things."

"Has he seen this Earthman?"

"He hasn't said he has."

"Well, he hasn't. Under the circumstances, I doubt that you can have faith in his word."

Abel put down his glass. He clasped his hands loosely in his lap and said, "Just the same, I'm sure the Earthman exists. I tell you, Fife, we should get together on this. I have Steen and you have the Earthman. In a sense we're even. Before you go on with your current plans, before your ultimatum expires and your *coup d'état* takes place, why not a conference on the kyrt situation generally?"

"I don't see the necessity. What is happening on Sark now is an internal matter entirely. I'm quite willing to guarantee personally that there will be no interference with the kyrt trade regardless of political events here. I think that should end Trantor's legitimate interests."

Abel sipped at his wine, seemed to consider. He said, "It seems we have a second political refugee. A curious case. One of your Florinian subjects, by the way. A Townman. Myrlyn Terens, he calls himself."

Fife's eyes blazed suddenly. "We half suspected that. By Sark, Abel, there's a limit to the open interference of Trantor on this planet. The man you have kidnaped is a murderer. You can't make a political refugee out of him."

"Well, now, do you want the man?"

"You have a deal in mind? Is that it?"

"The conference I spoke of."

"For one Florinian murderer. Of course not."

"But the manner in which the Townman managed to escape to us is rather curious. You may be interested . . ."

Junz paced the floor, shaking his head. The night was already well advanced. He would like to be able to sleep but he knew he would require somnin once again.

Abel said, "I might have had to threaten force, as Steen suggested. That would have been bad. The risks would have been awful, the results uncertain. Yet until the Townman was brought to us I saw no alternative, except of course, a policy of do-nothing."

Junz shook his head violently. "No. Something had to be done. Yet it amounted to blackmail."

"Technically, I suppose so. What would you have had me do?"

"Exactly what you did. I'm not a hypocrite, Abel. Or I try not to be. I won't condemn your methods when I intend to make full use of the results. Still, what about the girl?"

"She won't be hurt as long as Fife keeps his bargain."

"I'm sorry for her. I've grown to dislike the Sarkite aristocrats for what they've done to Florina, but I can't help feeling sorry for her."

"As an individual, yes. But the true responsibility lies

with Sark itself. Look here, old man, did you ever kiss a girl in a ground-car?"

The tip of a smile quivered at the corners of Junz's mouth. "Yes."

"So have I, though I have to call upon longer memories than you do, I imagine. My eldest granddaughter is probably engaged in the practice at this moment, I shouldn't wonder. What is a stolen kiss in a ground-car, anyway, except the expression of the most natural emotion in the Galaxy?

"Look here, man. We have a girl, admittedly of high social standing, who, through mistake, finds herself in the same car with, let us say, a criminal. He seizes the opportunity to kiss her. It's on impulse and without her consent. How ought she to feel? How ought her father to feel? Chagrined? Perhaps. Annoyed? Certainly. Angry? Offended? Insulted? All that, yes. But disgraced? No! Disgraced enough to be willing to endanger important affairs of state to avoid exposure? Nonsense.

"But that's exactly the situation and it could happen only on Sark. The Lady Samia is guilty of nothing but willfulness and a certain naïveté. She has, I am sure, been kissed before. If she kissed again, if she kissed innumerable times, anyone but a Florinian, nothing would be said. But she *did* kiss a Florinian.

"It doesn't matter that she did not know he was a Florinian. It doesn't matter that he forced the kiss upon her. To make public the photograph we have of the Lady Samia in the arms of the Florinian would make life unbearable for her and for her father. I saw Fife's face when he stared at the reproduction. There was no way of telling for certain that the Townman was a Florinian. He was in Sarkite costume with a cap that covered his hair well. He was light-skinned, but that was inconclusive. Still, Fife knew that the rumor would be gladly believed by many who were interested in scandal and sensation and that the picture would be considered incontrovertible proof. And he knew that his political enemies would make the greatest possible capital out of it. You may call it blackmail, Junz, and maybe it is, but it's a blackmail that would not work on any other planet in the Galaxy. Their own sick social system gave us this weapon and I have no compunction about using it."

Junz sighed. "What's the final arrangement?"

"We'll meet at noon tomorrow."

"His ultimatum has been postponed then?"

"Indefinitely. I will be at his office in person."

"Is that a necessary risk?"

"It's not much of one. There will be witnesses. And I am anxious to be in the material presence of this Spatio-analyst you have been searching for so long."

"I'll attend?" asked Junz anxiously.

"Oh yes. The Townman as well. We'll need him to iden-tify the Spatio-analyst. And Steen, of course. All of you will be present by trimensic personification."

"Thank you."

The Trantorian Ambassador smothered a yawn and blinked at Junz through watering eyes. "Now, if you don't mind, I've been awake for two days and a night and I'm afraid my old body can take no more antisomnin. I must sleep."

With trimensic personification perfected, important con-ferences were rarely held face to face. Fife felt strongly an element of actual indecency in the material presence of the old Ambassador. His olive complexion could not be said to have darkened, but its lines were set in silent anger.

He had to be silent. He could say nothing. He could only stare sullenly at the man who faced him.

Abel! An old dotard in shabby clothes with a million worlds behind him.

Junz! A dark-skinned, woolly-haired interferer whose perseverance had precipitated the crisis.

Steen! The traitor! Afraid to meet his eyes!

The Townman! To look at him was most difficult of all. He was the native who had dishonored his daughter with his touch yet who could remain safe and untouchable behind the walls of the Trantorian Embassy. He would have been glad to grind his teeth and pound his desk if he had been alone. As it was, not a muscle of his face must move though it tore beneath the strain.

If Samia had not . . . He dropped that. His own negligence had cultivated her willfulness and he could not blame her for it now. She had not tried to excuse herself or soften her own guilt. She had told him all the truth of her private attempts to play the interstellar spy and how horribly it had ended. She had relied completely, in her shame and bitterness, on his understanding, and she would have that much. She would have that much, if it meant the ruin of the structure he had been building.

He said, "This conference has been forced upon me. I see no point in saying anything. I'm here to listen."

Abel said, "I believe Steen would like to have his say first."

Fife's eyes filled with contempt that stung Steen.

Steen yelled his answer. "You made me turn to Trantor, Fife. You violated the principle of autonomy. You couldn't expect me to stand for that. Really."

Fife said nothing and Abel said, not without a little contempt of his own, "Get to your point, Steen. You said you had something to say. Say it."

Steen's sallow cheekbones reddened without benefit of rouge. "I will, and right now. Of course I don't claim to be the detective that the Squire of Fife represents himself to be, but I can think. Really! And I've *been* thinking. Fife had a story to tell yesterday, all about a mysterious traitor he called X. I could see it was just a lot of talk so that he could declare an emergency. I wasn't fooled a minute."

"There's no X?" asked Fife quietly. "Then why did *you* run? A man who runs needs no other accusation."

"Is that so? Really?" cried Steen. "Well, I would run out of a burning building even if I had not set the fire myself."

"Go on, Steen," said Abel.

Steen licked his lips and turned to a minute consideration of his fingernails. He smoothed them gently as he spoke. "But then I thought, why make up that particular story with all its complications and things? It's not his way. Really!

It's not Fife's way. I know him. We all know him. He has
no imagination at all, Your Excellency. A brute of a man!
Almost as bad as Bort."

Fife scowled. "Is he saying something, Abel, or is he
babbling?"

"Go on, Steen," said Abel.

"I will, if you'll let me talk. My goodness! Whose side
are you on? I said to myself (this was after dinner), I said,
Why would a man like Fife make up a story like that? There
was only one answer. He couldn't make it up. Not with *his*
mind. So it was true. It must be true. And, of course,
patrollers *had* been killed, though Fife is quite capable of
arranging to have that happen."

Fife shrugged his shoulders.

Steen drove on. "Only who is X? It isn't I. Really! I
know it isn't I! And I'll admit it could only have been a
Great Squire. But what Great Squire knew most about it,
anyway? What Great Squire has been trying to use the story
of the Spatio-analyst for a year now to frighten the others
into some sort of what he calls 'united effort' and what I
call surrender to a Fife dictatorship?

"I'll tell you who X is." Steen stood up, the top of his
head brushing the edge of the receptor-cube and flattening
as the uppermost inch sliced off into nothingness. He pointed
a trembling finger. "*He's* X. The Squire of Fife. He found
this Spatio-analyst. He put him out of the way, when he
saw the rest of us weren't impressed with his silly remarks
at our first conference, and then he brought him out again
after he had already arranged a military coup."

Fife turned wearily to Abel. "Is he through? If so, remove
him. He is an unbearable offense to any decent man."

Abel said, "Have you any comment to make on what he
says?"

"Of course not. It isn't worth comment. The man is
desperate. He'll say anything."

"You can't just brush it off, Fife," called Steen. He
looked about at the rest. His eyes narrowed and the skin at
his nostrils was white with tension. He remained standing.

"Listen. He said his investigators found records in a doctor's office. He said the doctor had died by accident after diagnosing the Spatio-analyst as the victim of psycho-probing. He said it was murder by X to keep the identity of the Spatio-analyst secret. That's what he said. Ask him. Ask him if that isn't what he said."

"And if I did?" asked Fife.

"Then ask him how he could get the records from the office of a doctor who was dead and buried for months unless he had them all along. Really!"

Fife said, "This is foolish. We can waste time indefinitely this way. Another doctor took over the dead man's practice and his records as well. Do any of you think medical records are destroyed along with a physician?"

Abel said, "No, of course not."

Steen stuttered, then sat down.

Fife said, "What's next? Have any of you more to say? More accusations? More anything?" His voice was low. Bitterness showed through.

Abel said, "Why, that was Steen's say, and we'll let it pass. Now Junz and I, we're here on another kind of business. We would like to see the Spatio-analyst."

Fife's hands had been resting upon the desk top. They lifted now and came down to clutch the edge of the desk. His black eyebrows drew together.

He said, "We have in custody a man of subnormal mentality who claims to be a Spatio-analyst. I'll have him brought in!"

Valona March had never, never in her life dreamed such impossibilities could exist. For over a day now, ever since she had landed on this planet of Sark, there had been a touch of wonder about everything. Even the prison cells in which she and Rik had been separately placed seemed to have an unreal quality of magnificence about them. Water came out of a hole in a pipe when you pressed a button. Heat came out of the wall, although the air outside had been colder than she had thought air could possibly get. And everyone who spoke to her wore such beautiful clothes.

She had been in rooms in which were all sorts of things she had never seen before. This one now was larger than any yet but it was almost bare. It had more people in it, though. There was a stern-looking man behind a desk, and a much older, very wrinkled man in a chair, and three others . . .

One was the Townman!

She jumped up and ran to him. "Townman! Townman!"

But he wasn't there!

He had gotten up and waved at her. "Stay back, Lona. Stay back!"

And she passed right through him. She had reached out to seize his sleeve, he moved it away. She lunged, half stumbling, and passed right through him. For a moment the breath went out of her body. The Townman had turned, was facing her again, but she could only stare down at her legs.

Both of them were thrusting through the heavy arm of the chair in which the Townman had been sitting. She could see it plainly, in all its color and solidity. It encircled her legs but she did not feel it. She put out a trembling hand and her fingers sank an inch deep into upholstery they could not feel either. Her fingers remained visible.

She shrieked and fell, her last sensation being that of the Townman's arms reaching automatically for her and herself falling through their circle as though they were pieces of flesh-tinted air.

She was in a chair again, Rik holding one hand tightly and the old, wrinkled man leaning over her.

He was saying, "Don't be frightened, my dear. It's just a picture. A photograph, you know."

Valona looked about. The Townman was still sitting there. He wasn't looking at her.

She pointed a finger, "Isn't he there?"

Rik said suddenly, "It's a trimensic personification, Lona. He's somewhere else, but we can see him from here."

Valona shook her head. If Rik said so, it was all right. But she lowered her eyes. She dared not look at people who were there and not there at the same time.

Abel said to Rik, "So you know what trimensic personification is, young man?"

"Yes, sir." It had been a tremendous day for Rik, too, but where Valona was increasingly dazzled, he had found things increasingly familiar and comprehensible.

"Where did you learn that?"

"I don't know. I knew it before—before I forgot."

Fife had not moved from his seat behind the desk during the wild plunge of Valona March toward the Townman.

He said acidly, "I am sorry to have to disturb this meeting by bringing in a hysterical native woman. The so-called Spatio-analyst required her presence."

"It's all right," said Abel. "But I notice that your Florinian of subnormal mentality seems to be acquainted with trimensic personification."

"He has been well drilled, I imagine," said Fife.

Abel said, "Has he been questioned since arriving on Sark?"

"He certainly has."

"With what result?"

"No new information."

Abel turned to Rik. "What's your name?"

"Rik is the only name I remember," said Rik calmly.

"Do you know anyone here?"

Rik looked from face to face without fear. He said, "Only the Townman. And Lona, of course."

"This," said Abel, gesturing toward Fife, "is the greatest Squire that ever lived. He owns the whole world. What do you think of him?"

Rik said boldly, "I'm an Earthman. He doesn't own *me*."

Abel said in an aside to Fife, "I don't think an adult native Florinian could be trained into that sort of defiance."

"Even with a psycho-probe?" returned Fife scornfully.

"Do you know this gentleman?" asked Abel, returning to Rik.

"No, sir."

"This is Dr. Selim Junz. He's an important official at the Interstellar Spatio-analytic Bureau."

Rik looked at him intently. "Then he'd be one of my chiefs. But," with disappointment, "I don't know him. Or maybe I just don't remember."

Junz shook his head gloomily. "I've never seen him, Abel."

"That's something for the record," muttered Fife.

"Now listen, Rik," said Abel. "I'm going to tell you a story. I want you to listen with all your mind and think. Think and think! Do you understand me?"

Rik nodded.

Abel talked slowly. His voice was the only sound in the room for long minutes. As he went on, Rik's eyelids closed and screwed themselves tight shut. His lips drew back, his fists moved up to his chest, and his head bent forward. He had the look of a man in agony.

Abel talked on, passing back and forth across the reconstruction of events as they had originally been presented by the Squire of Fife. He talked of the original message of disaster, of its interception, of the meeting between Rik and X, of the psycho-probing, of how Rik had been found and brought up on Florina, of the doctor who diagnosed him and then died, of his returning memory.

He said, "That's the whole story, Rik. I've told you all of it. Does anything sound familiar to you?"

Slowly, painfully, Rik said, "I remember the last parts. You know, the last few days. I remember something further back, too. Maybe it was the doctor, when I first started talking. It's very dim. . . . But that's all."

Abel said, "But you *do* remember further back. You remember danger to Florina."

"Yes. Yes. That was the first thing I remembered."

"Then can't you remember after that? You landed on Sark and met a man."

Rik moaned, "I can't. I can't remember."

"Try! Try!"

Rik looked up. His white face was wet with perspiration. "I remember a word."

"What word, Rik?"

"It doesn't make sense."

"Tell us anyway."

"It goes along with a table. Long, long ago. Very dim. I was sitting. I think, maybe, someone else was sitting. Then he was standing, looking down at me. And there's a word."

Abel was patient. "What word?"

Rik clenched his fists and whispered, "Fife!"

Every man but Fife rose to his feet. Steen shrieked, "I told you," and burst into a high-pitched bubbling cackle.

17. THE ACCUSER

Fife said with tightly controlled passion, "Let us end this farce."

He had waited before speaking, his eyes hard and his face expressionless, until in sheer anticlimax the rest were forced to take their seats again. Rik had bent his head, eyes screwed painfully shut, probing his own aching mind. Valona pulled him toward herself, trying hard to cradle his head on her shoulder, stroking his cheek softly.

Abel said shakily, "Why do you say this is a farce?"

Fife said, "Isn't it? I agreed to this meeting in the first place only because of a particular threat you held over me. I would have refused even so if I had known the conference was intended to be a trial of myself with renegades and murderers acting as both prosecutors and jury."

Abel frowned and said with chilling formality, "This is not a trial, Squire. Dr. Junz is here in order to recover the person of a member of the I.S.B., as is his right and duty.

I am here to protect the interests of Trantor in a troubled time. There is no doubt in my mind that this man, Rik, is the missing Spatio-analyst. We can end this part of the conference immediately if you will agree to turn over the man to Dr. Junz for further examination, including a check of physical characteristics. We would naturally require your further help in finding the guilty psycho-prober and in setting up safeguards against a future repetition of such acts against what is, after all, an interstellar agency which has consistently held itself above regional politics."

Fife said, "Quite a speech! But the obvious remains obvious and your plans are quite transparent. What would happen if I gave up this man? I rather think that the I.S.B. will manage to find out exactly what it wants to find out. It claims to be an interstellar agency with no regional ties, but it's a fact, isn't it, that Trantor contributes two thirds of its annual budget? I doubt that any reasonable observer would consider it really neutral in the Galaxy of today. Its findings with regard to this man will surely suit Trantor's imperial interests.

"And what will these findings be? That's obvious too. The man's memory will slowly come back. The I.S.B. will issue daily bulletins. Bit by bit he will remember more and more of the necessary details. First my name. Then my appearance. Then my exact words. I will be solemnly declared guilty. Reparations will be required and Trantor will be forced to occupy Sark temporarily, an occupation which will somehow become permanent.

"There are limits beyond which any blackmail breaks down. Yours, Mr. Ambassador, ends here. If you want this man, have Trantor send a fleet for him."

"There is no question of force," said Abel. "Yet I notice that you have carefully avoided denying the implication in what the Spatio-analyst has last said."

"There isn't any implication that I need dignify by a denial. He remembers a word, or he says he does. What of it?"

"Doesn't it mean anything that he does?"

"Nothing at all. The name Fife is a great one on Sark.

Even if we assume the so-called Spatio-analyst is sincere, he had a year's opportunity to hear the name on Florina. He came to Sark on a ship that carried my daughter, a still better opportunity to have heard the name of Fife. What is more natural than that the name became involved with his trace memories? Of course, he may not be sincere. This man's bit-by-bit disclosures may be well rehearsed."

Abel thought of nothing to say. He looked at the others. Junz was frowning darkly, the fingers of his right hand slowly kneading his chin. Steen was simpering foolishly and muttering to himself. The Florinian Townman stared blankly at his knees.

It was Rik who spoke, forcing himself from Valona's grasp and standing up.

"Listen," he said. His pale face was twisted. His eyes mirrored pain.

Fife said, "Another disclosure, I suppose."

Rik said, "Listen! We were sitting at a table. The tea was drugged. We had been quarreling. I don't remember why. Then I couldn't move. I could only sit there. I couldn't talk. I could only think. Great Space, I've been drugged. I wanted to shout and scream and run, but I couldn't. Then the other one, Fife, came. He had been shouting at me. Only now he wasn't shouting. He didn't have to. He came around the table. He stood there, towering over me. I couldn't say anything. I couldn't do anything. I could only try to turn my eyeballs up toward him."

Rik remained standing, silent.

Selim Junz said, "This other man was Fife?"

"I remember his name was Fife."

"Well, was he that man?"

Rik did not turn to look. He said, "I can't remember what he looked like."

"Are you sure?"

"I've been trying." He burst out, "You don't know how hard it is. It hurts! It's like a red-hot needle. Deep! In here!" He put his hands to his head.

Junz said softly, "I know it's hard. But you must try.

Don't you see, you must keep on trying. Look at that man! Turn and look at him!"

Rik twisted toward the Squire of Fife. For a moment he stared, then turned away.

Junz said, "Can you remember now?"

"No! No!"

Fife smiled grimly. "Has your man forgotten his lines, or will the story seem more believable if he remembers my face the next time around?"

Junz said hotly, "I have never seen this man before, and I have never spoken to him. There has been no arrangement to frame you and I am tired of your accusations in that direction. I am after the truth only."

"Then may I ask him a few questions?"

"Go ahead."

"Thank you, I'm sure, for your kindness. Now you—Rik, or whatever your real name is——"

He was a Squire, addressing a Florinian.

Rik looked up. "Yes, sir."

"You remember a man approaching you from the other side of the table as you sat there, drugged and helpless."

"Yes, sir."

"The last thing you remember is this man staring down at you."

"Yes, sir."

"You stared up at him, or tried to."

"Yes, sir."

"Sit down."

Rik did so.

For a moment Fife did nothing. His lipless mouth might have grown tighter, the jaw muscles under the blue-black sheen of the stubble on his cheeks and chin bunched a bit. Then he slid down from his chair.

Slid *down*! It was as though he had gotten down on his knees there behind the desk.

But he moved from behind it and was seen plainly to be standing.

Junz's head swam. The man, so statuesque and formidable in his seat, had been converted without warning into a pitiful midget.

Fife's deformed legs moved under him with an effort, carrying the ungainly mass of torso and head forward. His face flushed but his eyes kept their look of arrogance intact. Steen broke into a wild giggle and choked it off when those eyes turned on him. The rest sat in fascinated silence.

Rik, wide-eyed, watched him approach.

Fife said, "Was I the man who approached you around the table?"

"I can't remember his face, sir."

"I don't ask you to remember his face. Can you have forgotten this?" His two arms went wide, framing his body. "Can you have forgotten my appearance, my walk?"

Rik said miserably, "It seems I shouldn't, sir, but I don't know."

"But you were sitting, he was standing, and you were looking up at him."

"Yes, sir."

"He was looking down at you, 'towering' over you, in fact."

"Yes, sir."

"You remember that at least? You're certain of that?"

"Yes, sir."

The two were now face to face.

"Am I looking down at you?"

Rik said, "No, sir."

"Are you looking up at me?"

Rik, sitting, and Fife, standing, stared levelly at one another, eye to eye.

"No, sir."

"Could I have been the man?"

"No, sir."

"Are you certain?"

"Yes, sir."

"You still say the name you remember is Fife?"

"I remember that name," insisted Rik stubbornly.

"Whoever it was, then, used my name as a disguise?"

"He—he must have."

Fife turned and with slow dignity struggled back to his desk and climbed into his seat.

He said, "I have never allowed any man to see me standing before this in all my adult life. Is there any reason why this conference should continue?"

Abel was at once embarrassed and annoyed. So far the conference had backfired badly. At every step Fife had managed to put himself in the right, the others in the wrong. Fife had successfully presented himself as a martyr. He had been forced into conference by Trantorian blackmail, and made the subject of false accusations that had broken down at once.

Fife would see to it that his version of the conference flooded the Galaxy and he would not have to depart very far from the truth to make it excellent anti-Trantorian propaganda.

Abel would have liked to cut his losses. The psycho-probed Spatio-analyst would be of no use to Trantor now. Any "memory" he might have thereafter would be laughed down, made ridiculous, however true it might be. He would be accepted as an instrument of Trantorian imperialism, and a broken instrument at that.

But he hesitated, and it was Junz who spoke.

Junz said, "It seems to me there's a very good reason for not ending the conference just yet. We have not yet determined exactly who is responsible for the psycho-probing. You have accused the Squire of Steen, and Steen has accused you. Granting that both of you are mistaken and that both are innocent, it still remains true that you each believe one of the Great Squires is guilty. Which one, then?"

"Does it matter?" asked Fife. "As far as you're concerned, I'm sure it doesn't. That matter would have been solved by now except for the interference of Trantor and the I.S.B. Eventually I will find the traitor. Remember that the psycho-prober, whoever he is, had the original intention of forcing a monopoly of the kyrt trade into his own hands, so I am not likely to let him escape. Once the psycho-prober is identified and dealt with, your man here will be returned unharmed to you. That is the only offer I can make and it is a very reasonable one."

"What will you do with the psycho-prober?"

"That is a purely internal matter that does not concern you."

"But it does," Junz said energetically. "This is not just a question of the Spatio-analyst. There's something of greater importance involved and I'm surprised that it hasn't been mentioned yet. This man Rik wasn't psycho-probed just because he was a Spatio-analyst."

Abel was not sure what Junz's intentions were, but he threw his weight into the scales. He said blandly, "Dr. Junz is referring, of course, to the Spatio-analyst's original message of danger."

Fife shrugged. "As far as I know, no one has yet attached any importance to that, including Dr. Junz over the past year. However, your man is here, Doctor. Ask him what it's all about."

"Naturally, he won't remember," Junz retorted angrily. "The psycho-probe is most effective upon the more intellectual chains of reasoning stored in the mind. The man may never recover the quantitative aspects of his lifework."

"Then it's gone," said Fife. "What can be done about that?"

"Something very definite. That's the point. There's someone else who knows, and that's the psycho-prober. He may not have been a Spatio-analyst himself; he may not know the precise details. However, he spoke to the man in a state of untouched mind. He will have learned enough to put us far on the right track. Without having learned enough he would not have dared to destroy the source of his information. Still, for the record, *do* you remember, Rik?"

"Only that there was danger and that it involved the currents of space," muttered Rik.

Fife said, "Even if you find out, what will you have? How reliable are any of the startling theories that sick Spatio-analysts are forever coming up with? Many of them think they know the secrets of the universe when they're so sick they can barely read their instruments."

"It may be that you are right. Are you afraid to let me find out?"

"I am against starting any morbid rumors that might, whether true or false, affect the kyrt trade. Don't you agree with me, Abel?"

Abel squirmed inwardly. Fife was maneuvering himself into the position where any break in kyrt deliveries resulting from his own *coup* could be blamed on Trantorian maneuvers. But Abel was a good gambler. He raised the stakes calmly and unemotionally.

He said, "I don't. I suggest you listen to Dr. Junz."

"Thanks," said Junz. "Now you have said, Squire Fife, that whoever the psycho-prober was, he must have killed the doctor who examined this man Rik. That implies that the psycho-prober had kept some sort of watch over Rik during his stay on Florina."

"Well?"

"There must be traces of that kind of watching."

"You mean you think these natives would know who was watching them."

"Why not?"

Fife said, "You are not a Sarkite and so you make mistakes. I assure you that natives keep their places. They don't approach Squires and if Squires approach them they know enough to keep their eyes on their toes. They would know nothing of being watched."

Junz quivered visibly with indignation. The Squires had their despotism so ingrained that they saw nothing wrong or shameful in speaking of it openly.

He said, "Ordinary natives perhaps. But we have a man here who is not an ordinary native. I think he has shown us rather thoroughly that he is not a properly respectful Florinian. So far he has contributed nothing to the discussion and it is time to ask him a few questions."

Fife said, "That native's evidence is worthless. In fact,

I take the opportunity once more to demand that Trantor surrender him to proper trial by the courts of Sark."

"Let me speak to him first."

Abel put in mildly, "I think it will do no harm to ask him a few questions, Fife. If he proves uncooperative or unreliable, we may consider your request for extradition."

Terens, who, til now, had stolidly concentrated on the fingers of his clasped hands, looked up briefly.

Junz turned to Terens. He said, "Rik has been in your town since he was first found on Florina, hasn't he?"

"Yes."

"And you were in town all that time? I mean you weren't on any extended business trips, were you?"

"Townmen don't make business trips. Their business is in their town."

"All right. Now relax and don't get touchy. It would be part of your business to know about any Squire that might come to town, I imagine."

"Sure. When they come."

"Did they come?"

Terens shrugged. "Once or twice. Pure routine, I assure you. Squires don't dirty their hands with kyrt. Unprocessed kyrt, that is."

"Be respectful!" roared Fife.

Terens looked at him and said, "Can you make me?"

Abel interrupted smoothly, "Let's keep this between the man and Dr. Junz, Fife. You and I are spectators."

Junz felt a glow of pleasure at the Townman's insolence, but he said, "Answer my questions without side comments please, Townman. Now who exactly were the Squires who visited your town this past year?"

Terens said fiercely, "How can I know? I can't answer that question. Squires are Squires and natives are natives. I may be a Townman but I'm still a native to them. I don't greet them at the town gates and ask their names.

"I get a message, that's all. It's addressed 'Townman.' It says there'll be a Squire's Inspection on such-and-such a day and I'm to make the necessary arrangements. I must then see to it that the millworkers have on their best clothes, that the mill is cleaned up and working properly, that the kyrt supply is ample, that everyone looks contented and pleased, that the houses have been cleaned and the streets policed, that some dancers are on hand in case the Squires would care to view some amusing native dance, that maybe a few pretty g——"

"Never mind that, Townman," said Junz.

"*You* never mind that. I do."

After his experiences with the Florinians of the Civil Service, Junz found the Townman as refreshing as a drink of cold water. He made up his mind that what influence the I.S.B. could bring to bear would be used to prevent any surrender of the Townman to the Squires.

Terens went on, in calmer tones, "Anyway, that's my part. When they come, I line up with the rest. I don't know who they are. I don't speak to them."

"Was there any such inspection the week before the City Doctor was killed? I suppose you know what week that happened."

"I think I heard about it in the newscasts. I don't think there was any Squire's Inspection at that time. I can't swear to it."

"Whom does your land belong to?"

Terens pulled the corners of his mouth back. "To the Squire of Fife."

Steen spoke up, breaking into the give-and-take with rather surprising suddenness. "Oh, look here. Really! You're playing into Fife's hands with this kind of questioning, Dr. Junz. Don't you see you won't get anywhere? Really! Do you suppose if Fife was interested in keeping tabs on that creature there that he would go to all the trouble of making trips to Florina to look at him? What are patrollers for? Really!"

Junz looked flustered. "In a case like this, with a world's economy and maybe its physical safety resting on the contents of one man's mind, it's natural that the psycho-prober would not care to leave the guardianship to patrollers."

Fife intervened. "Even after he had wiped out that mind, to all intents?"

Abel pushed out his lower lip and frowned. He saw his latest gamble sliding into Fife's hands with all the rest.

Junz tried again, hesitantly. "Was there any particular patroller or group of patrollers that was always underfoot?"

"I'd never know. They're just uniforms to me."

Junz turned to Valona with the effect of a sudden pounce. A moment before she had gone a sickly white and her eyes had become wide and stary. Junz had not missed that.

He said, "What about you, girl?"

But she only shook her head, wordlessly.

Abel thought heavily, There's nothing more to do. It's all over.

But Valona was on her feet, trembling. She said in a husky whisper, "I want to say something."

Junz said, "Go ahead, girl. What is it?"

Valona talked breathlessly and with fright obvious in every line of her countenance and every nervous twitch of her fingers. She said, "I'm just a country girl. Please don't be angry with me. It's just that it seems that things can only be one way. Was my Rik so very important? I mean, the way you said?"

Junz said gently, "I think he was very, very important. I think he still is."

"Then it must be like you said. Whoever it was who had put him on Florina wouldn't have dared take his eye away for even a minute hardly. Would he? I mean, suppose Rik was beaten by the mill superintendent or was stoned by the children or got sick and died. He wouldn't be left helpless in the fields, would he, where he might die before anyone found him? They wouldn't suppose that it would just be *luck* that would keep him safe." She was speaking with an intense fluency now.

"Go on," said Junz, watching her.

"Because there was one person who did watch Rik from the start. He found him in the fields, fixed it so I would take care of him, kept him out of trouble and knew about him every day. He even knew all about the doctor, because I told him. It was he! It was he!"

With her voice at screaming intensity, her finger pointed rigidly at Myrlyn Terens, Townman.

And this time even Fife's superhuman calm broke and his arms stiffened on his desk, lifting his massive body a full inch off his seat, as his head swiveled quickly toward the Townman.

18. THE VICTORS

It was as though vocal paralysis had gripped them all. Even Rik, with disbelief in his eyes, could only stare woodenly, first at Valona, then at Terens.

Then came Steen's high-pitched laugh and the silence was broken.

Steen said, "I believe it. Really! I said so all along. I said the native was in Fife's pay. That shows you the kind of man Fife is. He'd pay a native to——"

"That's an infernal lie."

It wasn't Fife who spoke, but the Townman. He was on his feet, eyes glistening with passion.

Abel, who of them all seemed the least moved, said, "What is?"

Terens stared at him a moment, not comprehending, then said chokingly, "What the Squire said. I am in the pay of no Sarkite."

"And what the girl said? Is that a lie too?"

217

Terens wet his dry lips with the tip of his tongue. "No, that's true. I am the psycho-prober." He hurried on. "Don't look at me like that, Lona. I didn't mean to hurt him. I didn't intend any of what happened." He sat down again.

Fife said, "This is a sort of device. I don't know exactly what you're planning, Abel, but it's impossible on the face of it that this criminal could have included this particular crime in his repertoire. It's definite that only a Great Squire could have had the necessary knowledge and facilities. Or are you anxious to take your man Steen off the hook by arranging for a false confession?"

Terens, hands tightly clasped, leaned forward in his seat. "I don't take Trantorian money, either."

Fife ignored him.

Junz was the last to come to himself. For minutes, he could not adjust to the fact that the Townman was not really in the same room with him, that he was somewhere else on the embassy grounds, that he could see him only in image form, no more real actually than was Fife, who was twenty miles away. He wanted to go to the Townman, grip him by the shoulder, speak to him alone, but he couldn't. He said, "There's no point in arguing before we hear the man. Let's have the details. If he *is* the psycho-prober, we need the details badly. If he isn't, the details he'll try to give us will prove it."

"If you want to know what happened," cried Terens, "I'll tell you. Holding it back won't do me any good any longer. It's Sark or Trantor after all, so to Space with it. This will at least give me a chance to get one or two things into the open."

He pointed at Fife in scorn. "There's a Great Squire. Only a Great Squire, says this Great Squire, can have the knowledge or the facilities to do what the psycho-prober did. He believes it, too. But what does he know? What do any of the Sarkites know?

"They don't run the government. Florinians do! The Florinian Civil Service does. They get the papers, they make the papers, they file the papers. And it's the papers that run

Sark. Sure, most of us are too beaten even to whimper, but do you know what we could do if we wanted to, even under the noses of our damned Squires? Well, you see what I've done.

"I was temporarily traffic manager at the spaceport a year ago. Part of my training. It's in the records. You'll have to dig a little to find it because the listed traffic manager is a Sarkite. He had the title but I did the actual work. My name would be found in the special section headed Native Personnel. No Sarkite would have dirtied his eyes looking there.

"When the local I.S.B. sent the Spatio-analyst's message to the port with a suggestion that we meet the ship with an ambulance, I got the message. I passed on what was safe. This matter of the destruction of Florina was not passed on.

"I arranged to meet the Spatio-analyst at a small suburban port. I could do that easily. All the wires and strings that ran Sark were at my finger tips. I was in the Civil Service, remember. A Great Squire who wanted to do what I did, couldn't, unless he ordered some Florinian to do it for him. I could do it without anyone's help. So much for knowledge and facility.

"I met the Spatio-analyst, kept him away from both Sark and the I.S.B. I squeezed as much information out of him as I could and set about using that information for Florina and against Sark."

Words were forced out of Fife. "You sent those first letters?"

"I sent those first letters, Great Squire," said Terens calmly. "I thought I could force control of enough of the kyrt lands into my own hands to make a deal with Trantor on my terms and drive you off the planet."

"You were mad."

"Maybe. Anyway, it didn't work. I had told the Spatio-analyst I was the Squire of Fife. I had to, because he knew that Fife was the biggest man on the planet, and as long as he thought I was Fife, he was willing to talk openly. It made me laugh to realize that he thought Fife was anxious to do whatever was best for Florina.

"Unfortunately, he was more impatient than I was. He insisted that every day lost was a calamity, while I knew that my dealings with Sark needed time more than anything else. I found it difficult to control him and eventually had to use a psychic probe. I could get one. I had seen it used in hospitals. I knew something about it. Unfortunately, not enough.

"I set the probe to wipe out the anxiety from the surface layers of his mind. That's a simple operation. I still don't know what happened. I think the anxiety must have run deeper, very deep, and the probe automatically followed it, digging out most of the conscious mind along with it. I was left with a mindless thing on my hands. . . . I'm sorry, Rik."

Rik, who had been listening intently, said sadly, "You shouldn't have interfered with me, Townman, but I know how you must have felt."

"Yes," said Terens, "you've lived on the planet. You know about patrollers and Squires and the difference between Lower City and Upper City."

He took up the current of his story again. "So there I was with the Spatio-analyst completely helpless. I couldn't let him be found by anyone who might trace his identity. I couldn't kill him. I felt sure his memory would return and I would still need his knowledge, to say nothing of the fact that killing him would forfeit the good will of Trantor and the I.S.B., which I would eventually need. Besides, in those days, I was incapable of killing.

"I arranged to be transferred to Florina as Townman and I took the Spatio-analyst with me on forged papers. I arranged to have him found, I picked Valona to take care of him. There was no danger thereafter except for that one time with the doctor. Then I had to enter the power plants of Upper City. That was not impossible. The engineers were Sarkites but the janitors were Florinian. On Sark I learned enough about power mechanics to know how to short a power line. It took me three days to find the proper time for it. After that, I could murder easily. I never knew, though, that the doctor kept duplicate records in both halves of his office. I wish I had."

Terens could see Fife's chronometer from where he sat. "Then, one hundred hours ago—it seems like a hundred years—Rik began remembering again. Now you have the whole story."

"No," said Junz, "we have not. What are the details of the Spatio-analyst's story of planetary destruction?"

"Do you think I understood the details of what he had to say? It was some sort of—pardon me, Rik—madness."

"It wasn't," blazed Rik. "It couldn't have been."

"That Spatioanalyst had a ship," said Junz. "Where is it?"

"On the scrap heap long ago," said Terens. "An order scrapping it was sent out. My superior signed it. A Sarkite never reads papers, of course. It was scrapped without question."

"And Rik's papers? You said he showed you papers!"

"Surrender that man to us," said Fife suddenly, "and we'll find out what he knows."

"No," said Junz. "His first crime was against the I.S.B. He kidnapped and damaged the mind of a Spatio-analyst. He belongs to us."

Abel said, "Junz is correct."

Terens said, "Now look here. I don't say a word without safeguards. I know where Rik's papers are. They're where no Sarkite or Trantorian will ever find them. If you want them you'll have to agree that I'm a political refugee. Whatever I did was out of patriotism, out of a regard for the needs of my planet. A Sarkite or a Trantorian may claim to be patriotic; why not a Florinian as well?"

"The Ambassador," said Junz, "has said you will be given over to the I.S.B. I assure you that you will not be turned over to Sark. For your treatment of the Spatio-analyst, you will be tried. I cannot guarantee the result, but if you cooperate with us now, it will count in your favor."

Terens looked searchingly at Junz. Then he said, "I'll

take my chance with you, Doctor. . . . According to the Spatio-analyst, Florina's sun is in the pre-nova stage."

"What!" The exclamation or its equivalent came from all but Valona.

"It's about to explode and go boom," said Terens sardonically. "And when that happens all of Florina will go poof, like a mouthful of tobacco smoke."

Abel said, "I'm no Spatio-analyst, but I have heard that there is no way of predicting when a star will explode."

"That's true. Until now, anyway. Did Rik explain what made him think so?" asked Junz.

"I suppose his papers will show that. All I can remember is about the carbon current."

"What?"

"He kept saying, 'The carbon current of space. The carbon current of space.' That, and the words 'catalytic effect.' There it is."

Steen giggled. Fife frowned. Junz stared.

Then Junz muttered, "Pardon me. I'll be right back." He stepped out of the limits of the receptor cube and vanished.

He was back in fifteen minutes.

Junz looked about in bewilderment when he returned. Only Abel and Fife were present.

He said, "Where——"

Abel broke in instantly. "We have been waiting for you, Dr. Junz. The Spatio-analyst and the girl are on their way to the Embassy. The conference is ended."

"Ended! Great Galaxy, we have only begun. I've got to explain the possibilities of nova formation."

Abel shifted uneasily in his seat. "It is not necessary to do that, Doctor."

"It is very necessary. It is essential. Give me five minutes."

"Let him speak," said Fife. He was smiling.

Junz said, "Take it from the beginning. In the earliest recorded scientific writings of Galactic civilization it was already known that stars obtained their energy from nuclear transformations in their interiors. It was also known that, given what we know about conditions in stellar interiors, two types, and only two types, of nuclear transformations can possibly yield the necessary energy. Both involve the conversion of hydrogen to helium. The first transformation is direct: two hydrogens and two neutrons combine to form one helium nucleus. The second is indirect, with several steps. It ends up with hydrogen becoming helium, but in the intermediate steps, carbon nuclei take part. These carbon nuclei are not used up but are re-formed as the reactions proceed, so that a trifling amount of carbon can be used over and over again, serving to convert a great deal of hydrogen to helium. The carbon acts as a catalyst, in other words. All this has been known back to the days of pre-history, back to the time when the human race was restricted to a single planet, if there ever was such a time."

"If we all know it," said Fife, "I would suggest that you are contributing nothing but a waste of time."

"But this is *all* we know. Whether stars use one or the other, or both, nuclear processes has never been determined. There have always been schools of thought in favor of each of the alternatives. Usually the weight of opinion has been in favor of the direct hydrogen-helium conversion as being the simpler of the two.

"Now Rik's theory must be this. The hydrogen-helium direct conversion is the *normal* source of stellar energy, but under certain conditions the carbon catalysis adds its weight, hastening the process, speeding it up, heating up the star.

"There are currents in space. You all know that well. Some of these are carbon currents. Stars passing through the currents pick up innumerable atoms. The total mass of atoms attracted, however, is incredibly microscopic in comparison to the star's weight and does not affect it in any way. *Except for carbon!* A star that passes through a current containing unusual concentrations of carbon becomes unstable. I don't know how many years or centuries or millions of years it takes for the carbon atoms to diffuse into the star's interior, but it probably takes a long time. That means that a carbon current must be wide and a star must intersect it at a small angle. In any case, once the quantity of carbon percolating into the star's interior passes a certain critical amount, the star's radiation is suddenly boosted tremendously. The outer layers give way under an unimaginable explosion and you have a nova.

"Do you see?"

Junz waited.

Fife said, "Have you figured all this out in two minutes as a result of some vague phrase the Townman remembered the Spatio-analyst to have said a year ago?"

"Yes. Yes. There's nothing surprising in that. Spatio-analysis is ready for that theory. If Rik had not come up with it, someone else would have shortly. In fact, similar theories have been advanced before, but they were never taken seriously. They were put forward before the techniques of Spatio-analysis were developed and no one was ever able to account for the sudden acquisition of excess carbon by the star in question.

"But now we know there *are* carbon currents. We can plot their courses, find out what stars intersected those courses in the past ten thousand years, check that against our records for nova formation and radiation variations. That's what Rik must have done. Those must have been the calculations and observations he tried to show the Townman. But that's all beside the immediate point.

"What must be arranged for now is the immediate beginning of an evacuation of Florina."

"I thought it would come to that," said Fife composedly.

"I'm sorry, Junz," said Abel, "but that's quite impossible."

"Why impossible?"

"*When* will Florina's sun explode?"

"I don't know. From Rik's anxiety a year ago, I'd say we had little time."

"But you can't set a date?"

"Of course not."

"When will you able to set a date?"

"There's no way of telling. Even if we get Rik's calculations, it would all have to be rechecked."

"Can you guarantee that the Spatio-analyst's theory will prove to be correct?"

Junz frowned. "I am personally certain of it, but no scientist can guarantee any theory in advance."

"Then it turns out that you want Florina evacuated on mere speculation."

"I think the chance of killing the population of a planet is not one that can be taken."

"If Florina were an ordinary planet I would agree with you. But Florina bears the Galactic supply of kyrt. It can't be done."

Junz said angrily, "Is that the agreement you came to with Fife while I was gone?"

Fife intervened. He said, "Let me explain, Dr. Junz. The government of Sark would never consent to evacuate Florina, even if the I.S.B. claimed it had proof of this nova theory of yours. Trantor cannot force us because while the Galaxy might support a war against Sark for the purpose of maintaining the kyrt trade, it will never support one for the purpose of ending it."

"Exactly," said Abel. "I am afraid our own people would not support us in such a war."

Junz found revulsion growing strong within him. A planet full of people meant nothing against the dictates of economic necessity!

He said, "Listen to me. This is not a matter of one planet, but of a whole Galaxy. There are now twenty full novae originating within the Galaxy every year. In addition, some two thousand stars among the Galaxy's hundred billion shift their radiation characteristics sufficiently to render uninhabitable any habitable planet they may have. Human beings occupy one million stellar systems in the Galaxy. That means that on an average of once every fifty years some inhabited planet somewhere becomes too hot for life. Such cases are a matter of historical record. Every five thousand years some inhabited planet has a fifty-fifty chance of being puffed to gas by a nova.

"If Trantor does nothing about Florina, if it allows it to vaporize with its people on it, that will serve notice to all the people of the Galaxy that when their own turn comes they may expect no help, if such help is in the way of the economic convenience of a few powerful men. Can you risk that, Abel?

"On the other hand, help Florina and you will have shown that Trantor puts its responsibility to the people of the Galaxy above the maintenance of mere property rights. Trantor will win good will that it could never win by force."

Abel bowed his head. Then he shook it wearily. "No, Junz. What you say appeals to me, but it is not practical. I can't count on emotions as against the assured political effect of any attempt to end the kyrt trade. In fact, I think it might be wise to avoid investigating the theory. The thought that it might be true would do too much harm."

"But what if it *is* true?"

"We must work on the assumption that it is not. I take it that when you were gone a few moments ago it was to contact the I.S.B."

"Yes."

"No matter. Trantor, I think, will have enough influence to stop their investigations."

"I'm afraid not. Not these investigations. Gentlemen, we will soon have the secret of cheap kyrt. There will be no kyrt monopoly within a year, whether or not there is a nova."

"What do you mean?"

"The conference is reaching the essential point now, Fife. Kyrt grows only on Florina of all inhabited planets. Its seeds produce ordinary cellulose elsewhere. Florina is probably the only inhabited planet, on a chance basis, that is currently pre-nova, and it has probably been pre-nova since it first entered the carbon current, perhaps thousands of years ago, if the angle of intersection was small. It seems quite probable, then, that kyrt and the pre-nova stage go together."

"Nonsense," said Fife.

"Is it? There must be a reason why kyrt is kyrt on Florina and cotton elsewhere. Scientists have tried many ways of artificially producing kyrt elsewhere, but they tried blindly, so they've always failed. Now they will know it is due to factors induced in a pre-nova stellar system."

Fife said scornfully, "They've tried duplicating the radiation qualities of Fife's sun."

"With appropriate arc lights, yes, that duplicated the visible and ultraviolet spectrum only. What about radiation in the infrared and beyond? What about magnetic fields? What about electron emission? What about cosmic-ray effects? I'm not a physical biochemist so there may be factors I know nothing about. But people who are physical biochemists will be looking now, a whole Galaxy of them. Within the year, I assure you, the solution will be found.

"Economics is on the side of humanity now. The Galaxy wants cheap kyrt, and if they find it or even if they imagine they will shortly find it, they will want Florina evacuated, not only out of humanity, but out of a desire to turn the tables, at long last, on the kyrt-gouging Sarkites."

"Bluff!" growled Fife.

"Do you think so, Abel?" demanded Junz. "If you help the Squires, Trantor will be looked on not as the saviors of the kyrt trade but of the kyrt monopoly. Can you chance that?"

"Can Trantor chance a war?" demanded Fife.

"War? Nonsense! Squire, in one year your holdings on Florina will be worthless, nova or not. Sell out. Sell out all Florina. Trantor can pay for it."

"Buy a planet?" said Abel in dismay.

"Why not? Trantor has the funds, and its gain in good will among the people of the universe will pay it back a thousand-fold. If telling them that you are saving hundreds of millions of lives is not enough, tell them that you will bring them cheap kyrt. That will do it."

"I'll think about it," said Abel.

Abel looked at the Squire. Fife's eyes fell.

After a long pause he too said, "I'll think about it."

Junz laughed harshly. "Don't think too long. The kyrt story will break quickly enough. Nothing can stop it. After that, neither one of you will have freedom of action. You can each strike a better bargain now."

The Townman seemed beaten. "It's really true?" he kept repeating. "Really true? No more Florina?"

"It's true," said Junz.

Terens spread his arms, let them fall against his side. "If you want the papers I got from Rik, they're filed among vital statistic files in my home town. I picked the dead files, records a century back and more. No one would ever look there for any reason."

"Look," said Junz, "I'm sure we can make an agreement with the I.S.B. We'll need a man on Florina, one who knows the Florinian people, who can tell us how to explain the facts to them, how best to organize the evacuation, how to pick the most suitable planets of refuge. Will you help us?"

"And beat the game that way, you mean? Get away with murder? Why not?" There were sudden tears in the Townman's eyes. "But I lose anyway. I will have no world, no home. We all lose. The Florinians lose their world, the Sarkites lose their wealth, the Trantorians their chance to get that wealth. There are no winners at all."

"Unless," said Junz gently, "you realize that in the new Galaxy—a Galaxy safe from the threat of stellar instability, a Galaxy with kyrt available to all, and a Galaxy in which political unification will be so much closer—there will be winners after all. One quadrillion winners. The people of the Galaxy, *they* are the victors."

EPILOG
A YEAR AFTER

"Rik! Rik!" Selim Junz hurried across the port grounds toward the ship, hands outstretched. "And Lona! I'd never have recognized either of you. How are you? How are you?"

"As well as we could wish. Our letters reached you, I see," said Rik.

"Of course. Tell me, what do you think of it all?" They were walking back together, toward Junz's offices.

Valona said sadly, "We visited our old town this morning. The fields are so empty." Her clothing was now that of a woman of the Empire, rather than that of a peasant of Florina.

"Yes, it must be dreary for a person who has lived here. It grows dreary even for me, but I will stay as long as I can. The radiation recordings of Florina's sun are of tremendous theoretical interest."

"So much evacuation in less than a year! It speaks for excellent organization."

"We're doing our best, Rik. Oh, I think I should be calling you by your real name."

"Please don't. I'll never be used to it. I'm Rik. That's still the only name I remember."

Junz said, "Have you decided whether you're going to return to Spatio-analysis?"

Rik shook his head. "I've decided, but the decision is, no. I'll never remember enough. That part's gone forever. It doesn't bother me, though. I'll be returning to Earth. . . . By the way, I rather hoped I'd see the Townman."

"I think not. He decided to go off today. I think he'd rather not see you. He feels guilty, I think. You have no grudge against him?"

Rik said, "No. He meant well, and he changed my life in many ways for the better. For one thing, I met Lona." His arm went about her shoulder.

Valona looked at him and smiled.

"Besides," Rik went on, "he cured me of something. I've found out why I was a Spatio-analyst. I know why nearly a third of all Spatio-analysts are recruited from the one planet, Earth. Anyone living on a radioactive world is bound to grow up in fear and insecurity. A misstep can mean death and our planet's own surface is the greatest enemy we have.

"That makes for a sort of anxiety bred into us, Dr. Junz, a fear of planets. We're only happy in space; that's the only place we can feel safe."

"And you don't feel that way any longer, Rik?"

"I certainly don't. I don't even remember feeling that way. That's it, you see. The Townman had set his psychic probe to remove feelings of anxiety and he hadn't bothered to set the intensity controls. He thought he had a recent, superficial trouble to deal with. Instead there was this deep, ingrained anxiety he knew nothing of. He got rid of all of it. In a sense, it was worth getting rid of it even though so much else went with it. I don't have to stay in space now.

I can go back to Earth. I can work there and Earth needs men. It always will."

"You know," Junz said, "why can't we do for Earth what we're doing for Florina? There's no need to bring up Earthmen in such fear and insecurity. The Galaxy is big."

"No," said Rik vehemently. "It's a different case. Earth has its past, Dr. Junz. Many people may not believe it, but we of Earth know that Earth was the original planet of the human race."

"Well, perhaps. I can't say, one way or the other."

"It *was*. It's a planet that can't be abandoned; it *mustn't* be abandoned. Someday we'll change it, change its surface back to what it once must have been. Till then—we're staying."

Valona said softly, "And I'm an Earthwoman now."

Rik was looking out at the horizon. Upper City was as garish as ever, but the people were gone.

He said, "How many are left on Florina?"

"About twenty million," said Junz. "We work slower as we go along. We have to keep our withdrawals balanced. The people that are left must always maintain themselves as an economic unit in the months that are left. Of course, resettlement is in its earliest stages. Most of the evacuees are still in temporary camps on neighboring worlds. There is unavoidable hardship."

"When will the last person leave?"

"Never, really."

"I don't understand."

"The Townman has applied unofficially for permission to remain. It's been granted, also unofficially. It won't be a matter of public record."

"Remain?" Rik was shocked. "But for the sake of all the Galaxy, why?"

"I didn't know," said Junz, "but I think you explained it when you talked of Earth. He feels as you do. He says he can't bear the thought of leaving Florina to die alone."

AFTERWORD

The Currents of Space was written in 1951 and was first published in 1952. At that time, comparatively little was known of the astrophysics of nova formation and my speculation concerning "carbon currents" was legitimate. Astronomers know much more now, and it seems quite certain the nature of the currents of space have nothing to do with nova formation (though, as it happens, the analysis of interstellar clouds of dust and gas has become far more interesting now than ever I imagined in 1951). This is too bad, for my speculations concerning the currents of space were so clever (in my opinion) that I feel they *should* have been true. —Still, the Universe goes its own way and won't bend merely to pay homage to my cleverness, so I can only ask you to suspend your disbelief in respect to nova-formation and enjoy the book (assuming you do) on its own terms.

Isaac Asimov
November, 1982

ABOUT THE AUTHOR

Isaac Asimov was born in the Soviet Union to his great surprise. He moved quickly to correct the situation. When his parents emigrated to the United States, Isaac (three years old at the time) stowed away in their baggage. He has been an American citizen since the age of eight.

Brought up in Brooklyn, and educated in its public schools, he eventually found his way to Columbia University and, over the protests of the school administration, managed to annex a series of degrees in chemistry, up to and including a Ph.D. He then infiltrated Boston University and climbed the academic ladder, ignoring all cries of outrage, until he found himself Professor of Biochemistry.

Meanwhile, at the age of nine, he found the love of his life (in the inanimate sense) when he discovered his first science-fiction magazine. By the time he was eleven, he began to write stories, and at eighteen, he actually worked up the nerve to submit one. It was rejected. After four long months of tribulation and suffering, he sold his first story and, thereafter, he never looked back.

In 1941, when he was twenty-one years old, he wrote the classic short story "Nightfall" and his future was assured. Shortly before that he had begun writing his robot stories, and shortly after that he had begun his Foundation series.

What was left except quantity? At the present time, he has published over 340 books, distributed through every major division of the Dewey system of library classification, and shows no signs of slowing up. He remains as youthful, as lively, and as lovable as ever, and grows more handsome with each year. You can be sure that this is so since he has written this little essay himself and his devotion to absolute objectivity is notorious.

He is married to Janet Jeppson, psychiatrist and writer, has two children by a previous marriage, and lives in New York City.